NIGHTSONG

A. M. Leibowitz

Supposed Crimes LLC • Matthews, North Carolina

Many thanks to those who took the time out of their busy schedule to beta read (and re-read and suggest changes). Your dedication and support are above and beyond, and this novel would not exist without you.

Thank you to my family, particularly my children, who have provided names for people and locations. You are all better at this than I am, and I hope you know we'll be having many more conversations in which I will ask you to name things for me.

Finally, thanks to my readers. While reading the words may be a solitary activity, a book is a communal experience. I hope through these pages you learn that you are not alone, you are not wrong, and you are not broken.

Mark well, therefore, our souls,
rather than the poor players' garb
we wear, for we are men
of flesh and bone, like you, breathing
the same air of this orphan world.
- Prologue, *Pagliacci* (Ruggero Leoncavallo)

CHAPTER ONE

Nate Kingsley was on the theater's third floor in the classroom wing, washing dishes in the lounge. He heard a noise behind him and peeked over his shoulder. A beautiful young man with light brown hair and eyes to match bounced in, still in costume from the rehearsal going on downstairs. The elegant cape around his shoulders billowed out as he twirled across the room. After grabbing a peach from the fridge, he stood in the middle of the room, one hand on his hip, waiting for Nate to acknowledge him.

Once Nate turned around to look, Del cleared his throat. "Never get involved with a married man," he declared. With that sage advice, he flopped onto the couch in the lounge and swung his feet up, heaving a dramatic sigh.

Nate raised his eyebrows, trying to decide if Del was serious or not. He half suspected most of what Del said was exaggeration, but in this case, he didn't doubt there was some truth to it. Del had been on about this particular nameless man for several weeks. On the other hand, he had a reputation as being up for anything—or anyone—and he needed to maintain it, regardless of how true the story was.

"Learned your lesson the hard way, eh?" Nate asked, drying his hands.

Del flung his arm out. "Guess it wasn't meant to be a fairy tale ending."

Nate snorted and turned away. Del's relationship woes were notorious, and hooking up with a married man was only the latest in a string of poor partner choices he'd made, at least if he was looking for the mythical happily-ever-after. Nate would have felt sorry for him, but Del knew the man was married, knew he was closeted, and knew he had no plans to leave his wife or come out. Eyes wide open and all that. The truth was, Del *liked* drama. It's what made him good at what he did, even if it also made him ten kinds of irritating whenever he chose to act out his profession in his personal life.

Not that Nate should be talking. He'd wasted a lot of years on the wrong people himself. If he were making a list, he might as well start with his first boyfriend and end with the unrequited crush he'd had on his best friend, Trevor. The result of his own bad decisions had been losing one of them and nearly losing the other. Del didn't know any of that, however, and it left Nate free to needle him a little.

"You could have said no," he pointed out.

Del rolled his eyes. "Where's the fun in that? I had three months of getting fucked by the hottest man I've ever met. I can die happy, even if I'm disappointed it's over."

"You have a one-track mind." Nate crossed the room and began picking up trash left by the previous occupants.

"And you haven't gotten laid in...how long now? I've lost count." Del bounced off the couch. "You've been super bitchy lately, and for everyone's sake, it needs to stop. Obviously your own hand isn't enough."

"First of all," Nate said, turning around again, "don't call me bitchy. You know how I feel about that word. Second, my stress has nothing to do with my lack of sex, thank you very much."

That was mostly true. Nate had taken over as creative director of the tiny opera company less than a month prior, and not only did he miss taking lead roles, he also hated the endless and infuriating day-to-day problems. Del was the least difficult to work with because he didn't tend to bring his issues on stage, even if he did complain about them during breaks. Far worse were the couple who constantly broke up and got back together, the person who complained daily about not getting the right roles, and the one who made rude comments every time a particular cast mate was on stage.

Del huffed. "I get that you're a tortured artist and all, but I really do think you need to relieve all that pent-up tension."

"Why? Are you offering?" Nate sneered at him.

"Oh, honey, you could not handle me," Del replied, his voice smooth as butter. "I'm so not your type. Take it from me, though. You'll feel a lot better once you blow off some steam. No one can go this long without it building up."

"Not all of us are like you," Nate snapped. At Del's hurt expression, he relented. "I'm sorry. Listen, I know you mean well, but I don't need a man to make my life better. What I need is to get my own shit together and focus on work. After the holiday production, I'll have a break to deal with my personal relationship crises. Okay?"

"Okay, okay. I'll leave you to it." Del stretched, scratched his stomach, and flounced out of the room.

Once he was gone, Nate sat on the couch Del had vacated and put his head in his hands. Del was right about one thing—Nate had been taking out his frustration on everyone else as much as they'd been annoying the snot out of him. He wished he could go home, whine about it a little—fine, a lot—and let Trevor take care of him the way they'd done all through school. Except they were adults now, had been for a long time in fact, and Trevor was not interested in engaging with Nate in any tension-relieving activities. He had enough to balance with a new relationship and a baby on the way; never mind that he'd made it clear his and Nate's days of being each other's right hand were over.

Nate growled and flopped against the back of the couch. It was going to be a long day.

Tired and with aching feet, Nate opened the door to the apartment, ready to put away the few groceries he'd bought, grab a beer, and throw himself onto the couch to watch mindless something or other until the other guys he lived with arrived home. Instead of silence, he was greeted by the sound of angry voices drifting from the hallway by the bedrooms. He was torn between worry and a sense of deja vu. If they kept it up, their downstairs neighbor—affectionately referred to as Mrs. Crochety—would have something to say about it. He stepped into the apartment and peered around cautiously.

Sure enough, outside the bathroom, Jamie was having another fight with his on-again, off-again boyfriend. Everything about Nate's day felt like it was on repeat, from the backstage attitudes to Del's relationship drama to this. Nate tried hard for Jamie's sake not to hate The Boyfriend, whose name he intentionally didn't remember, but it was damn hard. The Boyfriend was whiny, immature, and entitled. None of them understood why Jamie liked being around him, especially on days like today.

Nate watched and listened for a few minutes, catching the gist of the argument. The Boyfriend was after Jamie about some plans he'd made which Jamie either didn't want to go through with or hadn't agreed to in the first place. Nate guessed it was the latter because Jamie wasn't one to break a commitment.

"Please," Jamie begged. "You know how I feel about it." He sounded like he was on the verge of tears.

The Boyfriend *tsk'd*. "For once in your life, think about how *I* feel."

"I am!" Jamie protested. "You can take someone else. I can't, okay? Please." He was shaking.

The Boyfriend obviously realized he wasn't getting anywhere because his next move was to step closer and put his hands on Jamie's shoulders. "Sh, baby. Come on. It's not as big a deal as you're making it. We don't even have to stay the whole time. Everyone wants to see you, and I want to show them how fucking hot you still are." He kissed Jamie's lips, despite the fact that Jamie was a stone in response.

He moved one hand down to Jamie's hip then slowly inched his fingers farther in until they rested on Jamie's crotch. Jamie flinched, but his muttered, "Stop it" went unheeded.

Nate hated getting in the middle, but once Jamie's *no* had been disrespected, he couldn't help it. "Hey, Jay?" he called, moving closer to them.

The other two fell silent. Jamie cleared his throat and responded, "Yeah?" as he turned toward Nate.

"Want to come help me in the kitchen for a sec?"

Jamie started to step out of the hallway, but The Boyfriend caught his arm. "Where the fuck do you think you're going? We're not done."

"I'm going to help Nate like he asked." Jamie jerked his arm away.

He entered the kitchen and wiped his face on his sleeve. His cheeks were blotchy and his eyes were bright, but he looked all right otherwise. Nate wouldn't have put it past The Boyfriend to hit Jamie, though he hadn't seen him do it yet. He held out the bag of groceries and leaned in as if he were discussing the cream cheese.

"Are you all right?" he asked, low.

"Yeah."

"Jamie."

"It's nothing, okay?" Jamie sighed. "But thanks for getting me out of there."

"Want to tell me what that was about?"

Jamie shrugged and stepped around Nate to open the fridge. He glanced over his shoulder and leaned closer. "Not now."

Nate nodded and put the last few items away. He tossed the reusable bag into a drawer and stalked over to The Boyfriend. Nate towered over him, and he wasn't afraid to use his height to his advantage. The Boyfriend shrank back a bit, though he was still scowling.

"Probably a good idea to leave," Nate said.

"Not without him." The Boyfriend nodded at Jamie. "He's coming with me like he promised."

"Hell, no. Didn't sound like he promised you anything." Nate crossed his arms and stared down at The Boyfriend.

The Boyfriend gave a whining huff and stormed out, pulling the door shut with force behind him. Jamie relaxed visibly and ran a shaking hand through his hair.

"Thanks," he said.

"He's an ass," Nate said.

"Please don't," Jamie snapped, his posture abruptly changing. "You don't understand."

"Understand what? I have no idea what you were arguing about, but damn it, Jamie, it gets fucking old."

"Oh? I'm sorry my life is ruining yours." Jamie pushed past Nate and took off down the hallway to his room. He slammed the door, leaving Nate alone in the kitchen.

Nate closed his eyes and breathed slowly. Great. Another friendship on the verge of collapse because he simply couldn't keep his mouth shut. He thought about Trevor and the mess he'd created there by accidentally-on-purpose outing him in a public and humiliating way. It had worked itself out, but it would be a long time before he could reconstruct their trust again. Now here he was, hurting Jamie too.

He smacked his hand on the counter. Enough was enough. He wouldn't lose someone else because of his overdeveloped sense of what was right. Nate went to Jamie's room and knocked on the door.

"What do you want?" Jamie asked.

"I want to make sure you're okay. I'm sorry I was a dick just now."

A moment later, Jamie opened the door. They stood there, Jamie craning his neck to look up at Nate, who was a good ten inches taller. Jamie's eyes were red-rimmed. Nate put a hand on Jamie's arm and squeezed gently. He let go, and with a nod, Jamie stepped back into his room and closed the door with a soft click. If Nate's eyes misted over too, no one else needed to know.

By the time Mack, their other roommate, came home, Jamie had mostly recovered. They had a private talk Nate didn't intrude on, and he hoped Jamie was telling Mack more than he'd told Nate even though he suspected he wasn't. They emerged from Mack's room a short while later, by which time Nate had food on the table. Mack gripped Nate's arm as he slipped past him to get a drink.

It should have been awkward, being there without Trevor. Technically, Trevor still lived with them. Most of his things were there, and he occasionally came back for a day or two at a time. He paid rent, and he wasn't planning on moving out officially until after Thanksgiving. But he was still trying to work through his complicated relationships with his boyfriend, Andre, and Marlie, who was having his baby and may or may not still have been his girlfriend. Nate was unclear on what sort of arrangement they had. He tried, and failed, not to judge them. It was only that he couldn't understand being in love with two people at once—he couldn't imagine wanting to share himself or a boyfriend that way.

Over their meal, they discussed the upcoming benefit event Mack was helping to plan. Andre volunteered part-time at his grandmother's health clinic and youth shelter. The clinic had a serious lack of funds, so the whole group was in the process of putting together the charity show. As they talked, Jamie slowly emerged from his earlier low and became more animated.

"So, Trev called," he said with enthusiasm. "He said Andre's friend from the bar—don't know if you remember him, he's the bouncer—is working on getting us a night. Probably sometime in November. Says he wants to do it before people get too busy with the holidays. So we have, like, six to eight weeks to plan this thing."

"That's not a whole lot of time," Mack commented. "I'm not sure I know enough people to participate." He snorted. "Could be mostly us playing for the whole night. I'm pretty sure no one wants that."

Jamie punched him in the arm, but he laughed. "We're not that bad. Are we?" He turned to Nate.

Nate shrugged. "You've improved." He was distracted, thinking about how Trevor had called Jamie and not him. Less than a year ago, things would have been different.

"Yeah, well, I don't think we're going to improve enough in six weeks to carry a whole benefit concert," Mack said.

"I can get some of my people to do something," Nate found himself saying.

"Opera?" Mack said, sounding incredulous.

Jamie socked him again. "That's a great idea!" he gushed. "People will love it. It's so...I don't know, kind of out there but in a good way."

"Gender-bent opera," Nate said, chuckling. "Yeah, we're definitely different."

"Well, there's two acts, then," Mack said. "I can have Andre ask Curtis about the regulars who perform on drag night, too. Surely some of them would be willing."

Nate hoped so. He'd seen them before, and they were good. An image of his favorite one sprang to mind—a queen with a full beard. Neatly trimmed, sure, but a beard nonetheless. She was gorgeous, too. Almost as tall as Nate and lean with long, long legs. He vaguely remembered her name was TaTa Latke, so he'd been expecting a bit more of a Jewish shtick. She didn't deliver it, though. The first time he'd seen her was during another benefit night at Grand Slam, the bar where Curtis worked. TaTa had been singing Annie Lennox songs. Nate kept it his little secret that he'd gone to see her regularly, especially after discovering her usual routine involved popular theater and her voice was incredible. She sometimes had a partner, a drag king. They were fun together, made hilarious by the fact that her partner was quite a bit shorter.

Mack broke into Nate's thoughts. "I wonder if Curtis could ask that guy who does Irish dance to come back. Holy fuckin' hell, he was hot. I've never seen anyone do that in a thong before. Damn, I'm sweating thinking about it."

His remark surprised Nate. Mack hadn't ever spelled anything out about his sexuality. He had a girlfriend, or possibly a friend with benefits, so Nate had made assumptions. Clearly he'd been wrong.

Jamie frowned. "He's one of my cousin's friends, actually. But he's kind of a snot."

"Who cares?" Mack argued. "Ask Brandon if he thinks his friend will do it." He grinned. "Preferably nearly naked again."

"Fine." Jamie scowled, and Nate wondered what had him so bent out of shape.

"Meanwhile, I'll talk to Gemma and Cassie about scheduling a few extra practices." They were in Mack and Jamie's band, keyboard and bass respectively.

Jamie nodded. "I'll see if Trevor can get Irina Clay-Jones, but I'm not sure if a rainbow-friendly bar alongside a bunch of drag queens and half-naked men is really the best place for gospel music." He snickered.

Nate laughed in spite of himself. "I don't know. There are plenty of queer Christians who might enjoy it. Plus, we definitely need some more lady talent up there, and I've been assured by people who like women that she's swoon-worthy."

"Amelia practically drools when she sings." Mack grinned. "God, sex afterward is so—"

Nate put up both hands. "Do not. Even. Say it."

Mack finished eating and put his dishes in the sink. He wasn't entirely being rude by not staying to help wash up. His regular job involved washing dishes, so they had an agreement it wouldn't be one of his household chores. Nate cleared the rest of the table, frowning when he noticed Jamie had barely eaten, but dismissing his surprise when he recalled what had happened earlier. He wouldn't have been in the mood either. Jamie helped him, leaving everything in the dish drainer. Nate spent a whole ten seconds contemplating drying them before deciding against it. Trevor would have been disappointed, but he wasn't there to complain or to clean up after them. They were doing better now that they couldn't rely on him, but their apartment had been a little scary for a bit.

Jamie escaped to his room, and Mack went out somewhere with Amelia, his whatever-she-was, leaving Nate alone in the living room. He flopped onto the couch and stretched out his long legs, leaning his head back. Before he had a chance to decide what movie to watch, he was fast asleep.

CHAPTER TWO

Israel "Izzy" Kaplan turned away from the radio and hollered over his shoulder, "Morales! Morales, get in here!"

A petite, dark-haired woman poked her head around the corner. "Yeah?"

"You're not going to fucking believe this." Izzy shook his head, chuckling. He couldn't hold back, and deep belly laughs rolled out of him.

"Kaplan, get it together." Val poked him in the side.

He composed himself, trying to keep a straight face despite the snicker filtering through. "We have a patient to pick up."

"And you're still sitting here because...?" She waved her hand at him.

"It's not an emergency."

"It's not like you to mock the homeless guy who keeps calling." Val's eyes narrowed in suspicion.

Izzy clammed up then cleared his throat. "Sorry. Not the homeless guy, either. You know I wouldn't make fun if it were. When haven't we gone to take care of him? It's something else."

Val huffed. "Yeah, okay. Get to the point already."

"We're supposed to go"—he laughed again—"pick up"—another snort—"a skeleton."

Val's face registered confusion. "Someone's been dead a long time."

"A real long time," Izzy agreed. "On the order of millions of years."

"Uh..."

He guffawed again. "We have to transport a fucking dinosaur. That's not a metaphor."

"Oh, you have got to be kidding me." Val grinned. "Well, my day just got about a thousand times more interesting. What are we waiting for?"

They pulled on their jackets and walked to the bay, both still snickering. The only reason given by dispatch was that the dinosaur was safer riding in an ambulance than being transported by cargo. In a weird way, it made sense. Izzy and Val were used to being gentle with the humans they brought to the emergency department. It would seem the researchers had drawn the conclusion they were more trustworthy than the local postal employees when it came to handling with care.

It wouldn't be the first time. Izzy had heard rumors of prior similar situations. He never thought he'd be the one driving an actual sack of bones, though. Being a smaller company, they didn't have the option to send a transport-only vehicle, so it was up to the two of them to get their charge to the hospital intact. At his side, Val blinked in the light and pulled her sunglasses down. They climbed in and set off for the research facility holding the dinosaur for pickup and transport to Mass General for x-rays.

Val messed with the radio, since they didn't have to worry about further calls while they were busy transporting Mr. Rex. Now he thought of it, Izzy hadn't asked what kind of beast their newest acquisition was. It could have been anything. Some song with a guy singing about what sounded like a hell of a blowjob came on. Izzy glanced at Val, who shrugged.

"What are you listening to?" he asked.

"It's like an off-brand Top Forty." She snickered. "They used to play this one on Christian radio, but now it's a mainstream hit because it's definitely not about the Good Lord."

"I can hear the lyrics. Did you just say this was on Jesus Radio?"

Val laughed harder. "Yes! It was popular in the spring. Pretty sure no one had a clue."

"Oh, I'm pretty sure they did." Izzy turned a corner. "I didn't know you were into religious music."

"You learn something new every day," Val quipped. "I grew up on that shit. I still like some of it, and this song is so great. Made even better after the guy singing it came out."

"He's gay?" Not that Izzy wouldn't have guessed, given that it was a man singing longingly about sucking off another man.

"Nah, he's bi." She grinned at Izzy's arched eyebrow. "And spoken for, unfortunately. Wonder if it's the guy from the song?"

"Hopefully." Izzy chuckled. "Why's it bad he's taken? Since I know you have no interest, were you planning to call the station in hopes of setting me up with him?"

"Shut up. I'm not that bad. Am I?"

"You are. But I love you anyway."

They pulled up to the parking attendant at the facility's restricted lot, and Izzy gave the details. The attendant raised the barrier, and they drove through. The buildings were arranged in such a way they looked like pods, grouped by letter with the buildings in each pod numbered. There was virtually no traffic in or out, and the whole place had a decidedly creepy feel to it like something out of a science fiction movie. Val called out letters as they passed, on the hunt for group J. They located it, and within it building 2, where they pulled up to a cargo bay.

It took close to an hour to load and secure the crate, which was large enough to fill the back of the ambulance. People in business casual attire and lab coats hovered the entire time they worked. Izzy didn't ask what kind of beast lay nestled in cedar shavings, preferring to rely on his imagination. He wondered if the public would ever see the dinosaur or if it would remain locked away in the lab to be studied until the bones turned to dust. He didn't ask that either.

At last he climbed back in beside Val, and they drove away from the facility. A van load of researchers tailed them. Val looked over her shoulder.

"Did you get a seriously weird vibe from those people?"

"Oh, yeah."

She shuddered. "Should I have stayed in back with our 'patient'?"

"Nah. I'm sure it's fine. Long as I drive carefully and don't go flying over a pothole or something."

She shrugged. "You're probably right. So, what were we talking about? Oh, yeah—my skills as a matchmaker."

"Don't flatter yourself, Yente," Izzy said with a snort. "You're worse than my mothers."

"Not possible."

Izzy eyed her sideways and burst out laughing. "Yeah, all right." He groaned. "It's fucking Friday. I'm supposed to have dinner with them tonight. Maybe you can work your magic before then? I think I trust your taste more than theirs."

"Nope. You're on your own. Sorry, man."

Izzy gave an amused shake of his head and merged onto the highway. Somehow, he would make it through dinner and his mothers' questions about when he might be ready to start dating again, citing his almost three years of being unattached since his divorce. At least Eema and Ma Rose were equal opportunity, as content to set him up with Sasha the Doctor as with Miriam the Cellist. They meant well, after all. One of these days, he might even take them up on the offer.

He kept his eyes on the road and half an ear on what Val was chattering on about, for the moment happy to enjoy an easy transport and good company. Any other thoughts about his mothers or matchmaking or his lack of love life were on hold for now, at least until they delivered Rexy to his appointment with the hospital radiology department.

When Izzy finally returned home after his shift, he made a beeline for the shower, half-stripping on his way and throwing everything into the hallway hamper. He adjusted the water and stepped under the spray, not muffling a drawn-out groan of relief as it hit his back. He thought thirty-six was far too young for his body to protest like this after every shift, desperately needing the hot water and the pounding of the massage setting on the shower head to quell the spasms in his lower back.

It had been happening all too frequently lately, both in his back and legs, and it bothered him. Not enough to have it looked at, but enough that he decided he had to get into better shape. He'd qualified for the Boston marathon and had signed up the day registration opened, and he needed to keep himself fit. He figured all the stiffness was his body's way of saying he hadn't run enough lately. It was true; he'd been working so many hours and had become a regular at Grand Slam over the summer as well.

He sighed at the thought of having to go back to being an occasional performer. Val wouldn't be pleased either. Izzy loved working with her, whether it was taking care of their hospital-bound charges or up on stage in drag. He hated the idea of disappointing her by backing out of their act. If he didn't whip his body back into shape, he wouldn't be able to dance in those heels, and even more than running the marathon, he couldn't bear the thought of giving up his night life. He needed to find more time, that was all. He pushed his concerns to the back of his mind. Right then, he needed to let the shower relax him enough to get a few hours' sleep. Being frustrated with himself wouldn't help.

In need of something to distract him, he thought about the opera he'd gone to see a few weeks ago. He'd already forgotten the name of the company, but they performed a gender-bent version of *Die Fledermaus*. All the roles were the same, but the cast had been in drag and used gender-swapped names. Izzy would need to dig out the program so he could see when their next opera would be. He did remember that much—they were doing Gilbert and Sullivan's *The Sorcerer*, and Izzy was curious how they would stage it.

Thinking about the opera brought to mind the gorgeous baritone who had played Falke. Everything about the man had given Izzy chills. He was huge—tall, muscular, broad-shouldered—and strikingly handsome, apparent even under the makeup. When he opened his mouth to sing, his voice was so rich and full it had nearly turned Izzy into a star-struck puddle right there in his seat. The friend who had accompanied him hadn't missed it and had teased Izzy mercilessly afterward. Izzy didn't even care. All he wanted was to see more of the sexy singer.

The memories caused Izzy's dick to react, and he gave in. A brief jerk-off in the shower would ease his tension, and he would be able to sleep off the haze once he got out. He didn't bother making it drawn-out or sensual. He simply stroked, one hand braced on the wall above the faucet. Enjoying the rush of impending release, he sped up his motion when he felt the pressure in his balls. He grunted, spurting toward the drain and then finally slowing his hand until he'd calmed down. After a minute, he straightened up, soaped himself, and rinsed everything away.

He shut off the water and stepped out, snagging a towel from the shelf over the toilet. Once he'd dried off, he wiped the mirror so he could see to neaten up his beard. It was one of the things which made his act unique—he didn't try to fully hide the person underneath. The beard was technically not a requirement for him, religiously speaking, but he felt a deeper connection with his ethnic and spiritual heritage by keeping it. He had to trim because of the fit of the mask for his full-time job, but he was allowed to keep it.

After finishing up and splashing water on his face, he pulled on a pair of boxer briefs and a t-shirt. A quick glance at his phone told him he had five hours until he needed to be at his mothers' house to share *Shabbat* supper with them. Eema might attend services beforehand, but he wouldn't go with her, and Ma Rose would likely stay home as well. Ma Rose wasn't quite as observant a Jew as Eema. Izzy headed for the bedroom, where he crawled under the blankets and sank into a deep sleep.

He was late. By the time he arrived at his mothers' house, Eema was lighting the candles. She stood before them, her head covered in an elegant scarf, wafting the light smoke of the candle as it drifted upward. Izzy closed the door as gently as he could then watched her, a smile on his lips. You could take a woman out of Orthodoxy, but you couldn't eradicate all traces from her life. Even as a little boy he'd been entranced by her graceful motion and the sound of her prayers as they left her lips. He was no less so now, despite all the times he'd seen her do it.

When she was through, she glanced over at Izzy. "You're late."

He chuckled. "I know, and I'm sorry. I overslept."

Eema glided over to him and reached up to pat his cheek. It was quite a distance; Eema was only five-foot-one, and Izzy was exactly a foot taller.

"You should get more sleep."

Leave it to Eema to state the obvious. Izzy knew better than to talk back to her, though. "I know. I'm trying."

"Good."

"Did you go to *Qabbalat Shabbat?*"

"Of course I did. You should come with me sometime. They have one for you young folk once a month, you know."

The statement carried the weight of its multiple implications, but Izzy only smiled. "Maybe I will, if I'm not working."

The table was already set, and Ma Rose brought out the last of the food, the homemade biscuits she'd been keeping warm. They sat down, and Izzy winced at the stiffness in his thighs. He really needed to get back into running. Unfortunately for him, Ma Rose's keen eyes didn't miss a thing. She arched an eyebrow.

"You okay?" she asked.

"Just a little stiff. It's nothing I can't cure with a good run." He picked up his fork and snagged a bite of chicken, using it to stall so he could speak without setting off a new round of questions. "I've been picking up extra shifts, so I haven't had as much time as I'd like." They were not to know he was referring to his night job.

"You work too hard," Eema chided. "Do something fun."

He laughed. "Running is fun! I need to be in shape for spring."

"Ah!" Ma Rose exclaimed, clasping her hands together. "I'd forgotten you registered for the Boston. You're in?"

"Yes. First time I've ever beaten the qualifying time by enough." He'd been as surprised as anyone when he clocked in under three in Chicago the previous year. It had been his best time in years.

They ate in silence for a while, and then Eema cleared her throat. "So, Lynne called me."

Izzy sighed. The subject of his ex-wife was always touchy. He didn't mind that she'd remained friends with his mothers; after all, the two of them had been able to become civil again in recent months. The ongoing news reel of her family life was draining, though. Izzy was glad she now had her family, but it did nothing to mitigate the emptiness and loss he felt.

"Oh?" he managed.

"You knew she was expecting again, right?"

"She hadn't said, no." The one thing Izzy hadn't been able to give her—or himself. He stabbed at a pea, not meeting Eema's gaze.

At least Ma Rose was in his corner. "Why are you bringing this up?" She waved a hand at Izzy. "You're upsetting him."

"Well, it was happy news!" Eema replied. "I like happy. And if it didn't work out between them, then at least—"

"Can you not talk about me like I'm not here?" Izzy snapped.

Both women looked toward him, and he shrank back. Eema must have had a reason for mentioning Lynne. It wasn't like her to bring up painful memories out of the blue.

"I'm sorry," he said. He took a deep breath. "It sounds like there's a story there."

Eema nodded. "So, anyway, she was at her appointment, and there was another woman there asking permission to put a flyer on the bulletin board in the lobby. Lynne asked to see it, and it was for a fundraiser show for a youth shelter."

Izzy frowned. "Okay, but what does that have to do with me?"

"Only that she told me all the details, and I wrote everything down. Maybe you'd like to participate."

Fork halfway to his mouth, Izzy froze. He slowly lowered his hand. "How—I mean—what are you talking about?"

"Your act."

"You know about that?" Izzy almost shouted.

"Of course I do." Eema smiled. "Did you think I wouldn't care about something so important to you?"

"I don't know," Izzy admitted. "I wasn't sure how you'd feel about it." He frowned. "How did you find out?"

"Do you remember Judith Rivken? Her daughter got married, and they had a party for her at a bar. I can't recall the name now."

"Grand Slam?" Izzy asked. He felt faint.

"That's the one," Ma Rose put in.

"Oh, shit," Izzy muttered. He propped his elbows on the table and put his head in his hands.

"That mouth!" Eema chided. "Anyway, we saw you."

Izzy groaned. "Did anyone else know it was me? And why the hell...heck...didn't you say something?"

"Well, I'm sure some of them guessed," Eema said. "Judith Rivken asked, and I told her I wasn't sure. Which is true, but Lynne confirmed it. That's why she called me about the fundraiser. She didn't realize you'd never told us."

"I can't believe this." Izzy sat back in his seat. "Mostly I can't believe you went to a bar, Eema." Despite his embarrassment, he chuckled. "How did you manage to get her there, Ma?"

Ma Rose laughed along with him. "It took a lot of convincing."

"I'll get you the information after dinner," Eema said, either oblivious to or ignoring the humor at her expense.

Dinner carried on, and conversation drifted. He'd known about the fundraiser, but he hadn't planned an act because he assumed it would mostly be people associated with the clinic. He would need to ask Rafael, the owner, if they were looking for more performers. If he could help out a youth shelter, he was all for it.

When they were through, Ma Rose stood up and made her way to the back deck while Izzy helped Eema clear the table. After Eema waved him off, he followed Ma Rose outside. She was seated in one of the patio loungers, cigarette in hand.

"That's gonna kill you one of these days," he remarked, plopping into the chair next to her.

"Not if your Eema gets to me first."

Izzy angled to look at her. "Everything okay?"

She shrugged. "What could be wrong for two old broads pushing sixty?"

They were quiet for a long time. Izzy lay back and looked up at the stars popping out in the deep purple sky. He inhaled the familiar, comforting scent of Ma Rose's cigarette while he listened to Eema moving around in the kitchen. He closed his eyes.

"She wanted to tell you before that we knew." Ma Rose's voice cut through the stillness.

"So, why didn't she?"

"I told her not to. Said you should tell us in your own time."

Izzy snorted. "Well, too late for that."

"Does your father know?"

"Why would he?" Izzy blew out a long breath. "It's not like he's going to drive here from New York to sit in a queer bar and watch me sing in a dress."

"He might."

Izzy turned his head to stare at Ma Rose. "Right. The man can't even be honest with himself after burying his own partner. You really think he'd be all right with me?" He swallowed. "With who I am?"

Ma Rose sighed. "There's a lot you don't know about him, Israel. Don't judge."

Izzy fell silent again. Ma Rose had been in his life for as long as he could remember. She was right; there was history among his parents, information they'd never shared with him except in bits and pieces. Maybe it didn't matter anyway. He focused on the current moment, wondering what had Ma Rose in a mood. Before he had a chance to ask, she spoke again.

"I'm fucking old, Iz," she said quietly.

"Nah, Ma. You're only as old as you feel, right?" He tried not to think about the way his thighs and back had been aching.

"Well, then, I feel old," she snapped. "I'm sorry. Just being moody." She laughed bitterly. "And I have no excuse anymore."

"I have no idea what you mean."

"I'm talking about the change," she said. "No more babies."

"You wanted to have a baby? At your age?" He cringed, realizing he'd confirmed for her that he, too, thought she was old.

"Of course not!" She stubbed out her cigarette. "I never wanted to be pregnant until I knew I'd never have the chance." She reached over and touched his hand. "I'm sorry, baby. I'm sorry we couldn't do more for you and Lynne. And I'm sorry Eema brought it up."

They'd never talked about it, the reason he and Lynne hadn't made it. Eema and Ma Rose had carefully danced around the subject, using phrases like "didn't work out" and "had some problems." But they'd never addressed the infertile elephant in the room, the ten years of marriage and countless doctor visits only to be told it was all his fault.

"You didn't do anything wrong," he said, hoping to comfort Ma Rose.

She smiled at him. "You're a good boy, Iz." She patted his cheek and changed the subject. "Are you going to do that fundraiser, then?"

"Yeah," he said. "I think I will."

"Good. We'll come see you."

"Ma!" he exclaimed, but he grinned, warmed all over by her support.

Ma Rose winked at him and lit another cigarette. Izzy lay back again, watching the smoke drifting toward the blackening sky.

CHAPTER THREE

On the commuter rail, Nate answered his cell phone halfway through his "You Draw Me In" ringtone. That was the song which had caused all the trouble—Trevor's Christian radio hit which was actually about the time Trevor sucked off his boyfriend in a bar bathroom. It was probably in poor taste to use it as Trevor's ring, given the fact that it was Nate's fault Trevor's life had gone sideways over the summer. Outing Trevor during the furor over the song hadn't been Nate's best move. Using it as his ringtone was his way of constantly reminding himself not to create drama anywhere but on stage if he wanted to keep his friendships intact. Trevor didn't know he was using it, seeing as he didn't call Nate while in his presence. What he wasn't aware of wouldn't hurt him.

The woman across the aisle from him on the train looked over and raised her eyebrows. Nate didn't know whether it was because she recognized the tune or because it was annoying her. He didn't care. He hit talk and put the phone to his ear.

"Hey," he said.

"Nate!" Trevor sounded excited about something. "You free for an early lunch?"

He was, in fact. He was going to the theater to have time alone for reading his notes on the scene they were blocking later, but he didn't have any other specific plans. It was his day off from his second job, which he assumed Trevor knew, as his schedule hadn't changed in nearly two years.

"Yeah, I'm free." Nate tried to sound casual, not like someone who was desperate to see his one-time best friend who he'd been missing since he screwed up.

"Cool. Where d'you want to meet?"

"I'm heading for the theater."

"I'm going the opposite direction. We had the early shift at the recording studio." Nate could almost hear Trevor making a face; he wasn't much of a morning person. "I'm at the Lighthouse now. There's a couple of places nearby where we could meet."

The Lighthouse was the shelter and clinic run by Andre's grandmother in North Quincy. Trevor probably had a reason to be there, something related to Marlie or Andre. Nate didn't pretend their relationship made any sense at all to him. If and when he ever found Mr. Right, he was a one-man kind of guy.

"Okay, fine. I'm nearly there, so I'll see you soon."

"Sounds good."

The call ended, and Nate sat there staring at his phone. The woman who had been eying him smiled in a knowing way, so Nate tried to give her a "what the hell" look. She laughed.

"Your ringtone," she said. "I love that song."

"I'm thrilled for you," Nate snapped back. He blew out his breath and tried again. Maybe Del was right about his moodiness of late. "Sorry. What I meant to say was, my friend wrote it. I was talking to him just now."

"Oh, my god! You know Trevor Davidson?" she positively squeaked. She got up and moved to sit next to him. "So, funny story. I sometimes like to put on Christian radio while I'm cleaning the house. My husband is one of those ex-evangelicals, so he doesn't listen to that kind of music normally, but he tolerates it for me. He basically said from the beginning that the song was about..." She had a lot to say on the subject, but Nate more or less tuned her out until she said, "...so when Trevor got outed on the radio, my husband was all like, 'yeah, could've told you that myself.'" The woman laughed. "And you know him personally?"

Nate gritted his teeth and said, "I was responsible for the whole mess."

Her eyebrows shot up. "No kidding."

"None at all," he told her. He leaned back against the seat, ignoring her even though she was still sitting far too close for his liking. He rubbed his temples, trying to clear the headache he now had brewing.

"Hey," the woman said, and Nate opened his eyes to look at her. "I'm sorry. I didn't mean to upset you. I was excited, that's all. You okay?"

Nate nodded. "I'm on my way to see Trevor now." Del's assessment of him returned, and he thought it might be time to do something nice for someone instead of being a cranky asshole. "Which stop are you heading for?"

"Quincy," she said.

"If you have time, you can come with me to meet him. We're having lunch there, near the Lighthouse. It's this clinic where his girlf—boyf—oh, fuck it, someone works there."

She looked amused at Nate's fumbling, but she said, "I know the Lighthouse. I live in Quincy. Sure, I'll walk with you." She smiled.

"Terrific." Nate thought he might have accomplished a not-too-terrifying smile of his own.

They were interrupted by hearing their stop called. Nate collected his bag from the overhead rack, and the woman stood up as well. As soon as the train stopped, Nate headed for the exit. He glanced over his shoulder to see if she had followed and slowed down, realizing she might have trouble keeping up. He had several inches of height on her. He was surprised when he turned around and almost ran into her.

She grinned. "I'm a marathoner," she said. "I'm used to keeping up the pace."

Nate laughed, feeling lighter than he had in a while. He surprised himself by discovering he liked this woman; she may have been one of Trevor's fangirls, but there was something about her which seemed refreshingly different from some of the others.

They stepped off the train and made their way from the station to the Lighthouse. It was quite a distance, and Nate tried to slow down in the interest of not forcing his companion to speed-walk there. She didn't seem to mind, clearly in good shape herself. They arrived at the clinic, where Trevor was waiting outside. He held up a hand in greeting to Nate.

"Hey," Nate said. "So...we met on the train, and this young lady wanted to see you in person."

Trevor's eyebrows rose, and his mouth dropped open. He recovered quickly and extended a hand. "Nice to meet you."

"Because of your song," she said.

"Oh." Trevor tensed visibly.

"I love it!" she enthused. "I was really excited to hear you're working with Irina Clay-Jones now. And that she's one of us." She grinned and winked at him.

Trevor's posture relaxed, and he smiled back. "Yeah, she's terrific. As cool in person as she is on the radio."

"Listen, I won't keep you from whatever, but it was so great meeting you." The woman pulled off her Red Sox cap. "Will you sign my hat?"

"Sure." Trevor took a pen from his pocket and drew his scrawling autograph at the edge of the brim. He handed it back.

"Hey, thanks!" She put the cap on and turned around, waving at them as she took off down the street.

Trevor turned to Nate. "Lunch?"

"Sounds good." As they walked, Nate asked, "How's everything?" He didn't know how to convey *I'm sorry for being a fuck-up* and *I miss hanging out with you*. He supposed he could have said those things, but they sounded needy and pathetic in his head.

"Pretty good." He frowned. "Marlie's had a bit of trouble with the pregnancy, and they were considering bed rest, but she seems to be doing all right for now."

"How about Andre?" It pained Nate to ask. It wasn't a secret he didn't have warm feelings for Andre.

Trevor eyed him, his suspicion obvious. "He's good. Why?"

Nate stopped walking. "I'm trying, Trev. He's someone you care about." He blew out his breath. "Why did you ask me to lunch?"

"Can't I want to catch up with you?"

"No. Not after everything that's happened."

Trevor grimaced. "Yeah, all right. I wanted to talk to you about the benefit for the Lighthouse." He started walking again, and Nate fell in step with him.

"You could have talked to me about it on the phone." He wouldn't bring up the fact that Trevor had called Jamie instead.

"Yeah, I could. But you know what? Maybe I wanted to see you, find out if we could put this shit behind us." He looked up at Nate.

Nate didn't say anything for a few minutes, thinking about his answer. He wasn't sure how to move on or even what had happened to cause the rift in the first place. It wasn't only his actions over the summer. The divide had been widening for a long time, even before they'd moved in together nearly a year ago.

"It'll be good to catch up without it hanging over us," Nate said.

Trevor appeared relieved, and Nate figured his response had been good enough. When they reached the quiet restaurant Trevor had chosen, Nate held open the door then followed him in. He took a moment while his eyes adjusted to the dim light, composing himself and preparing to lay the past to rest. The hostess showed them to their seats, and they slid into the booth. Nate could do this; he could have a not-awkward conversation with Trevor, hear about the fundraiser, and promise to be more involved. Trevor was right— the past was in the past.

He opened his menu. "So, what's good here?"

Lunch had been surprisingly relaxed once Nate let go of his worry. Good food, good conversation about the Lighthouse. Trevor had been pleased about Nate asking a few of his people to perform some familiar songs. There was no question Del would want to. Nate hadn't dared ask Trevor about the drag queens and whether they would be there, especially TaTa. He hadn't worked out how to casually bring it up in a way which didn't raise Trevor's suspicions.

Afterward, Trevor had left to meet up with some of the other musicians he worked with. Nate was at loose ends for a bit. He no longer felt much like going to the theater, not even to play with potential staging and certainly not to clean up after everyone. He checked the time. Kids from the Queer Youth Choral Society wouldn't be there for a couple more hours to practice. Nate reconsidered, deciding there wasn't any reason he couldn't go there and look through the theater's library for sheet music. He would need to come up with some kind of plan for their act at the benefit night. He headed for the train station with a few ideas in mind.

Nate leaned back in his seat, not even checking messages or social media on his phone. He closed his eyes for what he thought was only a moment but turned out to be a lot longer—which was how he realized he'd missed his stop. With a frustrated groan, he checked the station. He was a long way from the theater. He browsed his phone to see if he had any reason to be closer to this side of the city, glaring at the screen when he discovered he might as well backtrack. Sliding his phone back into his pocket, he stood up as the train slowed.

He exited onto the street, not in a hurry to ride the other direction right away. There were some coffee shops nearby, but Nate made himself at home on the steps of one of the buildings. He would eventually need to get back on the train, but he hadn't really wanted to be at the theater in the first place. He pulled out his phone and stared at the dark screen for a long time. Del's ribbing still rankled, even days later, but there was some truth to it. Nate was perfectly content to take care of business by himself, so that wasn't the problem. The real issue was the constant feeling of being alone while everyone around him was paired off.

Dating apps had never appealed, mainly because Nate wasn't generally interested in hooking up, but Del had assured him he knew a number of people who had found a long-term match that way. Maybe Nate could locate someone who was bored on his lunch hour and wanted a cup of coffee and some casual conversation. He was about to open an app when a shadow fell across him. He looked up, shielding his eyes. A well-dressed man carrying a briefcase was on his way up the steps.

Their eyes met, and recognition struck both of them almost simultaneously—Nate saw his own realization reflected in the other man's face. His mouth dropped open, and he scrambled to stand up.

"Nate?" The man gaped at him. "Nate Kingsley?"

"R-Rocco Alessi," Nate answered.

His heart sped up at the sight of his high school boyfriend. Rocco at twenty-four was even more strikingly handsome than Nate had remembered him at eighteen. A tsunami of memories, good and bad, hit him. Rocco had been his first everything—first official boyfriend, first sex, first "I love you," first person to smash his heart into smithereens. Even now, years later, he had the ability to turn Nate into a pile of awestruck goo with a single glance while simultaneously causing him to ache with dashed hope.

Rocco looked Nate up and down, making him flush for his jeans and faded t-shirt. "I wasn't expecting to run into you. It's been a long time. What have you been up to?"

There were a lot of years since the last time they'd seen each other, and Nate wasn't sure how to answer the question. "That could take a while," Nate said. "Six years' worth of life happened in there."

"God. That long?" Rocco sounded regretful.

Nate shrugged one shoulder. "Since high school."

"Wow, yeah." Rocco set his briefcase on the steps and put his hands in his pockets. "You still in touch with the old crew?"

"Not really, except for Trevor Davidson. You remember him?"

"Yeah." Rocco smiled darkly. "Heard what happened to him, too. Hell, I wish I'd known back then he was...well, anyway. Are you two a thing now?"

He sounded so casual about his interest in Trevor. Rocco was a far cry from the boy who had dumped Nate and told his parents he'd been confused. Nate swallowed a snide reply, recalling how it had been at least partly his responsibility. He'd wanted more than Rocco could give. Still, he didn't feel bad squashing any notions Rocco might have.

"No, there's nothing going on between us. Trevor's a friend, and he's seeing someone." Two someones, but Nate didn't have Trevor's permission to explain further.

"Hm. How about you, then? You with anyone?"

Nate couldn't interpret Rocco's tone of voice. "No," he said.

"Ah." Rocco paused then asked, "What are you doing here, anyway?"

Nate wasn't sure what Rocco meant, and it made him defensive, as though he had to stand up for his right to be in that part of the city. He started to say something of the sort in response, but he saw Rocco had caught his own error.

"Sorry," he said, his face reddening. "I didn't mean it like that. I just can't picture you working in the financial district—it doesn't seem like it would suit you."

It wouldn't, not like Nate's older brother. Dean was the one with all the business sense. Nate shook his head and said simply, "I missed my stop, and I was taking a break before catching another train. What about you?"

Rocco's confusion melted into an amused smile. "I work here. This is my father's building."

Nate glanced at the glass door and choked back a groan. *Giuseppe Alessi and Co.* was in bright gold lettering. "I wasn't even paying attention to where I sat."

"I'm glad you didn't. Definitely made my afternoon more interesting." Rocco laughed, sending a delicious ripple through Nate's belly. "Need a ride somewhere?"

"Uh..." Nate couldn't fathom why Rocco wanted to do him the favor. "I don't want to put out. Shit...I mean put *you* out." He could almost hear Del-in-his-head snickering.

Rocco's eyes lit up, and he looked like he was trying to hold back his laughter. "It's no trouble. I finished up a lunch meeting and was headed back to pick up some papers. I'm working from home the rest of the afternoon."

"Wouldn't want to hold you up."

"I told you, it's not a problem. Besides, we can catch up a bit more on the ride." Rocco's disarming grin appeared, the one he'd used to melt Nate when they were dating. It was still irresistible.

"Okay," Nate said. "That would be great, thanks."

Being underdressed for the occasion, Nate waited on the steps for Rocco to dash in and get what he needed. He reappeared a few minutes later, and they headed for the parking garage. It wasn't a long walk to Rocco's car, and neither of them said much on the way. Once they were settled inside the vehicle, Rocco turned to Nate.

"Where are you headed?"

"Dyer Theater."

"Oh, I know where that is. Still performing, huh? You always were into it." Rocco smiled at him then backed out of the parking space. "Won a lot of awards, if I recall."

"Yeah."

Not the right kind, though. Not like Dean. Nate wasn't an athlete. He hadn't earned a big basketball scholarship or been valedictorian. Instead, he'd earned the right to be compared to his brother until he was old enough to earn his own titles—ones that would never be good enough in their parents' eyes. He slid down in his seat, wondering why Dean was on his mind all of a sudden.

To avoid dwelling on him, Nate changed the subject. "What about you? What have you been up to?" He swallowed thickly. "Heard you got married." He kept it to himself that he'd heard it from a man Rocco had been involved with.

"I did," Rocco confirmed. "Got separated, too. Also got served with divorce papers." He kept his head facing forward, but Nate caught his glance out of the corner of his eye.

"I'm sorry." Nate's gaze flicked to Rocco's left hand. There was still a ring there.

Rocco didn't miss it. "Yeah, well, it's not final, but it's a matter of time."

Nate wondered if it meant Rocco was ready to be honest with himself. He didn't ask. They pulled up to the theater, and Nate made to get out, but Rocco put a hand on his arm. Nate's skin tingled where Rocco's fingers lay, and he strained not to shiver in pleasure at the touch and the memories it stirred.

"Wait," Rocco said. "Can I come see?"

It was a strange request, and Nate didn't know what to make of it. "You want to pay six bucks to park and look inside for five minutes?"

Rocco tilted his head. "Yeah. Why the hell not? I don't have much going on."

He removed his hand, causing Nate to regret the loss of contact. He settled back into his seat, and Rocco drove around to the theater's small parking lot. They entered the theater through the back, via the stage entrance. Nate led Rocco down the long, twisting hallway and up into the main lobby. It was a tomb in there—the only people inside were the ones working in security and ticket sales. Nate waved to the young woman at the booth, who waved back before returning to the book she had in her hand.

"Well, this is it," Nate said. "The Dyer Theater."

It was old, and while not in disrepair, it hadn't been updated in years. Nate was hardly showing Rocco the latest in theater design, modern and polished. He'd never felt embarrassed about where he worked before, but now, under Rocco's scrutiny, Nate's cheeks burned. He didn't want Rocco to feel sorry for him for working in a place that barely paid to keep the lights on.

"I like it," Rocco said quietly, and the words warmed Nate's belly. "Can you show me anywhere else in here?"

"Sure." Nate was about to ask why, but Rocco had become distracted by studying the old posters on the walls.

"Were you in these?" he asked.

"Some, yeah."

"Wow. This is...I don't know. I've never seen anything like it. I love the feel of the history here."

The words gave Nate a rush of pride. "Come on," he said. "I'll show you the upstairs."

The second floor housed storage for old costumes, props, and set pieces they might repurpose. Everything for the current show was down below, in the wing behind the stage where the dressing rooms were located. The top floor had all the classrooms.

Nate pushed open the door to the props room. When he'd taken over, the first order of business had been to collect a crew of volunteers and organize everything. There were floor-to-ceiling shelves, and everything was organized by type. Nate was proud of what they'd done with the room, making it easier to find what they needed.

"Here's where all the details happen," Nate said. "We have a really creative team who can make things out of nearly anything..."

He continued talking, pointing things out to Rocco. While he spoke, absorbed in explaining his work, he was distracted enough to miss Rocco coming up behind him until he felt warm breath on his neck. It sent delicious shivers up and down his spine.

"You've really done a lot with this, I can tell," Rocco murmured.

Nate turned to face him. "I've had a lot of help."

"I'm glad you're doing so well now." Rocco's voice was smooth, refined.

Nate moved in. "I do all right."

Rocco's hands moved up to touch Nate's biceps. "You do indeed. I'm sorry I let so much time go by after high school."

"Uh...me too." Nate was now having trouble forming words.

Rocco smiled, and there was something sad in his eyes. "You surprised me back then, you know. That someone like you wanted to hang out with me."

"Why wouldn't I? You were—" Startled, Nate stopped himself before he said something foolish, like "the hottest guy at school," especially since that was hardly what Nate had loved most about him.

Seeming to read Nate's mind, Rocco chuckled. "I know what everyone said about me back then. Of course, they didn't know..." He trailed off and shook his head. "Anyway, I thought you had a thing for Trevor, but then he was always with Marlie."

"Still is," Nate muttered.

"What?" Rocco gave him a strange look.

"Nothing. Go on."

"And then you let me kiss you." He laughed again. "Thought I was going to explode right then and there."

"I wanted to do it sooner, but I assumed you were straight. Or that you wouldn't give me the time of day, but then we had that Shakespeare class together and you asked me to help you."

Rocco shook his head and his expression turned wistful. "It was an excuse. You were Mr. Big Star. In every single school play, you already had that incredible voice. I played soccer and studied a lot."

"It worked out okay for us back then."

"Until it didn't," Rocco agreed, taking a step closer. "I've always regretted how we ended things."

Nate wanted to say he felt the same way, that he'd never fully gotten over the devastation of Rocco breaking his heart. Even so, he'd have taken him back in an instant if Rocco had only said the word. Now here he was, right in Nate's personal space and implying he was asking for his second shot. Nate couldn't speak for fear of shattering the moment. He opened his mouth, but no sound came out.

Rocco continued. "You were on my mind a lot. I wanted to ditch everything and come back to you, but I couldn't. Not then." He touched Nate's cheek then moved his hand around to the back of Nate's head.

If Nate had any confusion over Rocco's intent, it was gone the minute his other palm rested on Nate's hip. Nate moved forward slowly, his heart thumping so hard he was sure Rocco could hear it in the stillness of the room. Rocco had always had intense power over Nate's mind—and other parts of him—which were magnified in his adult self. It was impossible to tell how much of Nate's current state was due to lack of companionship, as Del had said, and how much was down to Rocco's appeal.

"Yeah," he replied, out of any other words for the moment.

He licked his lips and stepped closer. Del's advice rolled around in Nate's head, and he considered asking Rocco if he wanted to go somewhere else. Before he had a chance, Rocco leaned forward, and a moment later, they were kissing like it was their oxygen. Rocco backed Nate up until he hit an empty section of wall next to a shelf full of fake food. Nate angled himself, sliding down against the wall a bit so Rocco could reach. He only had about four inches on Rocco's height, but it was enough Nate had to adjust. Rocco didn't seem to mind, diving back into their kiss with a groan.

They bit and licked at each other, rolling their hips together with increasing pressure. Nate shoved Rocco's suit coat off his shoulders, and Rocco shrugged out of it without breaking lip contact. Rocco tore his mouth away and dragged Nate's t-shirt up and over his head while Nate yanked Rocco's shirt out of his trousers. Their kisses were interspersed with grunts and panting as they struggled to keep going and undress at the same time.

By the time they had both stepped out of their pants and underwear, Nate was sure he wouldn't even make it to actual coupling. It had been so long he thought he'd probably come the second Rocco's hand was on him. Fortunately, Rocco wasn't in any better shape.

"Wait." Rocco grunted and backed off, bracing his hand on the wall next to Nate.

After a moment, they resumed their kissing and groping, slowing down the pace a fraction. Nate was beyond ready. He reached down between them to grip them both. Rocco's hand on his wrist halted his progress.

"Turn around," he said. "I want to be inside you."

Nate shook his head, about to say they shouldn't, not there in the props room. Except he was long past the point of caring where they did it. This was good enough. Nate was still horny as hell and wanted Rocco. Having him inches away, ready to do glorious things to Nate, brought back another torrent of memories. He didn't know where it would lead them—back to the beginning, maybe, a chance to start fresh. Whatever else, it would take the edge off. He spun around and angled himself at a good height for Rocco, bracing his hands on the wall. Rocco rained kisses down Nate's neck and shoulders, kneading his ass cheeks and then running a finger down the crack. Nate groaned and pressed back against him.

"Shit...I don't have supplies in here."

"Hang on," Rocco murmured against Nate's neck. He backed off and bent down to grab his trousers, pulling out a squeeze tube of some kind of lip balm. "This'll do."

"Perfect," Nate said. "I'd hate to cut this short." He grinned over his shoulder, hoping to inspire Rocco to get on with things. "Condom too?"

"Damn it. No." Rocco leaned in close again. "No problem. I'll pull out. I'm always dry till I come."

Nate almost laughed at him for saying something so odd, but it turned into a lazy groan when Rocco swirled a slick finger around his hole. Any objections were forgotten the moment he pushed it inside, reaching around with his other hand to tug on Nate's erection until they were both back to panting. While Rocco worked him, Nate grabbed a cloth napkin out of a bin on the shelf next to them. Rocco's laughter was breathless.

"What the hell are you doing?"

"Don't want—" Nate groaned. "—to get jizz on the props shelves."

They were both still chuckling when Rocco withdrew his fingers to replace them with his cock. Nothing else mattered except being as close as possible to each other. Everything blurred into needy grunts and aroused groans, Rocco's chest pressed against Nate's back, damp with sweat. Rocco swore loudly and withdrew so fast it made Nate gasp. A moment later, wet heat hit the small of Nate's back.

Rocco's shaking, slippery fingers slid between Nate's ass cheeks, finding their way inside him again. Nate's breathing sped up until he was almost hyperventilating, and at last he let out one long, whining moan as he jerked himself to orgasm with Rocco still spasming against him.

Nate took shallow, shuddering breaths until the wall in front of him swam back into focus as Rocco pulled his fingers out. He blinked a few times to clear the spots then turned around. He wiped most of the mess away with the cloth napkin and handed it to Rocco.

"Thanks." Rocco tossed it aside and began picking up his clothes. "Somewhere I can tidy up a bit more?" he asked.

The sudden change from hot coupling to businesslike put a damper on Nate's post-coital mood. He turned his back to Rocco again so as not to let his hurt show. "Yeah, if you don't mind walking your bare ass down the hall. There's a couple of bathrooms. Don't worry—there's no one here during the day."

Rocco shrugged and stepped toward the door. He paused, gave Nate a heated look, and leaned in for a steamy kiss. He slapped him on the ass before leaving the props room. The affectionate gesture warmed Nate as he followed, gathering his trail of clothes on the way and feeling distinctly unfresh but relaxed and happy.

They didn't say anything while they cleaned up and got dressed. Nate stole glances at Rocco every now and again, but Rocco's attention was focused on straightening himself out. He buttoned his shirt and tucked it in, and Nate turned to face him. He wondered where they went from here. Coffee? Dinner for two? Nate had been too wrapped up in other things to figure out the particulars beyond the moment. He wondered if Del would be proud or exasperated that Nate got the sex out of the way before the awkward part.

"I should go," Rocco said, breaking into Nate's thoughts.

"Of course." Nate paused, searching for something which wouldn't make him sound clingy. "How about you call me? Wouldn't mind doing this again sometime."

Rocco sighed. "Look, this isn't really a good time for me. It was great catching up, but...well, I'm sure you understand."

"Understand what?" Nate frowned, his joy fading.

"I'm separated but not divorced, and I'm not out at work. I can't have something my ex can trace back and use against me, like an old boyfriend's phone number."

"Ah, right." The same old story, six years later.

"But you could call me at this number." Rocco pulled out his wallet and supplied Nate with a business card. Then he leaned in and kissed the corner of his mouth. "I'm glad I ran into you."

"Sure, yeah," Nate answered. "I'll walk you out."

They descended the stairs and followed their footsteps in reverse to the theater entrance. Rocco gave Nate one last suggestive glance before turning around and heading for the parking lot. Nate stared at his back until he disappeared around the corner.

He should have known it wouldn't be as easy as picking up where they'd left off. If he'd been using the rational part of his brain, he would have. He probably wouldn't have changed anything he'd done, but at least he'd have had the good sense not to get his hopes up too soon. Nate had never been good at no-strings sex. Not with Trevor, not with Rocco, and not with anyone else he'd had in his bed. Not that there had been many; at heart, Nate was a hopeless romantic who wanted to go to sleep and wake up next to the same person every day.

Something loosened in his chest. Rocco may not have given him much—all right, the orgasm was pretty good—but he'd cleared something up for Nate. He wasn't wired for casual or hookups, especially not with someone who wasn't in a position to be open about himself. He needed a different kind of connection. He looked down at the card still in his hand. Was Rocco worth the wait? Slipping the card into his pocket, Nate decided he might be willing to see him again and find out.

For no good reason, his mind wandered to TaTa Latke, and he sighed. She was a fantasy; Nate didn't even know the person under the costume and makeup. Rocco might not be ready to pick out curtains, but he was real. Nate went back inside and headed up the stairs toward the library, his mind on how soon he could call Rocco and ignoring the part of him which suggested he'd be better off letting Del set him up with someone else.

Chapter Four

Izzy ran. Pavement disappearing under his feet. Sweat dripping down his back. The pounding of his heart and the rush of air in and out, controlled and measured. Cool air against his damp skin, a light breeze. Shadows and sunlight alternating as he wove through the neighborhood.

There wasn't anything like the high of a good run, in Izzy's opinion. He'd been chasing his own personal best since he was eight years old and attended a summer camp with track and field events. He felt fully alive when he was running, every part of him engaged in the freedom of flying. Almost nothing gave him so much pleasure.

Except today. It had been too long since he'd had a lengthy run, busy with work and the club. He tried to take it easy, going for a shorter route and a slower pace. It didn't help; he was already sore after the first couple of miles, his back throbbing and his thighs stiff. Izzy slowed to a walk then stepped to the side under the shade of a building. He stretched again, feeling things pop he hadn't before. It all made him feel old and out of shape. He knew it wasn't true, since he'd at least kept up with all the other parts of his fitness routine. He'd even been running; it had simply been shorter distances. Still, he couldn't help the sense of betrayal by his body.

Izzy resumed his run, determined to get in at least five miles.

The plan to make up for his lax habits was to increase his distance every day until he was back up to his full abilities. Now it looked like it might take longer than he'd anticipated to get there. He poured himself into his run, concentrating on letting go of all the tension in his life of late. As he focused on his breathing, his stress leeched out with his sweat, releasing into the cool morning air. At last he relaxed and settled into a comfortable, steady pace. There it was, the energy he'd been lacking.

He returned to his apartment afterward to shower and change for work, feeling better than he had in some time. Even though he still felt the burn in his muscles, he took it as a sign he'd been right and that he simply needed to step up his training. If he followed the same steps he had before, he would be ready for the marathon in plenty of time, not to mention the two half-marathons he'd entered before then. He grabbed his bag and headed out to the station.

Half a day's work later, he and Val were enjoying a late lunch—or early dinner—together in the break room, finally back at the station after several draining calls. Some news show droned in the background, but Izzy ignored it. His mind was still on his conversation with his mothers about the charity show. He leaned forward and lowered his voice.

"Eema and Ma Rose told me about another benefit night at Grand Slam. Are you in?"

Val shrugged one shoulder. "Sure, if we're not on call."

"We're not, as far as I can tell from the schedule."

"All right." She straightened up. "On a different subject, I'm seeing someone."

"Oh?" Izzy grinned. "Who is she? Anyone I would know?"

"Nope. Met her through a friend." Val gave him a sly smile. "I could set you up. She has a sister and a brother."

"Her brother's interested in men?"

"I'll bet he could be persuaded."

Izzy rolled his eyes. "It doesn't work like that."

Val laughed. "I was kidding. I doubt Tamara's brother is available anyway. Her sister, though..." She trailed off with a wink.

She meant well, but Izzy shook his head. "I don't think so." He concentrated on his lunch, not wanting to look her in the eye.

"Hey," Val said. "I don't have to, you know. There's no hurry. I just thought maybe I'd offer."

"It's okay."

It wasn't so much that he wasn't ready. Izzy didn't feel any need to put himself on a timeline, and he was far enough removed from the slow and painful death of his marriage he could acknowledge what he was missing. Right now, though, he couldn't put into words how Lynne's second pregnancy had sent him right back to the headspace he'd been in while they were together. It would be easier to date someone who didn't have expectations about what it might one day mean for them, but he wasn't sure he was ready for that either. He hadn't been with anyone but Lynne since they got together. He didn't know if he remembered how.

Val tilted her head and watched him for a few minutes. "You usually play along or give me shit for trying to set you up. What's the matter?"

"It's nothing."

"No, it's not." Val sat back. "Come on, give."

Izzy decided he might as well tell her. "Lynne's pregnant again. Already."

"Oh, Iz." Val reached across the table and put her hand on his. "You all right?"

"I will be. It's not like I have to see her every day or deal with it. Eema told me about it, but Lynne didn't call me herself until a couple of nights ago. She said she would rather I not hear it from rumors, as though I'd still be welcome in her social circles now that we're not together. I don't even attend temple with my mothers anymore because of her family. Besides, it was too late."

"God. She really does have some nerve."

"It's not like that. We've tried to keep things friendly because we know too many of the same people. She's trying to do the right thing and spare me from other people gossiping. I'm not sure anymore whether I care what she's up to, but she hasn't caught on yet."

Val got up to throw away her trash. "This is why I suggested setting you up. She can't have this power over you every time something happens with her. You're not part of her life anymore, and she needs to wake up and realize it's not your concern."

"I know. Eema and Ma Rose mean well too, and I'm sure if I were involved with someone else, they would stop dragging me into it as well. I don't want to have to go meet people with that in mind, though."

"If this is all because you know the same people, maybe you need some new friends." Val arched an eyebrow.

Izzy looked away. He couldn't explain to Val the ways in which his family life was intimately tied to other members of his community, in part because of the choices his mothers made. They couldn't go back to where they'd come from and relied on their friends and neighbors from Temple Shomrei Sholom. Maybe he was exaggerating the extent to which he was unwelcome, but he didn't like being eyed with pity over the collapse of his union with Lynne. He'd grown up with these people, including Lynne's family. Even though he'd blanched at the idea of an entire group of his mothers' friends discovering his night life, he knew none of them would care or hold it against him. Judith Rivkin's daughter married another woman, after all, and Eema's rabbi and the *rebner*—his husband—had a houseful of kids and a menagerie of pets.

The realization Eema and Ma Rose's social circle was probably talking about his alter ego amused him. He turned a huff into a chuckle. "Maybe I do need to expand my world. Should I try online dating?"

"Ugh, no." Val punched his shoulder. "You saw how well that worked for me. I had to find my girlfriend the old-fashioned way."

"Good point. Speaking of that, when do I get to meet your new woman?"

"Soon," Val promised. "We'll all get together. Meanwhile, let's go plan for that other thing." She raised an eyebrow.

"Ah, yeah. Well, I did have a couple of ideas for it." He stood up.

Val linked her arm through his. "Tell me all about it so I can reject them all before I deliver the perfect act."

Still laughing, they exited the break room to find a quieter spot to work.

Nate was almost too blissed-out to notice when Rocco's phone rang. Through his sleepy haze, Nate felt motion next to him. He rolled over and admired the curve of Rocco's ass as the sheet slipped to reveal it when he reached over to the nightstand.

"This is Rocco." Pause. "Yes, that would be fine." Pause. "I'm with a client right now, but I can set it up after my meeting." His eyes flicked to Nate. "No, that's not possible." He covered the phone with his hand and whispered, "Be right back."

He rose from the bed and stalked into the bathroom. For a moment, it was quiet, and then he heard Rocco's muffled voice. He sounded angry, and Nate caught a few words like "let's not do this now" and "we'll discuss it later" and "it's not a good time."

Rocco opened the bathroom door and stepped out. "I'll call you back shortly." He ended the call and set the phone back on the nightstand then lay back down on the bed. "Sorry about that." He ran his hand over Nate's chest and kissed him.

Nate shrugged, but his gut twisted. Del's words haunted him, his advice on which men to avoid. He was nothing more than a "client" for now, someone Rocco could write off to his wife—whether or not she was really soon to be his ex—as a lunch meeting. How many other "clients" had Rocco had before, hotel bills he claimed were just drinks at the bar to entertain a business associate? Nate thought back to their first encounter, how easy it was to find Rocco and how he'd been eager to go with Nate even though he claimed he couldn't be caught with an old boyfriend's phone number. They'd been meeting up regularly for close to a month with no indication from Rocco where it was going. Nate recalled his acquaintance who had claimed a two-year affair with Rocco. He wondered how many others there had been.

It was a sobering thought, one which brought on a new rush of worries he dismissed. "It's fine," he said, even though he really wanted to ask Rocco a few pointed questions.

Rocco didn't miss the bitterness. "I already told you I'm not ready to be open about us. You'll have to give me some time. Once the divorce is final, it won't be such a hassle."

He leaned over and kissed Nate then began a slow path down his neck. Nate shivered, and Rocco's lip curved upward in response. He raised his eyes, keeping them on Nate's as he traveled lower. It hadn't even been fifteen minutes; there was no way Nate's dick would cooperate so soon, but it wouldn't stop Rocco from trying. Nate tipped his head back against the pillow and tried to relax into Rocco's touch.

He couldn't, though. Not when his mind was still on the phone call and how disjointed their relationship felt. All the hopes he'd pinned on imagining one day Rocco would tell him it was over, he was free of his ex-wife, vanished with a single conversation. The only reason Nate stayed was his futile effort to fall back in love with Rocco. In four weeks, the only thing he'd been successful at was putting off a genuine search for Mr. Right.

Maybe there was something wrong with him. Del seemed perfectly content to be in and out of anyone's bed, and he couldn't recall ever seeing Trevor so happy now that he was with both Andre and Marlie. Mack had whatever his arrangement was with his semi-girlfriend. Only Jamie was miserable, and that was probably because The Boyfriend was the definition of an asshole. Why was Nate the only one who felt dread at the thought of fumbling through the misadventures of dating and sex? Wasn't that what his twenties were supposed to be about? He ought to be bucking societal norms like Andre and Trevor or living a free-spirited life like Del, but neither of those things fit. He felt like an old man trapped in the body of a twenty-four-year-old.

Rocco must have realized he'd lost Nate's attention because he stopped kissing and flopped over onto his back. He rolled his head to the side to look at Nate. "What?"

"It's nothing."

"I'm sorry. I should have warned you about this. My ex put a lot of conditions on me until the papers are signed because of our kid." He ran a hand down Nate's chest. "It won't be long. I promise."

Nate wanted to believe him. Something didn't feel right, and it took a few minutes for him to puzzle out what it was. "You're not in love with me."

Laughing, Rocco sat up and swung his feet over the side of the bed. "Who said anything about that? We've been dating all of—what, three weeks at most?"

"Nearly four, and that's not what I meant." Nate rose as well and began putting his clothes on. He sat back down with his socks in his hand and stared at them.

Rocco paused, his fingers on his shirt buttons. "What did you mean, then?"

"You're asking me to stick it out with you until you're free, even though you don't love me." When Rocco didn't reply, Nate continued, "I've been out since I was fifteen, first to my family and then to everyone else. I don't want to hide who I am or who I'm seeing." Nate sighed and stood back up, leaving his socks in his place. He rounded the bed to stand in front of Rocco, running his hand down the crisp fabric of his dress shirt. "I like you, and god knows, the sex is hot. But I'm not the man for you. I wasn't when we were teenagers, and I'm not now. I want a lot more than being someone's secret."

"I wasn't thinking this had to be some forever thing." Rocco shook Nate's hand off and went back to buttoning.

"Maybe you weren't, but that's what I need to be able to hope for when I'm seeing someone." He paused and waited to feel angry or sad. Instead, he was disappointed, and only in himself for not seeing it sooner. "You're not ready for anything else, which is fine. Maybe if I were in love with you, I could wait, but I'm not. One day, you'll find someone who is willing. It just won't be me."

Rocco sat on the edge of the bed, and Nate joined him. "So, where does this leave us?"

"Hopefully parting on better terms than in high school. I do wish you well." Nate kissed his cheek.

"I'm going to miss having someone to talk to on my lunch hour." Rocco nudged Nate with his shoulder.

"You'll find someone else. I don't have a ton of experience here, but I think when you meet the right person, you'll know." He took Rocco's hand. "If you need someone to talk to about coming out, you know where to find me—even if you don't keep my number in your phone."

They were quiet for a while, and then Rocco patted Nate's thigh. He stood up and stretched before putting the rest of his clothes back on. Nate donned his socks and shoes then grabbed his wallet, keys, and phone to stuff back in his pockets.

"You go ahead," Rocco said. "I need a couple of minutes to make sure I'm presentable."

"Sure."

Nate stood in front of Rocco one last time and placed his hands on Rocco's shoulders. He leaned in and gave him a light kiss on the lips. Not the smoldering promise of a future date but the tenderness of a last time. Nate backed up, gave Rocco one final glance, and turned around to walk out the door for good.

The minute Nate opened his eyes, he knew something was wrong. The gritty, sandy feel when he blinked; the headache spreading down from his forehead; the fire under his skin. He was positive he had a fever, though he didn't own a thermometer to check. It wasn't surprising he'd picked up a bug, since he'd already sent multiple cast members home with illnesses. Working in close proximity made fertile ground for passing things around. He'd been feeling tired and a little off for a couple of days already. Still, he'd hoped he was wrong and he would escape the germs or at least meet them in weaker form. Apparently, no such luck.

He groaned and dragged the covers back over his head. He hoped this was more like a twenty-four-hour bug than the flu, but he suspected it was the latter. He didn't feel good, but he wasn't about to lose his non-existent breakfast, either. Despite the throbbing in his muscles even with minimal movement, he tried to go back to sleep.

Five minutes later, he was awake with a horrible realization—he was supposed to work at the cafe. He sat up too quickly, making everything hurt so bad he thought he really might throw up. He drew his knees to his chest and breathed until the feeling subsided. If he didn't work, he could lose his job. Being only part-time, he didn't have any of the benefits of some of the other employees, and he was likely to be the first one to go. He pushed the covers off and tried to get up slowly.

That was a mistake. Everything hurt like hell, and he dropped back onto the bed with a grunt. He flung his arm over his eyes. At the very least, he needed to find his phone and tell his manager he wouldn't be in for his shift. If only the room would stop spinning long enough to think.

Before he could formulate a plan for locating his phone, the door to his room opened and Jamie stuck his head in. "You okay?"

"No." There wasn't any point in hiding it. "I'm sick." Nate coughed for effect, even though it was unnecessary. His throat felt like someone had scraped it raw, and the fake cough made it worse.

Jamie backed up a few inches. "Do you need anything?" He sounded like he would rather not expose himself to whatever horrible microorganism had made itself at home in Nate's body.

"My phone. I can't find it."

"You left it in the living room last night. Hang on."

Jamie ducked out and returned a moment later, phone in hand, held by two fingers like it might give him Nate's flu.

"Oh, for chrissake." Mack came up behind Jamie. "It won't kill you to go in there and give it to him." He snatched the phone out of Jamie's hand and stepped in to hand it to Nate. "You look like shit."

"I'm sure I do," Nate replied. "Feel like it, too."

"You should have gotten a flu shot. You know, you ought to go see a doctor. They can give you something for it."

"No." Nate wasn't about to explain his lack of health insurance or the fact that he hadn't applied for assistance. He didn't even have a doctor at the moment. He certainly wasn't about to go to the clinic because that would involve Trevor finding out he was sick and fussing over him. "I just need to call in to work and then sleep it off. I'll be fine."

Mack shrugged, but he didn't push any further. He and Jamie

retreated to the other room to get ready for whatever they had going on, leaving Nate's door open. Nate called the cafe and then phoned a few of his coworkers until he found someone to cover his shift. He had to promise extra hours to them, but it was worth it considering he had no idea when he'd be well enough to return to the cafe. Somehow, he would figure out a way to work them in around his rehearsal schedule.

His next call was to Del, who was far too chipper for Nate's taste. Fortunately, Del was more than willing to take the cast through that night's rehearsal. Nate told Del to block scene three using the notes he emailed. With everything accomplished, he could finally get back to the business of sleeping it off. Even lying down, the energy required for a few phone calls had worn him out.

As he drifted in and out of awareness, his mind ran circles around the mess of his second breakup with Rocco. The fever and aches magnified all his misery over yet another way in which he'd managed to screw up his life. He'd known better—thanks to Del's advice—but had chosen to ignore the problems in favor of falling for Rocco's charm. He was sure he'd done the right thing, but it was difficult to see it when he was busy being miserable in every possible way. He pulled the covers back up, shivering, and tried to block out the intrusive thoughts.

Nate had no idea how long he'd been in bed when he heard the apartment door and someone moving around in the main room. He cringed; every noise set his teeth on edge. It was as though he could feel it in each individual skin cell. He rolled over and put a pillow over his head to muffle the sounds, hoping whichever of the others had gotten home early would be quiet.

A moment later, his door creaked. The sound made his head throb. "Hey," Trevor said.

Nate turned onto his back, groaning. "Go away." He cracked one eye open. "Why are you here, anyway?"

Trevor chuckled. "Nice to see you too. Jamie called me and said you could use someone to look in on you."

Of course he had. Jamie and Trevor were now apparently BFFs who called each other for every little thing. Even though Nate knew that was an exaggeration—and a somewhat mean one—he felt justified in his irritability. If he'd wanted Trevor there, he'd have called himself. Probably.

"He should have minded his own business." Nate moaned and rubbed his temples. "Ow."

"You want me to make you some soup?"

"No. Wait...yeah."

Trevor retreated from the room, closing the door this time. So much for not telling Trevor he was sick and having him fuss. Nate had been sure Trevor wouldn't be home. He'd been helping Marlie move into the house Andre had closed on a couple of weeks before. That had been a sore point—Trevor had wanted to include all of them on the mortgage, but Andre still considered everything too unsettled to do so and had kept only his name on it. Apparently they'd come to an understanding. Trevor wasn't officially moving out yet, but he never spent much time at the apartment anymore.

While Trevor cooked, Nate drifted off again. His sleep was fitful, and he didn't feel refreshed when Trevor emerged from the kitchen. He had a tray bearing a steaming bowl, a glass of water, and a bottle of pain relievers. He set the tray on the bedside table.

"You want me to go get you some of that flu stuff from the drug store? Jamie said you wouldn't go get it checked out, but at least we can try to make you more comfortable."

"I don't need to get it checked out," Nate growled. "It's nothing. Half the cast has already had it, and they're all fine. Rest, and this soup. That's all I need."

Trevor nodded. "I told Jamie you'd say that."

"So he asked you to baby me for a bit."

"Yes." Trevor grinned.

Nate humphed, which made his throat burn and his head pound. In a million years he would never admit it, but it was nice to know both Jamie and Trevor cared. Trevor's lips curved upward; he was obviously amused by Nate's failed attempt at annoyance. Nate ignored Trevor in favor of trying to eat a bit of the soup. It was pretty good, but Nate only managed a few mouthfuls. He took a couple of the pain relievers and swallowed them with the water. Laying back against the pillows, he tried to alleviate the ache in his limbs. He closed his eyes. The pain reliever began to work its magic, and Nate floated in the halfway space of not quite asleep.

"You want to go in the other room so you can watch a movie or something?"

Nate squinted at Trevor, not wanting to open his eyes too far. Even the dim light filtering through the blinds was too much. "No. Just need to sleep."

"All right. I'll be around, so let me know if you want something. I'll check in on you again later."

He retreated from the room, and Nate closed his eyes again. It wasn't all bad, having someone around to take care of him. If only he could get the headache to go away, he would be fine. A little sleep, just as he'd told Trevor. Everything would look better afterward. He settled down, pulling the covers up and drifting off.

Chapter Five

Only six of them were at Grand Slam to go over details for the upcoming benefit. All four roommates—if Trevor could still be counted—plus Andre and Julian sat around a table in the nearly empty bar. Julian was only there because he was their primary contact person. He'd done some work for the owners, creating an interactive website. If Nate had been able to scrape together funds, he'd have hired Julian to update the Dyer Theater's website; he was that good. Too bad they'd need a benefit of their own to raise the money.

"You look like you're feeling better," Andre remarked as Nate sat down between Mack and Jamie. By that point, everyone had seen the rough shape Nate had been in over the previous few weeks.

Nate grunted. "Finally. That was a damn nasty flu. Took out half my singers and screwed up all our rehearsals. We'll be lucky to have the whole thing ready to go by Thanksgiving."

Trevor sneered at him. "You didn't even have it confirmed, you ass."

"I went to the clinic!" Nate protested.

"Yeah, to see if it was strep, and only because I made you go. I thought you had scarlet fever."

Mack laughed. "Scarlet fever? Isn't that some disease people got in the olden days?"

Trevor smacked the back of his head. "It's a real thing! It's a rash you get from strep throat."

"I wouldn't know about any of it." Nate shrugged. "It wasn't strep anyway. I wasted my time having them poke my throat with a stick only to tell me it was just a virus."

"You should have gotten flu confirmed," Trevor said again. "The health department collects stats on cases."

The nurse at the clinic had asked Nate to do so and also recommended several other tests, including for mono, none of which he could afford. He wasn't about to take advantage of the clinic's pro-rated options, knowing how much financial need they had, but he didn't have the money for more prodding or a doctor or prescriptions to treat the flu. Rest, plenty of water, and his trusty pain relievers became his companions, and he'd been correct anyway—he was already much better. At least, that was what he told himself to quell his self-nagging at all the information he'd left out or his failure to get the tests. None of the others had a right to Nate's private thoughts, so he wasn't sharing.

Instead, he deflected with, "How the hell do you know so much about this, anyway?"

"Marlie."

Nate rolled his eyes. He'd forgotten Marlie was a nurse who sometimes worked at the clinic. She hadn't been volunteering the day he went in and sat in between two teenagers, both of whom had avoided eye contact and both of whom had looked like they wanted to be anywhere else. He had no idea why either of them was there, and he hadn't asked. All he'd wanted was a simple strep test and to get out of there as soon as possible.

"I'm completely fine now," Nate said. "No fever in a few days. I'm obviously on the mend."

Andre was eying him curiously, but he said nothing. Nate was sure he suspected something about the lack of health insurance, or maybe he was bothered by Nate going to his grandmother's clinic when it was in danger of being closed. Either way, it made Nate uncomfortable, and he feigned ignoring Andre until he looked away.

Denver, one of the three owners of Grand Slam and the bar manager, brought a tray with their drinks. She was a lanky, dark-haired woman with expressive deep brown eyes. She smiled as she bent over to set the glasses in front of them, her blouse gaping to reveal a hint of her small breasts. Her low ponytail slid over her shoulder. She didn't usually serve, but there were only a handful of other patrons there so early, and Andre and company were considered friends. From what Nate gathered, Julian wasn't the only reason Curtis, Rafael, and Denver were willing to help them out. Something about Curtis having needed assistance from the Lighthouse to care for his younger brother years ago.

"There you are, fellas. Rafael says the first round's on the house, but if you stick around after talking to him, you buy your own. I suggest you do—it's drag night, and that's always wicked fun."

She straightened up and winked at Nate before turning around and sashaying away with the tray. A flush crept up Nate's cheeks. Of course Denver would have noticed how often he came in. He wished he could stop her and ask if TaTa would be there. He could use some cheering up, and his favorite queen would definitely do it. Being sick and still trying to cope with both jobs had left him no time to dwell on his second breakup with Rocco. It wasn't so much that Nate missed him as much as a wish he hadn't wasted nearly a month of his time on an ill-advised relationship.

He sipped his drink, a nice seasonal Sam Adams, and let his mind wander away from the conversation. It was a bad idea, harboring an unrequited crush on TaTa. For all Nate knew, she was already spoken for. Besides, it wasn't as though she knew who he was. TaTa was safe, someone whose aesthetic he could admire from afar. It beat going back to Rocco or chatting with strangers over an app, but it wasn't any more real than his other choices. Once again, Nate was faced with his mixed feelings about relationships and his complicated history.

It took so much for Nate to feel a spark with anyone. He'd fooled around with Trevor, made good by the depth of their friendship. Then he'd fallen hard for Rocco. After it had ended the first time, he'd only had two boyfriends—one in college and one the previous spring. Now he was alone again, never having told the others about his second round with Rocco out of respect for the man's need to remain closeted. He tried to tell himself his reluctance was only because he'd been brought up in a sheltered, traditional life where everything was carefully scripted, but it didn't work. If there were any family he never wanted to emulate, it was his own.

Trevor nudged him. "All right? We lost you for a sec there."

"Yeah. Fine." Nate took another swig of his ale. "Still a little tired, I guess."

"No problem. We're making a schedule for the acts. Where do you want to go?"

Andre turned his laptop to face Nate, and Nate filled in a few cells on the spreadsheet for his cast members. He chuckled when he saw Cian Toomey listed as "sensual Irish dance." Not really how he'd have described it, but he wasn't the one making the list. Nate's breath caught when he saw the names of the drag performers, including TaTa. To cover for it, he coughed a little and said, "I see the Kreepy Krullers won't have to fill every slot."

"Shut up," Jamie said, kicking him under the table. "We're really not that shitty anymore!"

"You're not," Trevor agreed, and a look passed between them which Nate couldn't figure out. A flare of jealousy over their friendship threatened, but he stomped it out. Trevor was allowed to be close with people other than Nate.

"Thanks." Jamie blushed and looked away.

"All right," Andre said. "The schedule is done. We've grouped acts which can use the same equipment to minimize set-up time. Now all we need to do is some publicity. Obviously, this is already up on the website, but if you could all spread the word to any of your contacts, that would be appreciated. We'd love to pack this place."

"Elisa says she's already got her coworkers interested. They're planning an unofficial ladies' night out." Julian grinned.

"Dang. How did your wife convince a group of elementary teachers to show up?" Trevor asked.

Julian shrugged. "No idea."

Rafael emerged from in back, ready to outline the particulars for the benefit and how everything would flow. For the next hour, they concentrated on hammering out the details. By the time they were through and had ordered more drinks and some food, people were beginning to fill up the bar. Denver hadn't been joking when she said drag night was a good time. Nate knew from past experience how popular it was. He wondered again if TaTa was performing and how he might conceal his appreciation from the others.

He supposed he'd hide it the same way he was keeping it from them that he still hadn't quite regained his appetite after being sick for so long—unsuccessfully. He pretended not to notice Trevor and Mack sneaking glances at him while he picked at his food. Fortunately, Jamie was doing the same, so the attention wasn't all on Nate. Even so, he knew they were concerned. Jamie was already tiny, and his weird food habits were well-documented, so they didn't make much of an impression. Nate, on the other hand, had lost enough weight over three weeks that he'd considered buying new clothes. It couldn't possibly have gone unnoticed.

A hand on his arm shifted his focus to Andre, who was presumably passing on his way to the bathroom. Nate met his eyes and shook his head. A slight worried frown flickered across Andre's face before he nodded and continued by. Nate sighed and tried to force himself to feel hungry enough to eat a few of the potato wedges. They were good, making him consider having a couple more for a reason other than to appease the others.

Around them, the sounds of the bar increased in volume. The show would begin soon, and Nate intended to enjoy it—especially if TaTa was on stage. He relaxed; there was no sense in wasting a night out with good friends, good food, and good entertainment. He tuned back into the conversation around him, determined to make the most of the evening.

There was already a steady flow of people at Grand Slam when Izzy arrived, but it wasn't yet busy. Instead of going in the back way, he entered the main door. He greeted Curtis, the bouncer, who waved him on through. As he passed the bar, he stopped for a glass of water. Denver was busy with other patrons, but Jack, her second in command, popped over to chat. He was only there a couple nights a week, the rest of his time taken up with classes. Izzy slid onto a stool and asked for his drink.

"You on tonight?" Jack asked as he pushed the glass toward Izzy.

"Yeah." Izzy took a sip and drew in a deep breath, concentrating on the beer tattoo on Jack's left forearm.

Concern flickered in Jack's blue eyes. "Are you all right?"

"Sure. Just getting my game face on." Izzy forced a chuckle.

Jack wasn't fooled. "You look exhausted."

"Had to work earlier. I'll be good to go." Same conversation as with his mothers, only instead he was having it with the cute bearded bartender. It didn't seem fair that someone nearly fifteen years younger would have as much insight into Izzy as the women who raised him.

"All right. But if you need anything, let me know." Jack winked. "Bet I could help you wake up."

Izzy rolled his eyes, but he smiled. He never knew how much of

Jack's flirting was just for fun and how much of it he meant. No one was safe from his affection, but he was strictly hands-off while at work. It was all part of his persona.

"I'll be sure to come see you if something comes up." Izzy set his empty glass on the coaster and stood up.

Jack collected it and shooed Izzy away. "Better get moving, then. It's starting to fill up in here."

He made his way toward the dressing rooms backstage. More like storage areas, but Rafael had installed mirrors, sinks, and counters. They were still always too full, but that was part of the charm.

On the way past, Izzy happened to look up. A table to the side caught his eye. He stopped moving and stared. There were six men seated there, and in the center of the ring, Izzy recognized one of them. Sure, he was without his stage makeup and grand costume, but Izzy was certain it was him—the beautiful baritone from the opera. He looked a little washed out, but it might have been the lighting or the angle. Despite that, he was still gorgeous, with his sandy brown hair and strong features. Izzy stood watching him, his mouth open.

The small, slim black man seated one over from him stood, and they exchanged words. When the other man left, the baritone's eyes traveled toward Izzy. For a moment, Izzy was sure he'd been caught staring. But the other man's gaze wandered on, and Izzy let out a sigh. He turned to go and nearly smacked into the man who had just left their table.

"Sorry!" Izzy exclaimed. "Are you all right?"

"No harm done. You?"

"I'm fine, thanks." Izzy contemplated asking about the guy at his table, but when he looked back over, the baritone seemed to be deep in conversation with one of the others seated near him. It occurred to Izzy that maybe he wasn't available. Or maybe Izzy was wrong and his wishful thinking only made him believe it was the opera singer. He turned back to the man he'd almost run into and saw he'd turned away and was headed toward the bathrooms.

Izzy shook off his temporary distraction and continued to the back and into the dressing room. Inside, it was crowded and hot. Izzy chose a spot at the far end of the long mirror and dropped his bag at his feet. He fanned himself with a pair of gloves someone had left on the dressing table. Behind him, there were multiple conversations at once. Quickly, he shed his street clothes and began taking out costume pieces for his latest creation with Val, a.k.a. Chico El Sabroso.

He put on his costume—the tight black pants, the off-the-shoulders black shirt, and his heeled tap shoes. Those were different from the original, but they were a necessary part of the act. He admired the look briefly before beginning on his makeup, taking care to get the contours just right while being heavy enough for on stage. When he was through, he fussed with the curls on his blond wig until he was satisfied then lifted it onto his head. It was a perfect recreation, and Izzy couldn't wait to see Val's counterpart.

Having finished the rest, he picked up a tube of red lipstick and began applying it. The hand on his shoulder made him jump, and he yanked his hand from his mouth before he smeared the lipstick.

"TaTa!" a voice exclaimed, far too loud and far too close to his ear.

Izzy swiveled around in his chair. "Hey, Brunhilde."

Brunhilde the Great was nothing like most people expected. Nearly everyone who hadn't seen her assumed she would be a big-boned, blond Scandinavian. Instead, she was a petite Pakistani with a vibrant turquoise wig. She was a comedienne, mostly poking fun at her upbringing in an almost exclusively white suburban neighborhood. She was their regular emcee. As far as Izzy knew, it was her only gig. Her alter ego had a day job teaching social studies at a private Catholic school, along with a wife and three young kids. Like Lynne had done for Izzy once upon a time, Brunhilde's wife loved the act and often came to watch.

"How've you been, darling?" Brunhilde asked giving air kisses on both sides of Izzy's head.

"Not bad," Izzy replied.

He turned back to the mirror and finished putting on the lipstick, the final touch. Now she was fully transformed into TaTa. She puckered her lips into a pout and peeked up at Brunhilde's reflection, batting her false eyelashes.

Brunhilde laughed. "Lookin' good, sweetheart." She eyed TaTa up and down. Twirling a finger, she said, "I'm guessing you're not solo tonight, not dressed like that. Chico's here?"

"Yeah, he texted me on my way in. I haven't seen his costume yet, though, and he hasn't seen mine."

"Mm, saving it for the big reveal, huh? Well, I'll see you out there, sweetie."

Brunhilde patted TaTa's shoulder and made her way around

the room to greet the others. TaTa stood up, wobbling for only a second on the shoes. Her feet were numb, like she'd been sitting on them only without the prickling of blood returning to the area. She frowned. That wasn't right. She'd never had trouble walking in her taps before. She seemed stable enough after a couple of minutes, so she brushed it off as lingering fatigue from work. Once she was on stage, the energy of the music and lights would carry her just fine.

TaTa stepped out of the dressing room and into the slightly cooler area backstage. Chico was already there, and he waved her over. TaTa grinned when she saw him.

"Where did you get the letterman's jacket?" she asked.

"Consignment shop. It's not an exact match, but it'll do. As long as we do this thing justice, no one will care that the stripes are the wrong color."

The rest of the effect was striking, and TaTa couldn't wait for everyone to see it. In her opinion, creating the look was as much fun as the performance itself. They'd done all manner of costumes, and Chico was forever designing new looks for them. This one was one of TaTa's favorites.

They kept an ear out for the performers before them. Some, like TaTa and Chico, actually sang, but most lip-synced and a few performed other acts. Brunhilde had worked the crowd into peak enthusiasm, and it sounded like everyone was having a good time. TaTa's mind briefly wandered to the gorgeous baritone sitting with his friends. She wondered what he would think of her and Chico.

They were up next. TaTa stretched, leaning forward a little and tilting her neck. The sudden flash of pain down her spine almost made her cry out. Instead, she sucked air into her lungs. As quickly as it had come, the pain fizzled out, and TaTa breathed easily again. Chico glanced over and frowned.

"You okay?"

"Yeah. Just pinched a nerve or something when I stretched. I'm fine."

Chico eyed her but said nothing more. In the next moment, Brunhilde announced them, and before TaTa could blink, they were on stage. She left all other thoughts behind and focused on feeling the rhythm and delivering her lines as scripted. All her energy was concentrated on Chico and his chills multiplyin'.

It wasn't until Chico ooh-ooh-ooh'd his way across the stage to her that she lost her focus again. It was more subtle than the neck pain, but her ankles weren't holding up the way they should have, going numb like they had in the dressing room. For an instant, she almost broke character. Thinking fast, she changed a few of the steps and tried to make it look as natural as possible. Chico surely noticed, but he was professional enough to go with it. Fortunately, the audience was too distracted by Chico flinging his jacket off the stage.

Like when she was running, TaTa knew tensing up wouldn't help. She let her body relax, finding her rhythm again to finish strong. She turned the charm up to ten, and they delivered the end of the song with flare. TaTa looked out at the crowd as they applauded. She hadn't allowed herself the luxury of looking for the baritone while she concentrated on the music, but now her attention was on finding him. She spotted his table, and her lips curved upward when she saw him watching her. Their eyes met, and she winked. His mouth dropped open, and she wished she was close enough to see if she'd actually made him blush. She and Chico blew kisses and dashed off stage.

Not a minute too soon. Almost the instant they were behind the curtain, TaTa's left ankle finally gave out, spasming painfully. It buckled, and she went down hard. Chico and several of the other performers hurried to kneel down beside her.

"Are you all right, honey?" one of them asked. "Did you sprain it?"

"Get her some ice and something to prop it on," Chico said. He slid down to sit beside TaTa as the others dispersed to do as he'd asked.

"It's fine," TaTa said.

Chico leaned in and broke character. "Iz, you're not fine. Come on, it's just us. Talk to me."

Reaching up to pull off the wig, Izzy was back to himself. "It's nothing. I got a bit out of shape, and I started running again. I'm just getting used to it, that's all. I haven't built up enough muscle, and my ankle gave out. Obviously, I'm not twenty-two anymore. I really am fine."

The others showed back up with ice and a cushion from who knew where. Izzy propped his foot on it and applied the ice to give the impression it would help rather than probably making it worse. He couldn't say anything to Chico until they were both out of there and back in their street clothes.

"But—" Chico started.

"We'll talk about this later," he said, leaning his head against the wall behind him. *Much later.*

Chapter Six

Brunhilde leaned against the wall, chatting with Izzy as he applied his makeup. She had extra emcee duties for the evening, with all the different acts at the benefit night. It wasn't unfamiliar territory; Grand Slam frequently hosted all sorts of community events. Brunhilde was in her element, already buzzing with energy.

"So, are you and Chico all ready?"

Izzy swiveled to face her. "Just about. Can't believe they pulled off having so many acts tonight. Have you seen it out there? Bar's packed."

"These events usually are. Remember last spring when we did that Covers for Covers benefit? Let's hope this thing's as much of a success. I know a bunch of people who use the clinic over at the Lighthouse. Would be a shame if it closed."

"Yeah." Izzy was familiar with the place, having worked for a number of years in Quincy, and he hated the idea of the place having to shut its doors.

Brunhilde looked over her shoulder to where Rafael was waving from the doorway. "Oops, gotta go. Looks like they need me." She air-kissed Izzy's cheek so as not to smudge either of their faces. "See you out there."

As she sauntered away, Izzy kept watch out of the corner of his eye. He wouldn't have time to see all of the acts, unfortunately.

There was a bit of fumbling and several exchanges of "excuse me" in the doorway while Brunhilde exited and three other people came in. Izzy sucked in a breath when he saw them. One was the gorgeous baritone he'd seen the last time he performed as TaTa. Up close, the man appeared considerably younger than Izzy had thought when watching him from the stage. The second was a tiny wisp of a man so attractive it almost set Izzy's teeth on edge. He wasn't really Izzy's type, but he had the polished shine of someone who could have been paid for his good looks. Behind them traipsed a third man with dark hair and a lot of tattoos.

"We're all set," the small man said, bouncing enthusiastically. "Looks like it won't just be Mack and me up there playing."

Baritone laughed. "Good thing." Tiny socked him, but it looked good-natured, as though they were close friends.

"Have you seen Trevor?"

"Nope. I'm guessing he's out there somewhere with the others waiting to go on. You should get ready too."

Tiny and Tattooed slipped off just as Baritone put a hand to his pocket. He pulled out his phone.

"Hey." Baritone listened for a moment, his brow wrinkled. "Jesus, Del, you sound like crap. Are you kidding me? Stay home. Don't spread your delightful germs all over the place. I don't even want to think about how many people you'd hack all over on the train getting here." There was a long pause. Baritone shook his head. "I need you healthy for the last couple weeks of rehearsals before opening night. Get some sleep, and take a few days." He frowned. "Actually, you should probably see a doctor too." Pause. "Do not talk to me about what I should have done."

Izzy was relieved Baritone had told whoever it was to stay home. He couldn't afford to get sick with anything and risk ruining his voice. He chastised himself for being an unsympathetic clod, even if it was only in his head and not out loud. Turning back to the mirror, he adjusted his wig. A huff in the neighboring spot at the mirror caused him to look over, and his eyes nearly popped out of his head. Baritone was right there, a look of consternation on his face as he set his makeup kit on the counter.

"Well, shit." Baritone muttered something about having to figure out what to do to fill the spot Del had vacated on the program.

Without thinking, Izzy said, "What was he supposed to sing?"

Baritone turned toward him, and his mouth fell open. He

closed it, opened it again, and then stood there. He finally shook himself and said, "You-you're TaTa Latke. Oh, my god."

It was Izzy's turn to gape like a fish. The man he'd been thinking of as "his" baritone looked a bit awestruck himself. Izzy scrambled to recover. "Yes, that's me. And you are...?"

"Nate Kingsley. Oh, my god," he repeated. "I can't believe I'm standing here talking to you."

Izzy suddenly found the whole thing funny and let out a loud laugh, startling Nate and several other people nearby. "I could say the same. I've heard you sing."

"You have?"

"Yeah. I went to see *Die Fledermaus* multiple times." Izzy's cheeks heated.

"Oh, my god," Nate murmured. That seemed to be his go-to phrase.

"So, now that we've fangirled all over each other, want to tell me what Del was supposed to sing tonight?"

Nate sighed. "We were supposed to sing some duets. Why?"

"What's his voice range?"

"Tenor. Again, why?"

"I might be able to help you out, depending on what it was."

Nate pulled an amused frown. "You sing opera?"

Izzy laughed. "Not usually, but I have sung arias before. Besides, I wasn't sure you were going full-on opera tonight with this crowd."

"We weren't," Nate agreed. "It was supposed to be a mix."

"All right." Izzy pursed his lips. "You weren't planning to sing 'I'll Cover You,' by any chance?"

Nate shook his head, but he blushed. "No...well, we would have if anyone had asked for an encore. Why?"

Izzy rose to his feet and drew himself up to his full height, though he still had to angle up a bit to look Nate in the eye. He gestured down at himself then to his beard. "I couldn't pull off Angel, that's why."

The laugh bubbling out of Nate made Izzy a little weak-kneed. Nate's crooked grin remained in place as he said, "We really were going to sing one operatic duet, but I doubt you'd know it. Thanks for trying. I'll sing something on my own, and we've got a couple more people from the company here as well, though no other tenors."

"Hm." Izzy tilted his head and tapped his lips. "Are you familiar with 'Au fond du temple saint'?"

The look on Nate's face could have shot Izzy dead. "I'm a professional baritone. Yes, I know that one." He paused. "Wait...you know the tenor part?"

"I've been singing since I was in middle school. Yes."

"Would you be willing..." Nate shook his head. "I can't ask you to do that. You have your own music to perform, don't you?"

It was true, but at the moment, Izzy didn't care. There was nothing he wanted more than a chance to make music with the man in front of him. He wasn't entirely star-struck, but it was close. Nate was every bit as handsome up close, even if it was now obvious Izzy had at least ten years on him. His powerful voice stirred something deep within Izzy, and all he wanted was to hear those rich tones blending with his own. Just speaking made it obvious Nate had the ability to command a room, yet he seemed unsure and unaware of his own power. Izzy inhaled and let his breath out slowly before answering the question he'd almost forgotten Nate had asked.

"I do, but we're only responsible for one tonight because there are so many acts. It won't hurt my voice to sing another one."

"Oh, my god," Nate said again, at which Izzy had to suppress a laugh. "I can't thank you enough."

"Don't thank me until you've heard me sing it," Izzy muttered. "Maybe we should practice a bit. There's a stairwell out back which leads to the apartment upstairs. I'll ask Rafael or Denver if it's okay to go up there."

He stepped around Nate and headed for the door. Looking back, he saw Nate still watching him and gave him a grin and a thumbs up. The look of relief on Nate's face was comical, but at the same time, it was appealing. Izzy shocked himself wondering if that was the same blissed-out expression Nate wore after...no, Izzy definitely didn't need to go there. Not right before going on stage. He waved and stepped out of the dressing room.

Nate followed TaTa up the back stairs and into a narrow hallway. There was a two-stall bathroom, a cluttered office, and two more closed doors. Nate assumed one of them led to the apartment. The other door opened into what might once have been a studio room but was now lined with boxes. The only furniture was an old steel desk, shoved up against one wall, and an ancient swivel chair. TaTa led him into that room and flicked on the lights.

"It's just storage, but this is where they said we could practice. It's not completely silent, but it's not bad."

She was right; sounds of whatever performers were on stage drifted up, muffled by distance. This would do for a quick practice. Nate stretched, watching out of the corner of his eye as TaTa did the same. When he was through, he began warming up his voice. He'd only finished his resonance humming exercises and begun his scales when he caught TaTa watching. Nate paused.

"What?"

"You...it's...wow," TaTa said.

A nervous chuckle wormed its way out of Nate's throat. "Thanks, I think."

"No, it's good. Can you teach me what you're doing?"

"Sure. Just follow what I do. I usually hum first to get things moving, work on resonance."

For the next few minutes, Nate led TaTa in his warm-up routine. He tried not to come across as harsh, but he did make TaTa repeat some things when she missed the mark. Nate supposed the exercises would be good for her too, even though she didn't usually sing classical. When they were through, Nate sang a few lines from one of his more recent performances. It made him blush the way TaTa watched him the whole time.

They ran through "Au fond du temple saint" a couple of times, with Nate giving TaTa a few instructions on how to bring out the quality of her voice. For someone who wasn't professionally trained in classical music and opera, TaTa was good. With some voice lessons, she could easily perform alongside the members of Nate's company.

After they finished, Nate got an idea. "I was wondering...I had one other thing, which I was going to sing myself, but maybe you would consider singing the other part."

TaTa appeared taken aback. "Is it something I know?"

"No." Nate shook his head. "I wrote it with a friend, ages ago when we were still in college."

TaTa seemed amused. "College doesn't seem like it would have been ages ago for you." She cringed visibly. "Sorry. I have a tendency to open my mouth without thinking."

Nate laughed. "It's fine. You're right—it wasn't that long ago, but it feels like it sometimes." He wondered how old TaTa was. He'd assumed she was near his age, but up close, Nate saw the lines around her eyes and figured she was probably a good ten years older. "Anyway, I have sheet music for that one. Trevor, my friend, wrote it all down."

He pulled out the music from his bag and handed over a copy. TaTa scanned it, mouthing the words silently. Nate knew them by heart. For a long time, he'd clung to them as proof Trevor was hiding the same secret longing Nate was. He'd been wrong, though, and downstairs in the crowd were the two pieces of evidence. Nate could never have provided him with what he needed, and he doubted Marlie would have warmed to him as Trevor's partner in the way she had to Andre. It seemed strange, given that he'd been friends with her, but after everything he'd done, he couldn't blame her for her lack of trust.

Shaking himself free of those thoughts, Nate asked, "What do you think?"

TaTa's eyes gleamed. "I say we go for it. These words are beautiful, all about finding a way home and shelter." She tilted her head. "This doesn't seem like your typical song. It has more of a big Broadway musical feel to it."

Nate's face heated up all the way down his neck. "It was supposed to be. I wrote the music for my composition class, and Trevor helped me put words to it. We sang it at my senior recital."

"Let's do it, then," TaTa said.

They practiced until Nate was sure they had it right then made their way back downstairs. Jamie caught them at the bottom.

"You're on soon! We've been looking all over for you. Mack and I finished our set already."

Nate apologized for missing it, to which Jamie shrugged, and led TaTa back into the dressing room. He hurried inside to change and quickly apply stage makeup. When he was finished, he met up with TaTa and the accompanist backstage. From where they stood, Nate saw the act currently on stage and grinned. Jamie's cousin Brandon had obviously been successful at recruiting Mack's sexy Irish dancer, though he wasn't in a thong this time. Behind him, the electric fiddler played something so fast Nate was amazed he didn't set the instrument on fire.

Thunderous applause met them when the dance finished, and the dancer left the stage with the band trailing behind. He passed Nate, excusing himself with a brief grip to Nate's arm to keep upright as several people nearly plowed into them. Nate issued a non-committal response, which the dancer appeared not to notice.

What felt like only a moment later, the drag queen in the turquoise wig introduced them. Nate and TaTa were propelled onstage. For a second, Nate blinked in the glare of the lights. When he'd recovered his sight, he turned to TaTa and nodded. He motioned to their accompanist—who, fortunately, knew the piece—and they began.

The aria was well-received, and they were greeted by polite but enthusiastic cheers. Nerves bubbled in Nate's stomach. He hadn't performed Trevor's song in a long time. He wondered if Trevor would even hear it, since he hadn't performed yet himself. Taking a deep breath and letting it out slowly, Nate steadied himself. He glanced at TaTa, and she winked. She had the sheet music in hand, and Nate had given his copy to the accompanist. He motioned to her, and she gave a small nod in return.

They began the piece. It built slowly, starting out soft and then taking them soaring. Nate gave himself over to it completely, feeling every pang, every shredded hope as though it had been yesterday. He willed himself to keep going despite all the heartache it brought back. In his peripheral vision, he caught TaTa eying him. He rotated to face her, giving the impression of singing to each other. To her credit, she followed his lead and sang on, heading into the climax of the piece. Their voices blended, and Nate felt the moment she gave in as well. Everything around them faded, as though they were the only two people who mattered.

The final note hung in the air for a few seconds while the audience absorbed its full impact. A breath later, applause rang out, swelling as the music had. People rose to their feet, and everyone cheered. Nate turned to TaTa, who seemed as stunned as he was.

"We did it," she said.

They bowed, and Nate followed TaTa offstage with the accompanist right behind them. Before he could blink, Nate was surrounded by his friends. Jamie kissed his cheek. Mack gave him a squeeze and a fistbump. When they let him go, he was face to face with Trevor. They didn't exchange any words, but the look Trevor gave him said it all. The next moment, they were in each other's arms, and Trevor shook against him.

"I'm so sorry," Nate said.

"Me too."

Whatever had been broken between them had healed, and for the first time in months, Nate felt at peace. When they pulled apart, Nate glanced around for TaTa to thank her, but she'd already disappeared into the crowd. Nate made to follow, but he was swept away by his friends in the opposite direction. With any luck, he could catch her after the event to thank her again.

When the show finally ended, Nate's shoulders ached, but otherwise, he was in a good mood. From what he could tell, the night had been successful. By the time the crowd had thinned and he had extricated himself from multiple people offering congratulations, all he wanted was to escape into the relative quiet of the dressing room for a few minutes. A number of people had left already, but he hoped to catch TaTa before she went home. He slipped into the room and closed the door.

There were half a dozen people in there, wiping their faces clean and packing costumes away. None of them were TaTa. Nate slumped against the wall in defeat. Chances were, he'd never see her again. It hadn't even occurred to him to ask TaTa for her number; they'd all been so busy performing, and there had been what felt like a thousand people backstage. He didn't even know her real name. TaTa's words now came back to him, that she'd come to watch him more than once in *Die Fledermaus*. Nate could have kicked himself for his failure to act when he had the chance. They'd brought the crowd to their feet, but it was a one-time deal. Come the next day, they'd both go back to watching each other perform and admiring from a distance. Nate let out a slow, sad breath.

"You looking for someone?"

Nate glanced over at the short man by his elbow. He wasn't positive, but he thought it might have been the one who'd been wearing a neon turquoise wig earlier. "Sort of," he admitted.

"Maybe I can help. We all look a bit different without the makeup."

"Not much in this case," Nate said. "She has a beard, so I think I'd know her if she were in here."

"Oh!" The man grinned. "You mean TaTa. Hey, you're the one she sang with tonight, right?"

"Yes, that's me."

"TaTa's a regular here, so I'm sure if you come back another time, you'll see her."

"Sure, yeah," Nate agreed. He held in both his annoyance and disappointment at learning nothing more than what he already knew.

The man slipped past Nate and out of the dressing room. Frustrated, Nate turned to go. As he did, he glanced in the dressing table mirror and caught a glimpse of a small bag someone had left on the counter. No one in the room seemed to be looking for it, so

Nate stepped over and picked it up. He opened the zip, hoping for a clue to its owner. When he left, he could give it to Curtis, Rafael, or Denver. The first thing he pulled out was the sheet music he'd given TaTa for the second song they'd performed together.

Nate shoved the music back in the bag and carted it out of the dressing room. Maybe with this, Curtis would give him some contact information so he could call TaTa herself and return the bag in person. The thought made him smile as he made his way to the far corner of the bar where his friends sat. He slid into the booth beside Mack, who offered a crooked smile and slid a beer over to him.

Andre was discussing the profits of the night with his friend Julian. "Fifty thousand, Curtis said."

Julian whistled. "Should be enough for what the Lighthouse needs, right?"

Andre's smile faltered. "It is, but more likely it's enough to keep the place going until Grams can figure out how to close without too much of a mess left for us."

Trevor's head whipped around, and Marlie, who had been leaning against him, grunted. "Wait, what?" he asked.

"She's old, Trev," Andre replied. "I don't even know how she's done it for so long. Who's going to take over for her? I can't, and my sisters have enough to think about with their own families."

"Still, it seems a shame to close it down, especially after all our hard work." Jamie shook his head. Beside him, The Boyfriend had a thoughtful look, but he said nothing—for once.

"Nothing is set in stone. I don't know what the plan is, only that we need to take care of everything before we make a big decision." Andre sighed. "The Lighthouse has been part of my world for as long as I can remember. It's weird to think of it shutting its doors."

Jamie cleared his throat. "Your Grams helped me find Brandon." He turned toward his cousin, and the corner of his mouth lifted as he signed something to Brandon—presumably repeating what he'd said out loud. The Boyfriend offered a rare gesture of comfort, putting his hand on the back of Jamie's neck. Jamie leaned into the touch.

Mack shook his head. "Guys, really? Come on. We've had one of the best nights of our lives, and you're acting all gloomy. Be sad tomorrow, but tonight, we're celebrating!"

He slipped out of his seat and wandered over to the bar, where he leaned over to chat with Denver. Nate watched them flirt for a bit, knowing Denver wasn't interested in him. She only had eyes for Rafael and Curtis. Didn't seem to bother Mack, though. He left her some cash and sauntered back to the table while she got the drinks he'd ordered.

Trevor leaned over to Nate. "So, you and TaTa, huh?"

"What?" Nate gulped air and nearly choked on his spit. "There's no me and TaTa to speak of."

Andre laughed. "I think he meant singing, but wow."

"You owe me five," Julian said.

"What?" Nate repeated, glaring at the two of them.

"I do not," Andre said to Julian. "You and your ridiculous bets."

Julian snorted. "Worked out for you, didn't it?"

Andre didn't answer him and turned to Nate. "We all figured you had a thing for her when we were here for the last benefit and she did a cover of Annie Lennox. You actually got to sing with her tonight. Pretty damn good, if you ask me. She's got a voice on her."

"And she's hot," Trevor put in.

Marlie smacked him, but she was laughing. "Since when?"

"It's the beard," Trevor told her, and they both giggled.

He leaned over to kiss her. When he straightened up and glanced at Andre, even Nate saw the bald lust in Andre's eyes. What startled Nate was the absence of any negative emotion. Trevor kissed him as well, and Marlie had the same satisfied look on her face. Nate tore himself away from watching their interactions. Now was not the time to dwell on all the things he didn't grasp about their relationship.

"Anyway," he said, a little too loudly. "It was just a song. That's all."

Mack snorted. "You at least get her number?"

Nate slouched in his seat. "No. Look, it doesn't mean anything anyway, right? I don't really know her."

"Did you think we had no idea how many times you've come to watch her?" Mack asked. His mouth twitched with undisguised humor at Nate's expense.

"Maybe I came here for some other reason," Nate countered.

"Oh, please. You weren't here for the beer or the hookups," Mack replied. "After living with you for a year, I already know you're more the type to pop the top off a bottle and sit on the couch pretending to watch Netflix. You won't even bring a guy home until you know more about him than he knows about himself. Come to think of it, I think you've literally only brought one person home in the last year. What was his name again?"

"Piero, not that it's any of your business," Nate snapped.

He wasn't going to tell any of them about seeing Rocco. Only Trevor knew the history there, and even he didn't have the whole story. When Nate and Trevor had been fooling around, it hadn't been serious for Trevor, and Trevor had assumed it was similar with Rocco. Nate had never disabused him of the idea. He hadn't told Trevor how deep his feelings for Rocco had gone and how crushing it had been when Rocco used him as the scapegoat when he told his parents he'd been "confused." Similarly, Nate hadn't confessed his renewed relationship with Rocco or the hope he'd had it might work out for them this time.

Mack was about to say something else, but Nate was spared from having to answer any more questions. Denver brought over a tray of drinks, followed by Curtis. Nate leaned down and picked up the bag at his feet.

"I found this in the dressing room," he said, handing it to Curtis.

"Any idea who it belongs to?"

"It's TaTa Latke's."

A slow smile spread across Curtis' face. "And you'd like me to give you her number so you can return it."

"Uh..." Nate knew he was flushed red all over.

Curtis shook his head. "Now, you know I can't do that. But if you leave me your number, I'll pass it along with the bag the next time I see her." He winked at Nate and turned to the rest of the group. "Some night, eh?"

They carried on talking about the show, but it was all lost on Nate. He opened the bag and scrawled his number on the back of the sheet music. He prayed to an unspecified source that TaTa was as interested as he was because the thought of never seeing her—or performing with her—again was unbearable. He wondered if she was thinking about him then, remembering the way their voices had blended and held the audience captive. Whatever it took, he wanted to make magic with her again.

CHAPTER SEVEN

Izzy's morning run was uneventful, a rare time he woke up without his back aching like he'd been sleeping on a bed of rocks. While he ran, he contemplated buying a new mattress. His was older than his marriage to Lynne. Maybe then he wouldn't have so many days when it took twice as long to warm up before he could make his full loop. Today, though, was one of the good ones, and he planned to enjoy it. The air was chilly, hinting at things to come, and neither the sun nor most humans were up yet. Izzy enjoyed the relative quiet of his circuit through the city streets.

Finishing on a high note, Izzy headed back inside his apartment for a quick shower. He had some free time before going in to work at the station, so he pulled ingredients out to make *kasha varnishkes*. His wouldn't be quite as good as Eema's, but it would do, and there would be enough to take some to Val. She loved trading recipes and food with him. Val had introduced Izzy to a wide range of Puerto Rican food, and he had returned the favor. She was the only person outside his own family who would even take a bite the time he'd brought in homemade *gefilte* fish. Everyone else said it smelled like shit, and Izzy couldn't exactly disagree, even if it was ten times better than store-bought.

While he cooked, his mind drifted to the bag still sitting in his closet from the night of the charity benefit at Grand Slam. He'd been relieved when Curtis phoned him to say they had the bag. It didn't contain much, but he had various backup costume bits and a sewing kit in there. He'd stuffed the sheet music Nate had given him on top. When Curtis returned the bag to him, he'd winked and said Izzy should check the bag for what someone had left for him in there. To Izzy's surprise, it had been a hastily scrawled phone number and a name—Nate Kingsley.

Izzy's beautiful baritone, the one who had turned his insides to soup when he gave himself over to the music. At the benefit, Izzy had been afraid he would mess something up because he might be too awed by Nate's voice to sing a single note. He couldn't think what had possessed him to agree to sing together on the spur of the moment other than wanting to do anything to make sure Nate sang. When they'd practiced, Nate hadn't left room for fan worship. He was demanding, but in a way which left Izzy feeling both accomplished and eager to please.

Still, he hadn't called yet, and it had been almost a week since he'd gotten his bag back. He peeked at it again out of the corner of his eye while he stirred the onions into the kasha. Nate had left him the number expecting a call; why was he so nervous about picking up the phone and doing it? He sighed and turned down the heat to let the mixture simmer, and then he put on the water for the noodles. He crossed the room to his bag and extracted the paper. It wouldn't hurt to at least put it in his phone. The next day was Thanksgiving, which he would be spending at the station. Nate was likely to be with family, so Izzy thought he should wait and call him after the holiday. He entered the number into his phone and stuffed the sheet music back in his bag.

When his meal was done, he retreated with a plate to the living room. He ate while watching a lousy movie and wishing he had company to make snide remarks. A full stomach, a power nap, and a quick clean-up later, he was on his way in for work with a small container of the *kasha varnishkes* for Val in hand.

He'd texted her to tell her he was bringing lunch, so he wasn't surprised to find her waiting for him with her hand out to take the container. She popped the lid and sniffed.

"Mm. Smells good, Iz. What is it?"

"*Kasha varnishkes.* You'll like it."

"My turn next week." She sealed the container again.

They trooped inside to the common area they shared with the fire department. A few of the guys were cleaning the kitchen with internet radio on in the background. Val put the container in the fridge—carefully labeled with her name in black sharpie, not that it would stop anyone who wanted to take some. Of course, the *gefilte* fish had put most of them off wanting to taste things Izzy brought, so the *kasha* was probably safe.

"Tru and Henry went to the elementary school for safety day with a couple of the firefighters," she said. "They've got this whole thing going with a simulated smoke-filled house and emergency crews and stuff. The police are giving the kids stuff to take home for the missing children fingerprinting."

"Ah, yeah. Remember when it was our turn for that?"

Val laughed. "Do I ever, especially after that one kid puked on my shoe. I love it, though. That and the climb aboard at the public library. Those are fun."

"Except when we can't get one of the kids to give the rest a turn."

An upbeat song came on, and one of the other guys used the soup spoon he was washing as a microphone to lip sync-croon to the other. Izzy chuckled, until the others started joining in. They were terrible, but they were having fun. He plunked down in a chair to watch them. Val dropped down next to him and nudged his boot with her toe. He grinned at her, and she rolled her eyes.

Eventually, the others dispersed, leaving Izzy and Val alone. She thumbed through a medical supply catalog someone had left on the table. For no good reason, Izzy was restless. He had been since the benefit concert. It was probably a fool's errand, harboring a mix of crush and admiration on Nate. He had to be at least ten years younger, probably more. Izzy always tried to keep an open mind, but he couldn't help thinking their different life stages might be a problem. Izzy had already done the married and settled thing, and he wasn't in a hurry for a repeat performance. On the other hand, he wasn't looking for a pseudo midlife crisis fling, either. Something in the middle would suit him fine. Nate could be in the market for either end of the spectrum.

Val waved her hand in front of Izzy's face. "Yo. Lost you there, man."

"Sorry." He shrugged, not caring if Val knew he was daydreaming.

A slow, deadly smile inched its way across her face. "Thinking about the benefit at Grand Slam?"

Izzy jumped. "How did you know?"

"Every person there saw the way you and that hot opera singer made eyes at each other on stage. Was it really all an act?" She arched an eyebrow.

"Uh. Um," Izzy stammered.

"That's what I thought." She looked self-satisfied. "Did you get his number?"

"Yes."

"And you'll call him?"

Damn, she knew him too well. "Would it stop you from trying to set me up with your friends all the time?"

Val laughed. "Not unless you actually score a date. If you do, I'll gladly pay for it."

Izzy snorted. "Fine. I'll call him. No promises."

Before Val could reply, the alarm in the fire department's half of their shared space sounded. Both of them turned toward the noise, and Val was on her feet in an instant. Izzy stood more slowly, and Val eyed him.

"Give me a minute." He winced at the twinge in his back.

Val's brow furrowed. "You okay?"

"Yeah." He waved her off. "My back's been acting up. I should probably get it checked out, but I haven't had time."

"Definitely. You don't want to be out of commission." She scowled at him. "You never did explain to me what the hell was wrong with your ankle a few weeks back."

Izzy sighed. "Yes, I did. I told you I was getting back into running, and I was a little out of shape."

"You're not getting off that easily, Kaplan. I know you too well. Why the fuck haven't you seen a doctor about it? That's not the first time you've limped around like you have an injury."

"Maybe I'm just getting old," he snapped.

"Nice try." She headed for the door, and Izzy followed.

"I was fine at the benefit," Izzy said, but Val only snorted. "Fine. You win. I've been having these random things. I don't know, muscle spasms or something. Other weird shit, too." He scrubbed his face with his hand. "A couple of times, I haven't been able to feel the floor under my feet, and I'm getting tired a lot." He was absolutely not going to explain some of the more personal details.

"You should really—"

He held up a hand. "Don't say it. I know, I know. My mothers have said it too. It's probably nothing, but I'll make an appointment. I'm due for a physical anyway. Happy?"

"No," Val replied. "But this is as good as it's going to get. You all right for today?"

"Do I look like I'm having a problem?" He flexed for her.

She shrugged. "I wouldn't know. Until a couple of weeks ago, I wasn't aware of anything at all."

"I'm fine. I feel pretty good today, in fact. Ready to get out there."

Val nodded and turned around to continue walking at a brisk pace. Once her back was to him, Izzy massaged his lower spine, stretched again, and hurried after her for whatever adventures awaited.

Nate stepped inside his parents' house and shut the door behind him. He toted the bag of salad fixings into the kitchen, where his mother and sister-in-law were hard at work on the mashed potatoes and homemade cranberry relish. He gave them each a peck on the cheek, earning a huff from Mom and a return kiss from Corinne.

"Here, let me dry my hands so I can give you a proper greeting." Corinne wiped her fingers on a dish towel and stepped away from the counter to compress Nate in her strong arms. Corinne was nearly six feet tall herself, so she didn't have to stretch far.

Nate wriggled free. "Want a hand?"

"Sure."

Mom and Corinne were hardly traditionalists; the men would have been more than welcome to help, and at some point, Dad likely would—he was the only one who could make the gravy come out right. Dean, on the other hand, was a mess in the kitchen. He could cook, but he had a tendency to be more creative than a standard Thanksgiving dinner warranted. Chances were high they'd have ended up with their turkey covered in strange spices or their mashed potatoes baked into a casserole. It was for the best that he was out in the living room with his and Corinne's shorties, ages two and ten months.

Nate grabbed a knife out of the block and a cutting board from its nail on the wall. He returned to the island counter and began chopping vegetables. Corinne set a large glass bowl down next to him. A moment later, with the cranberry relish done, she set to work beside him.

The three of them made short work of the rest of the meal. Dad popped in to finish off the gravy, and in no time they were calling

Dean and the babies to the table. It was just the seven of them this year, with Nate's grandparents off in the Caribbean on a cruise with Nate's aunt and a couple of the cousins. He didn't mind the quiet, but with fewer people to hold the conversation, it was more likely Nate would end up being grilled on his life again. All his choices critically analyzed again.

Dean and Dad were going on about the housing market. Dad was a successful real estate agent, and he was talking about something regarding a client. Dean, who was himself emerging in the field, was listening raptly and adding his own thoughts whenever Dad paused for breath. Nate tuned them out, as none of it made much sense to him. He had nothing of value to contribute to that discussion or the one between Mom and Corinne about two-year-old Bridget's fussy eating stage. Instead, Nate thought about TaTa.

He hadn't heard from her, despite having gone to see her once since the benefit. Surely she'd have gotten her bag back from Curtis. Nate tried not to be disappointed. After all, he was only one of however many fans she had. Drag night at Grand Slam was one of the most popular, despite being mid-week. More than likely, TaTa wanted to keep business and pleasure separate. For all Nate knew, she was straight, though he hadn't thought so from the way Curtis suggested leaving a phone number. Curtis hadn't shared TaTa's real name with him, which might have meant she preferred to keep her circles separate.

Corinne nudged Nate with her foot, bringing him out of his musings and back to the table. He looked down and realized he'd stopped eating and was holding a full fork over his plate. Everyone else had gone quiet.

Mom sat up a little straighter. "So," she said, too brightly for Nate's taste—he knew what was coming. "How are things going for you?"

Nate put the bite of food in his mouth, chewing slowly to avoid answering right away. Nothing Mom ever said was exactly what she meant. She wasn't interested in the highlights of working for a small opera company which wasn't going anywhere. Nor did she care about the quirks of making fancy coffee for the residents of Weymouth to sip on their way into the city for work. If Nate was going to make a career out of performing, she wanted to hear that he was about to move to New York or travel the world as a guest artist.

The truth was, he had done a bit of touring over the summer, mainly in western Massachusetts and across New York State. It hadn't been fully satisfying, but it had been a good experience. It was his way of dodging the fallout from posting his anonymous comment on a blog and outing Trevor to anyone who bothered reading it—which, truth be known, hadn't been many. Unfortunately, the blogger *had* read it and chose to create a public spectacle. He couldn't tell his family that story, either.

He swallowed and set his fork down. "It's going fine. We added a few new people to the company, and we're about to open Gilbert and Sullivan's *The Sorcerer*." That was as much as he felt like giving them.

"That's great!" Corinne said. Nate gave her a tight smile; she was always supportive.

"Yes, that's lovely." Mom tilted her head. "You know, that theater is so old. Have you considered updating the building to something more modern? You might draw in a more upscale crowd that way."

Where in the world was Mom going with this? Nate frowned. "We like it. It has a classic feel to it, which suits us. There are classrooms—"

"Of course, dear. But you know, your father and Dean were just talking about some investors—"

Dean put his head in his hands as Nate snapped, "I don't need their help, Mom. We're doing fine."

Of course Dean's business sense and connections were in there somewhere. They always were. Dean was doing things his parents could be proud of, working hard and raising kids and preparing to move closer to their parents now they could afford it. Nate would never have the option, not that he wanted it. He wasn't going to share with her that the most he hoped for was to one day move closer to the heart of the city, in a neighborhood about as far from his snooty upbringing as possible. Weymouth was a nice pit stop, something affordable and temporary.

He attacked a bite of turkey and refused to engage in any more conversation about his job. They didn't care anyway. For them, a career in the arts was for other people, not for their own son. Music was a product, and they were the consumers, unless it was distinctly queer opera. No wonder Mom wanted him to consider a venue more palatable for rich heterosexuals.

Around him, he heard clinking of forks, but no one said

anything else. The phone in Nate's pocket buzzed, and he pulled it out, grateful for the distraction. Mom glared at him for checking it at the table, so Nate pushed back his seat as he answered. He stood up and walked into the kitchen.

"Hello?"

"Hey...is this Nate Kingsley?"

"Yes. Who is this?"

"Israel Kaplan."

"Who?" Nate frowned.

"Oh. Um, TaTa, from the bar."

Nate sucked in a breath. TaTa had a real name after all. He grinned. "I'm glad you called, Israel."

"You can call me Izzy. I'm sorry, I hope I didn't interrupt your dinner."

"You did, but you rescued me from the clutches of parents who ask too many questions they don't want a real answer to." From the dining room, Nate heard baby Margot's wail. "Hang on, let me go somewhere quieter."

He skipped up the stairs to what had once been his bedroom but was now an office. He shut the door and dropped into a plush chair.

"Was that a baby I heard?" Izzy asked.

"Yeah, my niece. She's ten months. So, how are you?"

"I'm good. I'm sorry it took me so long to call." There was an extended pause. "I was nervous."

Nate laughed. "For real? I'm not that scary, am I?"

"No." Izzy chuckled. "It's just been a long time since I've called anyone for a date. I feel like I've gone back about fifteen years."

Interesting. "That long, eh?"

"I'm doing this very badly, aren't I?" Izzy sighed. "I was with the same person for about twelve years, married for ten of those."

Nate liked the sound of that. Izzy was someone who preferred commitment, even if it hadn't worked out in the end. "I'm sorry."

"Don't be. It was...well, it was a lot of things." There was an extended pause. "Listen, I don't want to drag you down with that. I wondered if you'd like to go somewhere, maybe have dinner sometime."

"I would love to."

"Uh...Saturday? I'm not working this weekend because I worked the holiday." He lowered his voice. "I'm at work now, but there's nothing going on at the moment."

"Crap," Nate said. "I can't on Saturday. This is opening weekend for our new opera."

"Oh. Oh! How about if I go see your show, and then I'll take you somewhere afterward?"

"It would be really late."

"No problem. My job is weird hours, so I'm all over the place with sleep."

"It's a date, then. You can meet me in the theater lobby. I'll call or text you when I'm done wrapping things up after the show."

"It's a date," Izzy agreed. "Talk to you later, Nate."

They hung up, and Nate stayed in his chair with the phone in his hand. A date with TaTa—no, Izzy—to look forward to. Whatever strained conversation was going on downstairs in his absence was suddenly a lot less important. Nate rose to his feet, tucked his phone away, and headed back down to face the interrogation about his phone call he would no doubt have to endure. He could handle whatever they dished out; nothing was going to dim his mood this time.

CHAPTER EIGHT

Opening night was somewhere between a train wreck and a raging success. From the audience's perspective, it probably appeared fantastic. Del's voice was still raw, so his understudy took over for the time being. Nate was grateful Del was at least feeling better enough to give him a hand holding things together backstage. He wasn't sure what he'd have done otherwise. By the end, though, Del looked like he needed to sleep for a week.

After the final bows and once everyone had dispersed to the dressing rooms, Nate cornered Del. "You okay?"

Del nodded. "Still tired, but I expected it. I should be fine by the show next weekend."

"Good." Nate put a hand on Del's shoulder and pressed gently. "Thanks for all the help tonight. I need to take off. Have Evie and her stage crew minions got it covered from here?"

"She assures me they do." Del grinned. "Hot date?"

"Actually..." Nate ducked his head.

Del's eyes lit up. "Anyone I know?"

"I'm not sure. We met at the benefit. He filled in for you."

"Really? Well, don't keep him waiting! No wonder you've been in such a good mood. He must be—"

Nate held up a hand, laughing. "You know me better than that. This is our first date." Even Del's teasing about Nate's sex life—or lack thereof—couldn't dim his enthusiasm.

"Details Monday," Del stage-whispered before disappearing.

Without the distraction of the performance, Nate now had a case of nerves. He changed as quickly as he could then hurried out to the main lobby. He'd told Izzy to meet him at the far side near the concessions stand, since no one was likely to be hanging around there after the show. The crowd had thinned, and Nate easily weaved around the few stragglers. Nate was surprised to see Trevor, talking with a group of people. When Nate came closer, he caught sight of Izzy and stopped in his tracks. There was no way to miss him, despite never having seen him without a dress and a wig. His beard was a dead giveaway, as were those stunning dark eyes. The man was every bit as hot as Nate had imagined.

Izzy was tall—nearly as tall as Nate, only an inch or two shorter at most. He was slim but not wiry, all lean muscle. His short hair was dark and glossy, and he had smooth olive skin and full lips. He'd worn casual khaki trousers and a button-down shirt, the sleeves rolled up to his elbows and open at the collar to reveal a t-shirt. His jacket was slung over one arm. He was laughing at something Trevor was saying, his whole face alight with amusement. The sight took Nate's breath away.

Once he'd collected himself, Nate approached the group. Along with Izzy and Trevor, Andre was there, and two women Nate didn't recognize stood on Izzy's other side.

"Nate!" Trevor called out, and his warm greeting gave Nate a rush.

"Hey. What's everyone doing here?"

Trevor didn't answer right away. He grabbed Nate in an enthusiastic hug first. "That was incredible. You put together a great show. Hard to believe it's your first one as creative director. God, I am so proud of you."

"Thanks." Nate flushed, but he enjoyed the praise.

"We all came out to see it. Even Mack and Jamie, but they both had to leave for a late gig."

Trevor glanced at the bench behind him where Marlie sat. She waved. "Don't mind me," she said. "I needed to sit. I can't wait until I'm not lugging around a whole extra person."

Andre snorted. "Sure, right up until you realize you're gonna be lugging around a whole extra person for years."

"Not twenty-four-seven," Marlie shot back. Her smile turned wicked. "I can make you do it for me."

"That's not a threat," Trevor told her, and Andre looked sheepish, but he smiled.

Izzy turned to Nate. "We've all made introductions already, but you haven't. This is Val, my partner at work, and this is Tamara, her...girlfriend? Is it official now?" He turned to them, and both women nodded. "This is Nate."

The whole group made their way out to the parking lot behind the theater. Val and Tamara took off first, waving goodnight. Trevor had his arm around Marlie, and she appeared a little pale. Nate hoped she was all right; he didn't know anything about how pregnant people were supposed to look. He was about to say goodnight so he and Izzy could enjoy their date when Marlie winced and put a hand to her belly.

"You okay? Was it what we had for dinner?" Trevor rubbed her back.

"No," she said. "Contraction."

"The usual?" Andre asked.

"I don't think so. We should probably get home so I can call my doctor. I had one maybe seven or eight minutes ago—yes, I timed it— and a couple before that which were farther apart. We'll see."

"Isn't it a bit early?" Nate asked. He was sure Trevor had said Marlie was due around Christmas.

"Four weeks," Marlie said. "But we expected this might happen. That's why I was on bed rest for a while. Just didn't think it would be right now."

"Let's get you home, then." Trevor kept his arm around her as they walked out to the parking lot.

Marlie doubled over at their car, grunting in what sounded like pain tinged with frustration. In a blink, Izzy had left Nate to stand in front of Marlie. He looked her over.

"Can you describe it?"

"Squeezing. Longer and more intense than Braxton Hicks." She leaned against the car. "I don't feel good." All the color had drained from her face.

"We should call your doctor from here. They might tell you to wait, but with your history, they'll likely tell you to come in. You shouldn't go home first. Do you have the number with you?" Izzy asked.

"Yeah, in my phone."

By the time they got through to the doctor, Marlie looked to Nate as though she was in bad shape. Trevor and Andre were both trying to keep her calm, but Trevor also looked like he might be on the verge of freaking out. Nate hadn't been with his brother and sister-in-law for the birth of either of their children, but he'd heard all about it from Dean—and a completely different story from their mother, of course, despite the fact that she hadn't been there either. He took a deep breath and stepped over to Trevor.

Putting a hand on Trevor's shoulder, he said, "She's going to be fine, and so are you."

Trevor looked up, his face white as a sheet. "Something's wrong," he said. "I don't know...I just feel it."

Nate glanced back at Marlie and frowned. Trevor might have had a point. Marlie didn't look good; she was now almost gray. Izzy checked her over again then said something to Andre that Nate didn't catch.

"We should get her in now. I can drive so we can get in faster." His eyes met Nate's. "We can go somewhere afterward. I'm sorry."

"It's fine. Andre, are you going too?"

"Hell, yes."

Izzy was already helping Marlie into his car. Nate overheard him trying to keep it light by instructing Marlie not to give birth in the back seat. Trevor climbed in next to her and angled so he could see. A hand on Nate's arm startled him.

"Come on," Andre said. "You can ride with me."

By the time Andre parked and he and Nate made it inside, Izzy was waiting for them. He sent Andre up to the birthing unit, and he took off like a shot. Izzy turned to Nate.

"Still up for a late dinner?"

"Sure. I have my phone, so Trevor can call me if he needs anything."

Izzy's eyes crinkled when he smiled. "I take it you're pretty close, then."

"Yeah." Nate wouldn't have been able to say that even a few months ago, but he and Trevor had made their peace.

The only thing open was a pricey bar, but Izzy didn't seem to mind. They walked, and on the way, they spent the time going over the customary get-to-know-you questions. Nate already knew Izzy worked as an EMT, but he learned Izzy had grown up in Greater Sharon and that he had two mothers. Nate gave Izzy the run-down on his job as a barista, his childhood in Sudbury, and his family.

While they waited for their orders, Izzy opened a conversation about Trevor. "So, Trevor is with both Marlie and Andre. But they're not with each other, right?"

"No." Nate set down his fork. Something about the direction of the conversation had him on high alert.

Izzy nodded. "My ex-wife asked me if I ever wanted such a relationship, but I don't know if she was genuinely open to it or only thought she was obligated to offer. I wasn't interested."

"Ex...wife?" Nate recalled Izzy saying he'd been married, but he'd assumed Izzy meant to a man.

Izzy twirled his spoon. "Look, I should probably be upfront with you. I was married to a woman, and it wasn't out of obligation or being closeted. We loved each other at the time we got married, and our relationship didn't end because I like men."

Nate eyed Izzy, uncomfortable with himself for making assumptions. In his mind, Nate was aware there wasn't anything wrong with being bisexual, but he couldn't help the flash of tension in his gut. He had sworn after his ill-fated relationship with Rocco and his unrequited crush on Trevor that he wouldn't get involved with anyone closeted or bi again. He knew he was being ridiculous. Trevor's issues had very little to do with being bi and everything to do with not feeling comfortable being himself. Andre and Marlie both brought out the best in him. Rocco's problems were a lot more about his family than anything else. Since Izzy seemed to be suffering from neither of those afflictions, there wasn't any reason for Nate to worry.

Izzy must have caught on to Nate's thoughts because he said, "I didn't feel a need to make a big announcement. I guess I shouldn't have assumed my ex-wife was enough detail."

"I'm confused," Nate replied.

"You had kind of that look—the one some guys get when they're trying to figure out what I mean."

"So you're definitely bisexual?" Nate gnawed on his lip.

"Is that a problem?"

Nate didn't answer immediately. This was only their first date, and already he was wondering if Izzy was going to be like Trevor. Except it hadn't sounded that way from how Izzy spoke about his ex. Nate supposed it was a detail they would need to discuss later. At the moment, Izzy only wanted to know whether Nate had a problem with his sexuality. It was an easy question to answer. "No, it doesn't matter to me."

"Good. Not everyone has been decent about it."

Nate cringed. "I'm sorry."

Izzy laughed. "No problem. You didn't tell me to pick a side or ask if I was sure I'm not really gay, so I figure it's all good."

"God. People have said that?" Even Nate knew better. His problems with Trevor were his to own, and at their core they were unrelated to Trevor's bisexuality.

"A few, yeah. I think most don't care, but they don't want to talk about it, either." He paused, and Nate knew there was more coming. "I told you before, my ex suggested something more open between us. I should tell you that's not what I want, and if it's your thing, this probably won't go anywhere." He pursed his lips. "I'm sorry if I'm saying too much. I told you, it's been a while."

Nate was too startled by Izzy's forward exposition to say anything for a moment. Nearly all his friends were in various forms of non-monogamy, and he felt like the odd one out. All except Jamie, and everyone knew exactly how well that was working. It was nice to meet someone who was on the same page as Nate. When he'd gathered his thoughts, he said, "No, it's not for me either."

The food arrived, and they fell into an easy silence while they ate. As they both relaxed, Izzy asked Nate a thousand questions about his singing and how he'd ended up performing. They segued into discussing music, and Nate was so caught up in it he didn't notice how long they'd been sitting there. Around them, the sounds of other late diners thinned until only a few people remained in the pub. By then, Nate had made up his mind to ask Izzy for a second date.

Before he could say a word, his phone vibrated. He pulled it out and frowned when he saw it was Andre. Excusing himself to Izzy, he stood up and stepped away to take the call.

"Nate!" Andre sounded panicky. "Please, I need you. Something's wrong with Marlie. She's not doing well, and the baby's in distress, and I–"

"Where's Trevor?" Nate asked.

"He's with her. Damn. I'm scared for all of them."

He wasn't saying what Nate was sure was on his mind—that he was scared for himself, too. Trevor had said Andre was having a rough time dealing with Marlie's pregnancy because his wife and unborn babies had died in an accident. If Marlie and the baby were in trouble, it would have brought back a flood.

"What do you need?"

"Please...just come back to the hospital."

"Okay, okay. I'm on my way."

He ended the call and returned to the table. Izzy was in the process of signing the charge slip. He looked up and smiled, but it dropped away.

"What's wrong?" he asked.

"I'm sorry. I need to get back to the hospital. Andre said something about the baby being in distress, whatever that means. He's freaking out, and I get why. His wife was pregnant with twins when she died." He glanced at the bill. "At least I should pay for my half."

Izzy shook his head. "No, this was a date. My treat." He stood up and kissed Nate's cheek. "A first date, I hope?"

"Yeah."

"Can I at least walk you there?"

"Are you sure?"

"Of course. Come on, let's go."

Izzy went in with Nate despite his protests that he could just leave him at the hospital entrance. Nate stopped inside the automatic doors.

"You don't have to do this," he said.

"I know. But if there's anything I can do to help, I'm here. I brought them in." He didn't tell Nate the truth, that he wanted more time with him. If that meant spending the night at the hospital waiting for a baby to arrive, Izzy was all right with that. He'd had worse dates, and at least this was familiar territory.

They entered the lobby and used the directory, following the signs to the birthing unit. The family area at the end of the hallway was quiet. Besides Andre, the only other people were an older couple. Andre picked up and put down a magazine three times before he finally stood up. When he saw them, he rushed over.

Andre grabbed Nate and held onto him for a long time. Izzy hovered awkwardly for a moment then stepped farther into the room and took a seat in one of the plastic chairs.

Andre let Nate go. "Thanks for coming."

"Why aren't you with Trevor and Marlie?"

"We planned it this way. Her mom and sister were supposed to be her birth attendants, and he and I were supposed to wait here. Something about it being better for dads not to be in there. I don't know. She does research on this stuff. But then all this happened, and then something with the baby's heart rate, and they were talking about her needing an emergency c-section, and Trevor went with her because the others aren't here yet..." He was babbling.

"Andre, stop."

Nate put his arms on Andre's shoulders, and Andre took several noisy breaths. He stepped back, but his panic was replaced with a frown. "I can't just sit here," he snapped. He turned around and stormed out, heading for the nurse's station.

Nate flopped down next to Izzy. "Damn. I'm sorry about all this. You don't have to stay if you'd rather go home."

"It's fine." Izzy set his hand on Nate's knee.

"I hope you weren't planning—"

Izzy didn't find out what Nate had been about to say because Andre reappeared, scowling. He stalked over to them and sat down. Izzy could practically feel the heat of his fury, but Andre said nothing.

"What happened?" Nate asked.

"They won't tell me anything—not even where they are."

Nate frowned. "Why not?"

"I'm not the baby's father, nor am I legally married to either of the parents. They didn't leave my name anywhere so I could get information." Andre sighed. "I want to be pissed at them too, but I know it was urgent."

"They might tell me something." Izzy ducked out and walked briskly to the nurse's station.

The young woman putting notes into the computer looked up and smiled. "What can I do for you?"

"I'm trying to find out where a patient is. She's having a baby here. I'm the EMT who brought them in. I happened to be at the scene when she went into labor."

The nurse raised her eyebrows, clearly taking note of the fact that he wasn't in uniform. Technically, it was bad form to respond to an emergency in one's personal vehicle, but he'd been on site, so he figured he might get a pass.

"It's not visiting hours."

"I'm not the one who wants to see them. The father's boyfriend is here, and no one will tell him anything or let him back there."

"Well, there must be a reason for that." The nurse was still eying him suspiciously.

"All I know is that she's possibly having a c-section, and the baby's father hasn't come out to talk to him. Would you mind at least finding out if they're all right?"

After a lengthy pause, the nurse said, "I'll see what I can do." She ducked out from behind the desk and stepped around Izzy. He watched her retreat down the hall and leaned on the desk. His back hurt again, and he was tired. He hadn't gotten much sleep between arriving home and heading out to watch the opera. Stretching, he groaned when he felt the pops.

It seemed like forever before the nurse returned with information. "They're in room twenty-three, but it's restricted. All I can tell you is that everyone is stable right now. I asked them to send the baby's father out as soon as possible."

Heaving a sigh, Izzy returned to the family lounge. When he entered, both Nate's and Andre's eyes were on him immediately. Izzy shook his head, and they both deflated.

"The nurse said everyone is doing all right for now. She gave me a room number, but they're not letting anyone else in. I have no idea how long it'll be."

"Did she even ask Trevor or Marlie if they wanted me there?" Andre demanded.

"I have no idea. My guess is no."

Andre flopped back against the seat. It wasn't Izzy's place to say anything to a man he'd only just met, but he understood it must be difficult. Andre was an outsider to the relationship at the moment, and there wasn't anything to be said which would make it any better. It wasn't even the same as Eema telling Izzy about Lynne and her husband expecting again. Izzy's only stake in it was once having been married to Lynne. He thought it must feel different when it was one of your own partners. Complicated didn't even begin to describe Andre's situation.

He mulled over what Nate had said about Andre losing his wife and babies, wondering what happened. Izzy wanted to say something, but any words he might have shared would have been inadequate. His loss was different than Andre's, even if in a sense they were kin. Izzy kept silent. He slouched in the chair, sandwiched between Nate and Andre. Without a sound, he shifted to put an arm around each of them. He might have been a complete stranger to Andre, but he could at least offer some comfort. Andre tilted his head up to look at Izzy, then with an anguished sigh leaned in.

They all must have fallen asleep at some point because the next thing Izzy was aware of was Andre shifting next to him and soft voices. Andre vacated the seat, and Izzy opened his eyes. He turned his head to see a pair of women talking quietly with Andre by the door. Eventually, they stopped. The women came farther in and sat down, but Andre hovered near the doorway.

It seemed as though hardly any time passed before Andre stood a little straighter. A moment later, Trevor came in. He looked exhausted, and the first thing he did was collapse against Andre, shaking. Andre slipped his arms around Trevor's waist.

"Okay?" he asked.

"Yeah." Trevor dropped his head to Andre's shoulder. After a few seconds of silence, he raised his head. "I'm sorry. I'm so sorry."

A look of pure panic crossed Andre's face. "Marlie—the baby—"

"She's fine, and the baby's fine. She's asking for you."

Without another word, Trevor folded Andre into his arms and held on. Unexpectedly, relief flooded Izzy as he sat watching them. It was his turn to close his eyes, squeezing them shut against the rush of grief for what he would never have. Beside him, Nate stirred and came to life, looking up at him. Izzy breathed slowly, focusing on Nate instead of his own jumbled thoughts. Now wasn't the time. Both of them turned their attention back to Trevor and Andre.

"Hey," Trevor said. "Are *you* okay? I'd forgotten how hard this would be for you, and I didn't mean to shut you out."

Andre withdrew and pressed a kiss to Trevor's temple. "I'll be all right. I just need a minute with you."

They rested their foreheads together, eyes closed and hands clasped, breathing steadily. At last Trevor let go and raised his hand to cup Andre's cheek.

"I'm..." He paused and cleared his throat. "I'm a daddy." A shaky laugh rumbled out of him.

"So you are," Andre murmured, placing his hand on top of Trevor's.

"We're dads. Together." Trevor's voice was full of tenderness.

Nate leaned across Izzy. "What did you name the baby?"

Trevor grinned. "Aidan."

Andre coughed. "For real?"

"Hey!"

"It's cool." Andre put his hands up. "I like it." He kissed Trevor.

Trevor stepped around him to talk to the two women. Izzy deduced they were Marlie's mother and sister. He shoved Nate off him and stood up. Gray light filtered into the room through the long window, and Izzy realized for the first time how long they'd been there.

"Thanks for staying," Andre said. "Unless you want to hang around for another few hours until visitors are welcome, you might as well go home."

Nate stood as well, yawning and stretching. "You sure you don't need anything else?"

"Naw, I'm good."

Trevor returned. "Ready?"

"As I'll ever be," Andre said, squeezing Trevor's fingers.

They stepped out and retreated up the hallway, brushing against each other shoulder to fingertip. Nate ran a hand through his messy hair and turned to face Izzy.

"Ready to go?"

"Sure."

They made their way back to the parking garage, and Izzy drove Nate home. When they arrived, they sat in Izzy's car for a few minutes. Despite his exhaustion and having spent the whole night in a hospital waiting lounge, Izzy didn't want their time together to end.

"Crap," Nate said. He leaned his head on Izzy's shoulder. "I'm sorry I ruined our first date."

"Hey, don't worry," Izzy reassured him. "You needed to be there for your friends."

Nate snorted. "Yeah, but I didn't need to drag you into it." He raised his eyes. "Thanks for coming along."

"No big deal. I was the one who offered to drive them, remember?" Izzy pulled out his phone. "How about we try again? You like movies?"

"Sure."

Izzy scrolled. "Hm...action, comedy, or artsy gay film?"

Nate snickered. "I love action movies, but I can watch those with Trev. None of the other guys like the artsy stuff, not even Jamie."

"Okay. Well, the Queen Anne Theater is walking distance from my apartment. They have a double feature on Sunday nights. You're not performing, right?"

"Nope," Nate replied. "Just Fridays and Saturdays for the next three weeks until holiday break."

"Good. Want to meet me at my place?"

Nate's smile was tired but pleased. "Sounds like a plan." He yawned widely. "God. I'm so tired."

"Get some rest. I'll call you this week, okay?"

"Yeah." Nate's smile was lazy and sleepy, and Izzy couldn't help wondering if he would get to see it in a different context.

The thought made Izzy's head spin, and he was sure it wasn't the exhaustion. He leaned in. "Can I?"

Nate nodded, and Izzy followed through with the kiss. It started off light, a hint of what was to come. As he began to retreat, Nate chased his mouth with a much hungrier kiss, and Izzy went with it. For a long time, they sat in Izzy's car, doing nothing but kissing. With a gasp, Nate pulled back.

"I'm sorry!"

"It's all right," Izzy tried to reassure him.

"No, I mean—I shouldn't—" Nate shook his head.

"I didn't mean to rush you."

"It's just...we have this neighbor, and she's kind of nosy." There was something else, but whatever Nate was covering for, Izzy wouldn't get it out of him yet.

"No problem." Izzy kissed his cheek. "I promise, I'll call you."

"You'd better." The disarming grin was back, but there was something behind it. Relief, maybe.

Nate got out of the car and stepped back. He waved over his shoulder as he walked inside his building. Izzy waited until the outer door closed before driving home to sleep and hopefully dream about his beautiful baritone.

Chapter Nine

Nate closed the lids on several containers and stacked them in a reusable Stop and Shop bag. Jamie picked up a second bag with milk and orange juice in it. Mack leaned against the wall by the door, arms and legs crossed.

"Why are you two acting like hens all of a sudden? Since when do you care about babies?" he asked.

"Not any babies," Nate replied. "Trevor's baby. I promised we'd bring them a meal."

"Yeah, but don't they have family or church people to do that shit?" Mack continued complaining.

"Right, they do. I asked Andre to give them my number so we could sign up." He grabbed the Stop and Shop bag along with a stack of sloppily-wrapped presents.

Jamie followed Nate to the door. "Besides, this is Trevor." He bounced a little.

The pang of jealousy was less now, since Nate had started seeing Izzy, but it was still there. He didn't know when the closeness had developed, but he hated how it made him feel. It shouldn't have been a big deal, but Nate knew whatever friendship the two of them had was born during the months he and Trevor were at odds. Jamie had filled in the blank space. Nate reminded himself he had no right to be angry at either of them.

Besides, it was good to see Jamie smiling. These days, he was a ghost, disappearing into his room all the time and always looking worn out. Something wasn't right, but he wouldn't talk to Nate about it. It was bad enough even Mack seemed worried, and Mack had known him for years. At least for today he was enjoying himself.

"Do you even know anything about babies?" Mack demanded.

"No," Jamie said with a cheerily dismissive wave of his hand. "I've never really been around any. I'm kind of excited to see what one is like up close."

Nate snickered. "They're cute but boring. I have two nieces. At this stage, they pretty much just eat, sleep, and poop. Oh, and cry."

"That's the part I'm worried about," Mack muttered. He heaved a sigh. "Fine. Let's go."

They took Mack's van across town to Andre's house, a good-sized Cape on a hilly street. Trevor let them in through the garage, and they trooped up the stairs to the main living area.

Inside, Marlie was on the couch, propped up with several pillows behind her. She was breastfeeding the baby and seemed wholly unconcerned that three men had arrived. Nate, used to Corinne nursing her babies, didn't even blink. He walked past to set his bag in the kitchen, chuckling to himself at Mack's and Jamie's mild embarrassment and the way they both turned away.

While Nate unpacked the bag, he heard Marlie say, "They're breasts, guys, not nuclear reactors."

It only made Nate laugh harder. Andre stuck his head in, his eyebrows raised, and Nate tilted his head at the group in the living room. Andre laughed and shook his head, ducking back out of the kitchen.

When Nate had finished, he came back to find Marlie finishing up and tucking her breasts back under cover. Mack was busily looking anywhere else, but Jamie had given in and was hovering, anxious for a turn holding Aidan. Marlie handed him over, and Jamie's whole face shone with delight. He looked awed, and for some reason, it made Nate feel protective of him. Whatever he was dealing with, at least having Aidan in his arms was a temporary reprieve.

After a few minutes of cooing at the sleepy bundle, Jamie handed Aidan over to Andre, who took him to the rocker-recliner and sat down. Fatherhood suited him, and Marlie looked at him with such fondness. Nate wondered if he would ever have anything like what their little family did.

He enjoyed the picture of domestic bliss for another minute then followed his roommates and Trevor out to the kitchen to heat up the food. The four of them fell back into a rhythm they had learned when they all lived together, setting out plates and scooping portions from the containers. Jamie got down glasses and poured drinks.

While they worked, Trevor said, "So, Nate, how are things going with Izzy? I really meant to send you something to give him for helping us out, but with the baby and all, we haven't even written thank you notes for all the gifts."

Nate didn't answer immediately, unsure what he should say. He liked Izzy a lot, but he couldn't put into words what was holding him back. They'd been on a handful of dates since the disastrous first one, and kissing Izzy made him feel like a cross between being drunk and having a sugar rush. But that was as far as they'd gone. Every time, Nate stopped them before they got to the point of figuring out whose apartment they were heading to.

"It's going fine," he said, hoping to put Trevor off more questions.

"You haven't brought him home, though," Mack said, looking up from slicing a tomato for the salad.

"We've only been out a few times." Nate popped a dish into the microwave.

Mack shook his head. "I can't understand it. You haven't been out with anyone in months, you finally get together with the guy you've been after, and you're going at a snail's pace. Why?"

"Why not?" Nate shot back. "Maybe I'm taking things seriously this time."

Trevor dropped the spoon he was holding. "This time? What do you mean? I thought you and Piero were pretty serious. You brought him to see the band play and to the apartment a bunch of times."

Shit. Nate's hand shook. He hadn't meant to say anything. At least he didn't have to tell them who Rocco was. "Not Piero. It's nothing. I was seeing a guy for a while a couple months ago, but it didn't work out."

"What?" Trevor stared at him. "You didn't say anything." His face paled. "When was this?"

"Started in September. I broke it off a few weeks before the benefit. It wasn't a good situation."

"In what way?" Trevor frowned.

Nate cursed Trevor for being nosy and himself for opening up the floor for questions in the first place. "He was married. Separated. I don't really know for sure. It doesn't matter anymore."

The microwave beeped, but the four of them stood there, ignoring it. Nate ran a hand through his hair. He knew exactly what Trevor was thinking—that Nate had made a poor decision because of what had happened between them. He wasn't entirely wrong. If everything hadn't turned bottom-up in their friendship, if Nate hadn't screwed it all up, he wouldn't have hooked up with Rocco the day he'd had lunch with Trevor. He certainly wouldn't have kept hooking up with him in hope of something more.

Jamie finally broke the tense silence. "Why didn't you tell us?"

"Why should I have? It's not like Mack announces it every time he's with someone new." Nate pulled the plate out of the microwave and replaced it with a second one.

"Because you—" Jamie stopped and pursed his lips. "There was a lot going on with you those few weeks, and we all saw it, but we thought it was just because of the shit with Trevor and that song. And then you were sick, and...well, we didn't know, that's all."

He was being evasive, but hell if Nate could figure out what Jamie wasn't saying. They'd all been closed off regarding the trouble between him and Trevor, in exactly the same way no one ever tried to talk to Jamie about The Boyfriend.

"It was over by then."

Nate was with Izzy now, but he couldn't seem to let go of everything else. Mack might have been almost teasing about Nate being too slow, but he wasn't wrong. Izzy was a dozen years older, and he had no reason to stick around for Nate if he wasn't able to move their relationship along. What if he was wrong and Izzy wasn't with him because they had anything in common? Maybe he had expectations about what a twenty-four-year-old should be like.

He looked around at the other three, and their expressions were almost identical, somewhere between worry and sympathy. None of them seemed to have any trouble enjoying the ride. Not that they talked a whole lot about sex—more joking than anything deep. Still, the others seemed much more open about it all. Nate wondered again if something was wrong with him that he didn't want to dive right in again. Or rather, that he wasn't missing being physical. That might have been more concerning if the others knew.

"Hey," Trevor said. "It's fine. I don't know if you remember this, but Andre and I had to slow down for a while. If you need time, take it."

"I didn't know that," Nate said. He felt marginally better, enough to voice his fear. "I hope Izzy is willing to wait."

"If he isn't, he wasn't worth your time."

Nate nodded, and they all resumed preparing dinner for Andre, Trevor, and Marlie. In a few more minutes, everything was on the table. Knowing they needed some space and quiet, Nate, Jamie, and Mack bid the others good night and returned to Mack's van.

On the ride home, Nate was silent, barely listening to Mack and Jamie talking in the front. He leaned back against the seat and closed his eyes, thinking about Izzy. He knew it wasn't fair to compare Izzy to Trevor or Rocco, but he'd already had his heart crushed twice. Was it so bad to want more time to find out if this thing with Izzy would last? Nate tried not to think about how he'd done his share of breaking hearts too, especially Piero's.

When they arrived back at the apartment, Nate barely heard Jamie announce he was off to see The Boyfriend, and he dismissed Mack's offer to hang out. All Nate wanted was sleep and to avoid thinking about what he was going to do to make sure he didn't end up in yet another failed relationship.

Izzy's teeth chattered despite his warm jacket and the heat on in the rig. Outside the window, light snow flurries drifted down. He tried to concentrate on anything except visions of the multi-car crash on Quincy Shore Drive. He and Val were headed back to the station to finish their paperwork and have a much-needed cup of coffee. For all the years he'd been an EMT, he would never get used to children involved in accidents.

Beside him, Val was silent, and Izzy knew it affected her, too. She didn't even turn on the radio, so there was nothing to drown out the screams of the girl with the broken leg. Izzy shuddered and kept his attention on the road. A few more hours and he could shower and meet up with Nate for another night of movies. The thought was enough to distract him from his weariness and distress.

"What's with you?" Val asked.

Izzy startled. He hadn't realized he'd shown any emotion. "Meaning?"

"That was fucking awful, you looked for a second like you were gonna lose it, but then you smiled."

"Oh." Izzy snorted softly. "Thinking my date tonight might be enough to get my mind off things."

"Ah." Val shifted in her seat. "Nice to have someone to go

home to. And how's that going, by the way?"

"It's fine." Izzy glanced over at her. He couldn't hide much from Val anymore, so he didn't try.

"Mm-hm. Come on, give. I need something to wipe my memory of that little girl back there."

Izzy rounded a corner, slowing down so he wouldn't cause his own accident on the now-slick road. He used it as an excuse to stall on his answer. For the past few weeks, he'd seen as much of Nate as time and their respective schedules allowed. He appreciated the outlook on the new "family centered" hours he'd been assigned. Everything would be official as of January, but for those who had been around the longest, they were already rolling out some of the changes. It all meant Izzy now worked every Sunday, but the twelve-hour shifts ended at six. He had those nights free to see Nate, plus he was always free to perform at Grand Slam.

So far, they'd been to the Queen Anne double feature twice already. He'd also been to see Nate's show again, and Nate had come to watch him once at Grand Slam. Afterward, he'd hung around and they'd enjoyed a couple of beers together. It all reminded Izzy of evenings spent with Lynne, but in a good way. It was nice to have someone there for him, even if they went their separate ways afterward.

Which left Izzy where he was now. Nate didn't seem to be in a hurry. Since their heated kiss outside Nate's apartment, they'd shared several more, but that was as far as it ever went. It surprised Izzy. Nate seemed hesitant, almost nervous, and Izzy couldn't puzzle it out. He was sure he wasn't Nate's first boyfriend, but he hadn't asked, either. If Nate was inexperienced, Izzy was happy to take things slowly. He only hoped he wouldn't be a disappointment to a man so young and vibrant. Izzy was hardly old, but the way his body had been behaving lately, he certainly felt like it.

Izzy slowed down for the traffic light ahead. Once he'd stopped, he glanced at Val. "We've been seeing each other for a few weeks, and Nate hasn't even suggested going to his place or mine. We get close, and he backs off."

"Well, that's got to be frustrating," Val acknowledged. "I guess I thought that's why you were with him. He's young and energetic, and you're practically bordering on DILF territory."

For a moment, Izzy said nothing, too shocked to respond. He turned his glare on Val. "Fuck you, Morales." He snapped his attention back to the road, gripping the wheel tight. The light changed, and he pulled through the intersection.

"Oh—oh, shit. Iz, I'm sorry. I didn't think when I said that." Val put her hand on his arm.

He shook her off. "I'm not that old, and thanks for reminding me what I can't have."

"It was an expression." She scowled. "I said I was sorry. Jesus, this guy must be getting under your skin."

Izzy blew out his breath. "A bit, yeah. I'm not in a rush, and I don't mind waiting. I'm just surprised. I haven't done this in a long time, the dating thing. Hooked up a time or two, but it wasn't that much fun."

Val grinned. "You really like him."

"A lot, yeah." Izzy pulled into the bay and parked.

"Have you asked him about it?"

"No," Izzy admitted. "I didn't want to scare him off."

"Maybe you should try making a move."

Izzy disembarked, and Val followed suit. He pulled his jacket tighter. "What do you suggest, oh wise one?"

"You're going to a movie, right?" She grinned. "Make like a teenager."

Izzy groaned. "You're kidding me. Besides, what if he doesn't want to?"

"You ask him first, of course. C'mon, Iz. It's not that hard." She laughed. "But you can work on it."

"Fine, whatever. I'll think of something."

"I'll bet you will." Val gave him a playful shove. "Let's get this paperwork done, Romeo. That way you can focus on your man."

Shaking his head, Izzy followed her inside the station. Maybe Val was right. Only one way to find out.

They met outside the Queen Anne theater for the third week in a row. So far, they'd been treated to a romantic comedy, an action thriller, a strange fantasy, and a sob-worthy drama which turned out to have a happy ending after all. Izzy read the titles on the marquee and cringed. He swore softly just as Nate arrived at his side.

"What's up?" Nate asked. "Sorry I'm late."

"It's all right." Izzy pointed to the marquee. "I've seen both of these before. The second film is great, but the first one is...um...not really a date movie."

"Why not?" Nate frowned. "We sat through last week's movies, the weird-ass surreal thing and the one where everyone needed a box of tissues to get through it."

"It's kind of a love story, I guess. Won a lot of awards last year. But it's really sad, and not in a good way." He hoped that would be enough to put Nate off.

It wasn't. Nate raised his eyebrows. "Sad like one of them dies? I guess I don't mind, even if the Tragic Queer trope is a bit outdated."

Izzy studied him for a moment, wondering how to explain why he didn't want to watch the movie on the list. "Both of them, actually. They have AIDS. The story tracks them as they get sicker." Izzy had bawled his eyes out the first time he'd seen it. He remembered the way his father's partner had looked the year before he died, and his memory of the year his father lived with them slowly regaining his health was even more vivid.

"Oh." Nate was quiet for a minute. "Are you saying you'd rather not?"

Izzy put a hand on Nate's arm. This was one way in which their experiences were miles apart. He didn't want to explain about his father. "It's a little too close to people I've known," he said softly.

Nate's eyes went wide. "I'm sorry."

"It's all right." It wasn't, but there were too many things he couldn't talk about with Nate right then.

"I've never…I mean, I don't know anyone…"

Izzy wanted to tell him he probably did, but he didn't want to sound like an adult lecturing a child. How had a man working only with other queer people never known anyone? Instead, he said, "It's still probably a poor choice. The other one looks good, though. We'll have to pay full price—it's one charge for both movies—but we could go somewhere else first, then see only the second film. Have you eaten yet?"

"I had dinner with my roommates."

"Dessert, then? I know a great coffee shop around the corner that has chocolate covered matzoh."

"What?" Nate snickered.

Izzy elbowed him. "It's good, trust me. But if you don't want that, they also have rugelach. Have you ever tried it?"

"Uh…no. What is it?"

"Mm, something like a cinnamon roll but better, at least if it's done right. I've had it where it's dry as dust and just plain gross, but this place makes it really well."

"Lead the way," Nate said, sweeping his arm.

In the end, they settled on the coffee shop's decadent version of rugelach. When they had eaten their cherry-almond filled pastries and Nate had nearly sent Izzy over the moon with his reaction, they returned to the theater for the second movie. Nate insisted on paying for their tickets this time.

They slipped in the back as the credits were rolling on the first film. After his eyes adjusted, Izzy looked around. There were only seven other people in the theater. Three were seated together in the front row, and the others were all alone, scattered around. Izzy opted for seats all the way at the back, right under the booth. The theater still had a couple of old-style two-person seats. Perfect. He took off his jacket and set it in his lap. Nate followed suit.

Leaning in, Izzy said, "This one is good. A romantic drama but without some tragic death scene at the end, unlike the first one."

"You watch a lot of indie films?"

"Yeah. My moms were pretty big into that kind of artsy thing. Not just queer culture, either. We've seen all kinds of lesser known movies."

"My parents wouldn't even know what to do with any of it." Nate sounded envious.

There were a few ads between the films and a classic newsreel, which was fun. The feature film started. Izzy glanced over and saw Nate was absorbed in watching the relationship unfold between the main characters. Izzy slid an arm around him, enjoying the way their legs pressed together, and Nate relaxed against him. When the couple on screen shared their first kiss, Nate shifted slightly in his seat. He tilted his head, and Izzy met his gaze. He might as well do as Val suggested, taking advantage of the moment. His heart thumped, and a nervous tickle rolled through his gut.

He slid his hand against Nate's and whispered into his ear, "They're really sexy together, aren't they?"

Nate turned his eyes back to the screen. He licked his lips. "Yeah."

His obvious excitement turned Izzy on. "You ever make out in the theater?"

"It's been a while."

"Mm. Me too. Would you be interested?"

Nate's breath hitched. "Yeah."

Izzy blew in Nate's ear then kissed his way down Nate's neck. Each press of his lips was soft and slow, drawing it out. On the screen, something less physical was happening, but Izzy was only half paying attention, more interested in the way Nate's eyes drifted closed and his inhalations quivered with excitement. When Izzy turned his face, Nate was ready for it. Their lips met, closed-mouthed and sensual. They kept quiet, not wanting to draw attention to themselves. With the movie in the background, they kissed and kissed.

Nate opened for Izzy, rewarding him with the hot slide of his tongue against Izzy's. Even then, Izzy didn't increase the pace. He was extending the sweet torture, intending it as a promise of where he hoped this was heading later on. Nate put a hand to Izzy's cheek, fingering his short beard. Izzy caressed the back of Nate's neck and then moved his hand lower, running it over Nate's shoulder and down his chest. He squeezed gently, and Nate's breath caught. Izzy had to hold back the sound trying to work its way out of his throat.

Izzy's hand wandered lower still until it was tucked in Nate's lap beneath his jacket. He used only a little pressure, and the light touch caused Nate to shiver against him. His breaths turned into panting, and he closed his mouth. His effort to keep silent drove Izzy wild. Used to his temperamental body, Izzy wasn't surprised to still be mostly soft in contrast to the firm swelling in Nate's jeans. But Nate's enthusiastic response was intensely pleasurable in a way which did startle him.

Nate reached over, trying to return the favor, but Izzy batted his hand away. "I want to focus on you for now," he murmured.

Nate relinquished control to him. Fooling around in the theater made Izzy feel naughty and a little embarrassed, but he would do anything to keep seeing and hearing Nate in such rapture. He kept touching Nate until a hand on his wrist halted his motion.

Nate whispered, "Stop. I don't want to come in my jeans."

Izzy moved his hand away but nuzzled Nate's neck. "Have you ever?" he asked.

Tipping his head back, Nate said, "Yeah. When I was a teenager."

"Tell me about it."

"Why?"

"Because—" Izzy bit back a groan. "Because it gets me hot."

"Oh, fuck." Nate took several breaths before he answered. "In high school. Went to see some...ungh...superhero movie with my friend."

The point was to work them both up, to enjoy the state of arousal and the anticipation. If Nate didn't want to come that way,

Izzy would respect his wishes. Later on, if Nate was interested, they could continue at Izzy's apartment. He moved his hand farther away, intending to make it clear. Nate surprised him by adjusting his position slightly and moving Izzy's hand back to his crotch.

"Is this what you want?" Izzy murmured. "Thought you said you'd rather not."

"Please," Nate said. "Changed my mind."

"All right. Go on," Izzy whispered. He popped the button on Nate's jeans and ran the zipper down. His hand worked its way inside, over the top of Nate's underwear.

"M-My friend and I had both just broken up with people. We were trying to get our minds off it."

Nate cracked an eye open, and Izzy followed his gaze to the screen. The men were kissing again, moaning, and this was probably the film's big sex scene. Nate leaned his head closer to Izzy and continued telling the story, speaking softly into Izzy's neck. The whole time, Izzy kept steady pressure and friction on Nate's trapped dick.

"We started off watching the film...Oh, my god, yeah, don't stop...After a while, we were both bored. We...fuck...started making out." The groans on screen were louder now, and Nate was pushing against Izzy's hand. "We missed most of the second half." A pinched-off whine emerged from his throat when Izzy ever so slightly altered angle and pressure. "It was late—after midnight— when we left. We were both on edge." Nate gasped as Izzy moved his hand faster. "He asked me to sleep over—I knew he meant to finish what we'd been doing." Nate's head slammed back against the seat as his hips thrust forward. "Instead, we started kissing in his car. He got on my lap. We didn't even make it to taking anything off before we both came in our jeans." He jerked against Izzy's hand. "Shit...I'm going to..."

The couple in the movie got there, one of them making several loud, heated grunts. Nate let one soft moan escape just as he arrived as well. He gripped Izzy's arm as he pulsed into his underwear. Izzy held still until Nate's shudders finished and he slumped down in the seat. He pulled his hand out and carefully zipped Nate's fly. He left the button undone.

"Holy shit," Nate murmured. He shook his head.

Izzy kissed his temple. "Your story was better than the movie."

Nate chuckled. "But we missed them screwing," he complained.

"Nah. It's not that great." Izzy squeezed his thigh. "Also, we can watch it streaming if you really want to see it."

"I feel kind of gross with jizz cooling in my pants."

"Go on," Izzy said. "Clean up a bit and come back. I'll fill you in." He grinned. "Not that we're really watching it anyway."

Nate stood and wrapped his jacket around his waist. He paused and whispered, "Sure you don't want me to..." He gestured.

"Positive. Next time?" He winked.

"Oh, yeah. I owe you one."

Nate slipped out the theater doors, and Izzy slouched down in the seat to half-watch the movie. His head was no longer buzzing with the excitement of making Nate feel good. Instead, he felt guilty for not being honest with him about returning the favor. Sooner or later, whatever tricks his body was playing would catch up to him. If he was lucky, Nate would still stick around, but he wouldn't be surprised if it were a deal-breaker.

Before he had time to think about it any further, Nate slid back into the seat beside him. He grinned and threaded his fingers with Izzy's. They cuddled closer and turned their attention to the film. Izzy decided he could get used to this.

Chapter Ten

The moment Nate opened the apartment door, he knew something wasn't right. He couldn't put his finger on it. The living room was dim, the only light coming from the back near the bedrooms. He flicked on the light by the door and listened. There were voices coming from one of the bedrooms, and Nate relaxed a little. It was weird that the living room light was off if there were people there, but obviously one of his roommates had company and had failed to tell the others. Nate strode farther into the house and put his bag down by the couch.

The talking stopped, and Nate was about to turn on the television when he heard a muffled yell. On his feet in a flash, he dashed down the short hallway to the bedrooms. There was a light coming from Jamie's room, and Nate shoved the partially open door wider with his foot. Both heads turned at once toward the sound, and Nate took in the scene.

The Boyfriend had his hand raised as though he'd been about to hit Jamie. He lowered it when he saw Nate and stepped back, his posture relaxing and his face turning from angry to neutral. It was a second too late; he wasn't fooling anyone. Nate glowered at him. This time, instead of shrinking back as he had before, The Boyfriend stood his ground.

"This is none of your business," he said.

"You hurt Jamie, you make it my business," Nate snarled.

The Boyfriend turned to Jamie. "Tell him."

Jamie's voice was so soft Nate almost didn't hear him. "No. It's over."

"Yeah, right." The Boyfriend rolled his eyes. "We all know how this is going to go. You say we're done, you come crawling back, and we do this all over again. You can't admit it, but you need me."

Jamie said nothing, and The Boyfriend made a production of his irritated huff. "Whatever. When you change your mind, then you can come over."

The Boyfriend had turned the flouncing exit into an art form. Nate and Jamie watched him go in silence, listening for the slam of the apartment door. When he was gone, Nate turned to Jamie.

"I've kept my mouth shut for your sake, but I'm done. He's a complete turd, and he treats you like shit. Tell me what's going on now."

"I can't." Jamie was shaking so hard he was almost vibrating.

Not wanting to freak him out by touching him, Nate crossed the room and sat on the bed. "He was about to hit you. Has he done that before?"

Jamie shook his head. "He's been awful, but not like this."

It was a wonder Jamie's legs held up as he walked over and joined Nate. He almost collapsed, and Nate shifted so Jamie could lean on him. Jamie shivered against his side, still trembling and taking deep, shuddering breaths. There was something—or, more accurately, a lot of somethings—Jamie was hiding. The whole situation felt off in a way Nate couldn't pinpoint. He'd witnessed The Boyfriend being manipulative, whiny, and entitled, and he wouldn't have been surprised to find out he'd gotten physical about it. Jamie had denied it, but there was no doubt he was terrified. Nate wondered what other methods of control The Boyfriend had been using.

No sense in pushing Jamie to talk about it at the moment, though. "What do you need right now?" Nate asked.

"I have to get out."

"Out of here? This apartment?"

"No. Away from Sage." He tilted his face up. "I have to get my stuff from his place. Will you help me?"

Nate was temporarily confused until he realized that must have been The Boyfriend's real name. "I will, and so will Mack. But not tonight."

Jamie nodded. He was quiet for a moment then said, "Did—did I ruin your date? I thought maybe you would bring Izzy here."

"No." Nate sighed. Now was not the time to talk to Jamie about why, even after their intimate moment in the theater, Nate still wasn't ready for anything else. "We saw a movie and went our separate ways. But even if he'd been here, this is not your fault. Okay?"

That only earned him a shrug. At least Jamie had stopped quivering. He uncurled and stood up. Without responding directly to Nate's statement, he said, "I'm going to go take a shower and go to bed."

He grabbed a towel and some clothes then turned his back to Nate, making it clear the discussion was over. If Nate thought Jamie would talk to Mack, he never would have said anything else. He'd have let Mack handle it and left them alone. Mack had known Jamie far longer.

"Jamie, please at least tell me what he's done to you."

Jamie spun around. "You don't get it! I already told you I can't. Leave me alone!"

Nate stared after him as Jamie flew into the bathroom and slammed the door. He sat frozen to the spot, trying to piece together what he could have said differently. He had no experience, either in talking to Jamie specifically or in being a friend to someone in Jamie's situation.

The shower started, breaking Nate out of his trance. He rose from the bed and glanced around, hoping for some clue about what had happened or how to help Jamie. Nothing stood out to him, so he retreated from the bedroom. For a few minutes, he stood outside the bathroom door, listening. He wasn't sure what for, only that he wanted to know Jamie was all right.

The only sounds were the spray of the water and the occasional clunk of a soap bottle. Satisfied, Nate went to his own room. He lay down on the bed, hands behind his head. For a moment, he considered calling Izzy. He changed his mind, realizing there wasn't anything Izzy could do, and Nate didn't want to break Jamie's fragile confidence in him. Instead, Nate allowed his mind to wander back to his date.

Izzy had given him more than a highly pleasurable but mildly embarrassing thrill in the theater. He'd left Nate with a lot to think about. Izzy had freely admitted to being turned on by Nate's story about getting off with Trevor. He obviously had no reservations about sharing his personal kink with Nate. Which put Nate in the position of wondering whether he'd be safe telling Izzy his own.

Even alone in the dark, the thought sent heat to Nate's cheeks and ears. He rolled over, stopping his thoughts in their tracks before yanking the covers up and burying his face in the pillow. No, Izzy didn't need to know, at least not yet.

Nate and Mack took Jamie to get his things from The Boyfriend's apartment a few tense days later. Even another night out watching Izzy perform hadn't relaxed Nate, and Jamie had been mostly hiding out in his room the whole time. He'd even refused to go visit Trevor and the baby when Nate offered.

Jamie called ahead, since he didn't have a key of his own. When he emerged from his room afterward, he was pale and wouldn't say anything beyond giving Mack directions how to get there. They piled into Mack's van and drove to Quincy.

Nate would have liked to ask Izzy for help, but Izzy was working his twenty-four-hour shift. He wouldn't be off until the following morning, and then he'd need to sleep. Nate wouldn't even be able to call him for reassurance. It made him pause, the discovery that he wanted to be able to talk to Izzy and process what he couldn't expect Jamie or even Mack to hear. He tucked that idea away for later.

Jamie knocked on The Boyfriend's door, and he opened it to let them in. The apartment was nicer than Nate had expected, causing him to wonder how he paid for it. Nate didn't know what The Boyfriend did for a living.

"I boxed all your shit for you," The Boyfriend said, sneering. "You're welcome."

"Thanks," Jamie replied without a hint of sarcasm. "Um. I want to look around and make sure."

"Nice vote of confidence. But whatever. I don't care."

Mack's expression was frosty, and it was obvious he was trying not to say anything. Jamie stepped around them and examined the room. He seemed to be taking in the details of the apartment more than looking for anything The Boyfriend had "forgotten" to return to him. Nate began picking up the few boxes The Boyfriend had collected and stacking them by the door.

Jamie stepped out of the bathroom with a stick of deodorant. Nate wondered what possible sentimental value it could have had, since it wasn't as though Jamie didn't have any at home or couldn't replace it. He didn't question it when Jamie threw it into one of the boxes. He hadn't taken anything else.

The Boyfriend watched him, and the same thing must have occurred to him as to Nate. He frowned, but he said nothing until Jamie had finished and turned around to face him.

"Could we talk about this?" The Boyfriend asked. "Without your bodyguards?"

Nate took a step forward, about to tell him anything he needed to say to Jamie, he could say in front of them. Mack put a hand on him to hold him back. He leaned up and in to say quietly, "Leave it."

Jamie glanced at them before replying, "Fine."

They stepped into the bedroom at the back of the apartment and closed the door. For a long time, Nate heard them talking quietly, but it seemed all right. He was about to offer to take the boxes out to the van and let Mack handle things when Jamie came out. Before he spoke, the voices in the other room rose. Nate heard bits and pieces, both of them saying things about how they couldn't solve their problems in some particular way. He could only guess at what they meant.

When Nate heard Jamie yell, "No!" he moved in an instant toward the door. As he arrived, there was a crash from inside the room. Nate shoved open the door. Jamie was lying on the floor, his body positioned at an odd angle. The Boyfriend looked up from where he was crouched next to Jamie. A bedside table had been overturned, and the lamp lay in pieces beside it.

"Please," The Boyfriend said. "He's not waking up."

"What?" Nate rushed over and checked Jamie out. He was breathing, but he was definitely unconscious, not sleeping. "What the hell happened?"

"I don't know," The Boyfriend said, his voice breaking. "We were arguing, and—"

"Get out of the way." By that time, Nate had pulled out his phone and pressed 9-1-1.

"I just wanted to talk to him. He didn't want to listen."

The Boyfriend looked shaken enough Nate decided not to press him on why he thought that was a good idea, given how Jamie had broken up with him and said it was the last time. Instead he turned his attention to explaining the situation to the dispatcher. He tried to remain calm while giving as many details as he had from standing there.

When he ended the call, Nate rounded on The Boyfriend.

"Why the hell didn't *you* call?" he demanded. His worry for Jamie made him angry.

"I was going to!"

"Well, you didn't. What happened? Did you hit him?" Nate glared.

"No! I would never."

"I saw you last night." Nate used his height as an advantage, displaying his fury.

The Boyfriend shrank back. "I don't know! We were fighting, and then I—" He bit his lip. "He shoved me. Just onto the bed. So I grabbed him and I pushed back. That's all, I swear! Not hard enough to do anything. But then he hit the table. He passed out or something, and I couldn't wake him up."

Nate had a feeling there were some details The Boyfriend had left out, especially since Jamie's lip was split. He didn't get a chance to answer because the next thing he knew, there was a knock on the door. Nate frowned at The Boyfriend until he slunk out of the room to answer it.

Voices in the hallway preceded footsteps, and next thing Nate knew, the last person he expected rounded the corner. Izzy and his partner—Val, Nate remembered—strode into the room. Val immediately began checking Jamie over. Izzy's eyes flicked to Nate, but he returned his attention to The Boyfriend. He began asking him the same questions Nate had, and The Boyfriend gave the same non-answers in response.

Izzy seemed to have the same feelings about it Nate did because he turned to Nate. "Were you here the whole time?"

"Yeah." Nate glanced over at Jamie, wondering how much he should tell Izzy. He nodded his chin at The Boyfriend. "We came to get Jamie's stuff from him."

"Who is he?"

Nate paused. Jamie had said The Boyfriend's real name the night before, but he blanked. "That's his ex."

The Boyfriend scowled. "My name is Sage. Maybe if you bothered to learn it—"

"Oh, fuck off," Nate spit out.

Izzy held up a hand. "Both of you. I'm going to have to ask you to stop. Do you know if Jamie was taking any kind of medication?"

"Are you asking if he's on drugs?" Sage exclaimed. He appeared to be searching for a way to make himself look less responsible.

"No," Izzy answered, using the patient tone of someone used to dealing with unhelpful family members. "I need to know if he's on any prescriptions that you know of. Although if there's something else, now's the time to tell me."

Nate tried to recall if Jamie had mentioned it, but nothing came to mind. "I don't know," he told Izzy. "He hasn't been doing well, though."

Val had Jamie's shirt up and was listening to his chest. Nate gasped at how Jamie looked. His ribs were visible, and he had greenish bruises all along his torso. Nate spun to glare at Sage.

"You asshole," he snarled. "What the hell did you do to him?"

Sage's expression twisted from panic to anger. "I didn't do anything to him. You might want to ask Jamie what happened. Oh, wait. You can't because he's fucking unconscious!"

Nate would happily have taken Sage on right then, but more footsteps alerted him to people in the living room. A moment later, two police officers entered, followed by Mack. He spotted Val and Jamie on the floor. "Oh, god damn."

There were too many people talking at once. Sage was still protesting his innocence—and really, there was no evidence he wasn't, outside of his ongoing snotty behavior. From all appearances, Jamie had fallen and hit the table. Neither Nate nor Mack had witnessed what had come before that, even if they'd heard the two of them arguing. Mack was trying to get to Jamie, but the officers were herding everyone away. Nate watched it all unfolding as though he'd separated from his body. Everything slid past him in a confused mass. Nate backed up against the wall, breathing hard. He closed his eyes.

"Hey." Izzy's cool hand on his neck brought him back.

"Please," Nate begged, even though he didn't know what he was asking for.

"We're going to take your friend, okay?"

Nate nodded, and Izzy said something else about it which Nate didn't catch. He stepped out of the bedroom, followed by Mack, Sage, and the police. Izzy and Val loaded Jamie onto a backboard and carted him past and through the apartment. The officers, having decided this was a medical emergency and not a crime scene, trailed after Izzy and Val, leaving Nate alone with Mack and Sage. Without any evidence or Jamie's statement, there wasn't anything else to be done about Sage.

"You asshole," Mack told Sage. "You're lucky we don't want any more trouble. Stay the hell away from Jamie."

Mack shoved Nate toward the apartment door, and they collected Jamie's boxes. They left before Sage had a chance to say or do anything else. After they loaded the van, Mack turned to Nate.

Mack leaned against the wall. "How much do you know?"

Nate frowned. "I feel like none of us ever tell each other anything. The other night, I came home to Jamie breaking up with him for the thousandth time. He asked me to help him get his stuff, but when I wanted to know what happened, he wouldn't say. Got pissed at me. What's going on with him?"

"I don't know anymore." Mack ran a hand through his hair. "Fuck, I need a smoke."

Nate couldn't stand being around Mack when he lit up, but he followed him around the side of the building anyway, wanting to hear whatever it was. Mack pulled out a cigarette and his lighter, taking his time and making Nate impatient. At last he drew in his first puff and exhaled the smoke. Nate leaned away and forced himself not to cough.

"I never feel like it's my job to push people," Mack said. "I don't know when I should say something or not. I finally did. Sage is a creep, and it was killing Jamie." He took another drag on his cigarette before he continued. "He virtually stopped eating again right before he told Sage it was over for good. I knew that fucker wasn't going to let it go."

"Again?" The word stuck in Nate's mind, looming larger than the other things Mack had said.

"He does that sometimes." Mack said it like he was talking about one of Jamie's hobbies.

"I didn't know."

"Well, now you do."

Nate leaned against the wall, thinking about all the times he'd seen Jamie do what Mack described, but he hadn't thought much about it. Or he had, but he'd been too wrapped up in his own troubles. Something else surfaced, and he turned his head to look at Mack, who had his eyes closed as though he was enjoying his last smoke ever.

"Did Sage do...that...to him?"

Mack cracked an eyelid. "The bruises?"

"Yeah."

"Brilliant deduction, Sherlock."

"No need to be an ass. I didn't realize."

"Sorry." Mack didn't sound as though he meant it, but then he exhaled the kind of sigh which meant he too felt guilty for not doing something sooner. "He hid it well. Don't know how long it had been escalating like that. I always just thought Sage was kind of a douche but not the type to rough anyone up. Jamie would never say what was going on, not directly."

Nate remembered months ago when he'd begun to wonder. Would Jamie have listened back then or any of the previous times? Maybe they could have gotten to him before it reached this point. Mack didn't say anything else. Whether Jamie's problems were because he hadn't been eating properly or because he'd done something else didn't matter. Neither Nate nor Mack could answer which it was. Mack stubbed out his cigarette.

"Come on," he said. "I'll drive the van. We need to get to the hospital so Jamie's not alone when he wakes up."

It sounded more hopeful than Nate felt, but he followed Mack to the van anyway. His mind drifted to the casual way Izzy had addressed him, had touched his neck in the hallway. He wondered if Izzy would still be there or if he had to finish his shift. Silently, Nate prayed to whatever powers there were that Jamie would be all right. He slid into the van next to Mack and watched out the window as they pulled away into the night.

Izzy had just finished his twenty-four-hour shift, and he knew he needed to rest. He should shower and eat something too, but instead he contemplated checking in on the young man he'd brought in. There wasn't any proof those bruises on him were delivered by his boyfriend, but Izzy had seen it too often over the years to ignore it. Why none of his roommates had done something was beyond Izzy's ability to understand.

He tried to tell himself that the only reason to check in on him was to make sure he was all right, but he knew the truth. He hoped to see Nate. There hadn't been time to talk while he was taking information about Nate's friend. Nate might have gone home, but it didn't seem like leaving his friend alone in the emergency department was the sort of thing he would do. After all, he'd stayed all night to wait for a baby that wasn't his. So instead of going home, Izzy headed for the hospital.

There was a chance they'd already sent Nate's friend home, but Izzy suspected not. He remembered the man's first name was James, but he couldn't recall the last name. He texted Val, and she responded with all the information she had. Izzy entered through the hospital lobby. After obtaining James Cosgrove's location, Izzy navigated the hospital's corridors to the unit.

A nurse in a hijab at the desk looked up from her chart when Izzy approached. He was glad he still had on his uniform because she greeted him as one professional to another. After asking which room, he followed her directions down a long hallway and around a corner. The door was ajar, and a low murmur of conversation drifted out. James had company, but Izzy didn't know who was in there. It didn't matter; even if it wasn't Nate, he could at least look in and find out how everything was going. He took a deep breath and pushed the door open farther.

Inside, James lay on the bed, connected to an IV. He still looked pale but much better than the previous night. Two other people were with him—Nate and his friend who'd had the baby. Trevor, Izzy recalled after a moment of thought. Trevor had hold of James' hand, and all three of them were talking quietly. It took a moment before anyone noticed Izzy in the doorway, but at last Nate looked up. Surprise registered on his face, followed by a shy smile.

Izzy hadn't counted on the effect Nate's blue eyes would have on him. He had to work harder to appear casual, leaning where he was and not reacting to being close to the man who had stolen his heart all those months ago when he first heard his powerful voice. Izzy kept his face neutral, holding back his desire to rush to Nate and kiss him. They were in his friend's hospital room, after all.

"Izzy," Nate finally said.

"I, um, came to check up on your friend." He nodded to the bed.

James appeared puzzled, so Nate said, "He was one of the EMTs who brought you here."

"Oh." James' confusion gave way to a nod and a half-smile.

"And he's my boyfriend." Nate's blush did nice things to Izzy's stomach.

"Oh," James repeated, but there was a lot contained in the single syllable, and the smile widened.

"I'm glad you're all right. I'm Izzy." He approached the bed and held out his hand.

"Jamie." He accepted Izzy's hand. "Wait...*you're* Izzy? Wow, you look a lot different up close."

Izzy grinned. "It's the wig, isn't it? I do look plain without it." The others laughed, and Izzy relaxed. "So, how are you doing?"

Jamie shrugged. "I'm okay. They're keeping me for a bit." He didn't elaborate, and Izzy didn't press.

The nurse from the desk, whose name tag read Alia, stepped into the room. Trevor excused himself, saying he had to head to work. He ruffled Jamie's hair and bid the others goodbye. In the meantime, Alia busied herself checking Jamie's blood pressure.

Izzy turned to Nate. "How about we let the nurse get on with her job and go grab coffee?"

"Sure."

Nate followed Izzy out of the room and pulled the door almost closed. They retraced Izzy's steps back to the elevator and went down to the cafeteria. Izzy got them both a cup of what was probably terrible coffee while Nate found a place to sit. The sounds of people chattering around them faded into the background. Izzy took a sip of his too-hot coffee and burned his tongue, providing both a stalling tactic and a diversion. He set the cup down.

"Your friends have a knack for ending up in the hospital," Izzy remarked. "I hope that doesn't mean I'm doomed."

Nate stared at him for a moment. He slowly closed his mouth, blinked, and said, "And you have a knack for showing up when they do. Does that mean I'm doomed?"

"Damn." Izzy cringed. "Sorry. I'm used to joking around about this stuff. Cuts the tension of all the shit I see on the job." He cleared his throat. "Is Jamie okay?"

"No," Nate said. "I hope he will be, but he needs to stay away from his asshole ex in order for that to happen."

"Did he—I mean—" Izzy remembered the ex in question and the way he'd been evasive.

"Sage lied, not that that's anything new. Jamie hadn't been eating properly as it was, and he was dehydrated and undernourished. They had a fight, Sage shoved him, and he ended up passing out because his body couldn't take one more thing. So I guess in a sense, Sage was being sincere when he said he barely touched Jamie. But the fact that he put his hands on him at all isn't good." Nate growled in the back of his throat. "Asshole," he repeated.

"I take it this wasn't the first time."

Nate's brow furrowed. "I can't tell anymore what's been going on. We all knew what a tool Sage was—it's why none of us ever used his real name—but Jamie won't talk about what happened. Sage wasn't beating him, if that's what you're asking. It's something else, but I have no idea what."

Izzy sat back. "I hope he can get some help."

"Me too." Nate paused. "I guess all I can do is pray at this point."

"Do you?" Izzy raised his eyebrows. "Pray, I mean."

Nate gave a short, sharp laugh. "Not really. It was an expression. I haven't prayed seriously in years. Why?"

"Just curious." Izzy shrugged. He and Nate hadn't ever talked about it. He assumed Nate knew he was Jewish, but Izzy had no information about Nate's religious history.

"Do you pray?" Nate asked. "I mean—I don't actually know anything about being Jewish. Crap. There I go, shooting off my mouth." He blushed again, a sight Izzy was sure he would never tire of.

Izzy smiled. "It's fine. Yes, I'm Jewish, and I do pray. I'll be happy to say a blessing for Jamie's healing."

"Thanks."

Nate put his hand on top of Izzy's, and Izzy rotated his so he could squeeze Nate's fingers. They were quiet for a few minutes, leaving their hands joined on top of the table while they sipped their awful coffee. Izzy set his empty cup down. He needed a gentle segue into the conversation he ought to have with Nate about where they were heading. He was far too old to want to be strung along with a casual nothing. If there was no hope for something more with Nate, he had to know before either or both of them dragged it out too long.

"Do you have plans for the holidays?" he asked.

Nate shrugged. "Probably midnight mass with my family."

Izzy cringed. "You're Catholic?"

"Sort of. Well, I mean, you're never really not Catholic anymore, not when you're born into it. I don't think people truly understand that."

"I definitely get it." Izzy nodded. "Same for me, but I'm still observant. It's as much cultural as religious for you, right?"

"It is," Nate agreed. "Ten years of Catholic education, until I got kicked out of school."

"What? You?" Izzy almost laughed. Nate hardly seemed like the sort to get in trouble.

Nate did laugh. "They didn't care all that much that I'm gay. It was more how back then, I really enjoyed making a show of it. I had a flair for the dramatic, which shouldn't be a surprise. They found me 'distracting to other students.' My parents weren't happy, but

I'm glad I went to public school. That's how I met Trev. Best friends for nearly ten years." He sounded proud.

The closeness between Nate and Trevor made sense now. "But you're not religious anymore?" Izzy asked.

"Nah. I still go at Christmas and Easter, though. What about you? I mean, you don't celebrate Christmas, right?"

"No." Izzy chuckled. "When I was a kid, I asked my mothers if we could. They were clear on the answer."

"But you get Hanukkah. Isn't that kind of a big deal? Eight days of presents."

"Ha! Not at all. Hanukkah isn't even a major holiday. The only reason it gets much attention is to compete with Christmas. We'll light our candles, of course, but we don't do gifts. I'm too old to play dreidel and eat jelly donuts." He paused, thinking about what he and Lynne had missed out on. To curb his sadness, he changed topics slightly. "You could come over," he suggested.

Nate didn't reply immediately. He looked as though he was searching for a response. After a moment, he said, "I'd like to see your traditions, yeah."

Was that all he wanted? Izzy brushed it off. "Wouldn't be on night one. You already said you're going to mass, and even I know Christmas Eve is the twenty-fourth."

"Yeah." Nate wiped his hands on his jeans. "I—"

Izzy sighed. "Look, if you don't want to do this anymore, it's fine, but please tell me."

Nate stared at him for a moment, and Izzy wondered if he'd said the wrong thing. When Nate had recovered, he shook his head. "I'm..." He rubbed his forehead. "I haven't had a lot of success with dating, and I didn't want to rush into staying over."

There was a story there, and Izzy wondered if he would ever hear it. He took Nate's hand again. "There's no hurry."

"I want to." The blush was back, and it was obvious he wasn't saying what he really meant. "We could spend First Night together?"

"I'm performing at Grand Slam. You could come watch, and then...we'll see?"

Nate's posture relaxed. "I'd like that."

"Good." Izzy stood up. He put a hand on Nate's shoulder, not wanting to draw attention to themselves with anything else. "Maybe we can go out again in between?"

"Yes, definitely." Nate grinned up at Izzy before pushing back his chair and rising to his feet.

They threw out their trash, and Izzy bid Nate goodbye. He watched Nate head back toward the elevators, on his way back to Jamie's room. Izzy waited until he was gone before he turned around and headed back to the parking lot. He thought about their plans, deciding there wasn't any other way he'd rather ring in the new year.

CHAPTER ELEVEN

Christmas passed uneventfully, and Nate enjoyed his break from rehearsals. They wouldn't start until the second week of January, which gave him enough time to talk to Del about the spring performance. He wanted to run a few things past him, particularly since Del had a lot of good ideas for what direction Nate might take with future shows.

Nate's parents were the same as always, and he chose not to subject Izzy to their snooty presence. He would have liked to introduce him to Dean, Corinne, and the kids, but it could wait. He'd gone with Izzy to his mothers' house instead and been treated to a surprisingly subdued menorah lighting. They were charming women, at least up until they took a thorough interest in Nate's Catholic upbringing. He'd endured an evening of having to either deny or acknowledge nearly every Catholic stereotype. Izzy seemed to find the whole thing amusing, and even Nate had to admit there was some humor in it. He'd never cross-examined his parents on their religious customs; it had always been background noise more than something Nate thought deeply about. He supposed he was lucky Izzy's moms didn't seem the type to flip out that Nate wasn't Jewish.

With the arrival of New Year's Eve, Nate's nerves were at maximum level. He was preparing to go to Grand Slam to watch both Izzy and his roommates. The drag show was on early in the evening, and Mack and Jamie's band had the prime slot for the midnight countdown. It was a big deal that they'd grown enough in skill for Rafael to allow them the privilege. It was an even bigger deal that Jamie seemed well enough to perform.

He hadn't spoken a word about what happened, either with Sage or at the hospital. He did seem to be eating again, more or less, so Nate left him alone about it. Jamie had taken some time off from work—a minor miracle, considering he rarely used any of his vacation days. He'd also gone to see Trevor, Marlie, and Andre a number of times. Nate wasn't keen on babies himself, but Jamie seemed fascinated with Aidan. Apparently, their time together was highly therapeutic.

Nate didn't normally have a lot of interest in clothes. He wore a uniform at the cafe and a costume when he was on stage, but the rest of the time he was a jeans and t-shirts kind of guy. Izzy didn't seem to mind Nate's lack of wardrobe variety, and he dressed in much the same way. Nate wondered if for both of them it was a need for comfort and relaxation more than anything else—a stripping off of public persona, in a way.

To Jamie's credit, he tried to help. He was trendy, and he loved dressing people. He'd even done it with baby Aidan, much to everyone's amusement. Unfortunately, Nate didn't own anything other than his uniform clothes, his casual attire, and a lone suit which he wore when he attended church to appease his mother. Jamie eventually gave up and instructed Nate not to wear a printed t-shirt or anything with holes in it. Nate tried on three before choosing a bright blue one, and he borrowed a pair of Jamie's earrings which matched nicely.

He shouldn't have been nervous. It was only Izzy, after all, and it wasn't as though Nate was a teenager or a blushing virgin bride. He'd never been so anxious about a first time. Even when he and Rocco had done it in high school Nate hadn't been so tense. He thought back to those days and snorted. He'd told Trevor about it, but only the funny part where Rocco's mom had been upstairs and they'd faked watching some baseball game to cover the sound. Nate hadn't told Trevor that it had kind of hurt, Rocco had been upset and humiliated at causing Nate pain, and it had been over almost faster than either of them could blink.

It had been good, though. Nate remembered eating the lasagna Rocco's mom had served them, thinking how grown-up he felt and how close to Rocco afterward. Even sloppy, terrible teenage sex carried magic for Nate because he'd been in love. He'd fudged that for Trevor's benefit too, implying he'd had sex because he was a typical, always-in-the-mood adolescent. It hadn't been true then, and it wasn't true now.

Guilt and embarrassment gnawed at him for making Izzy wait so long. None of his friends had ever seemed to hold back. Hell, Trevor had started a relationship with anonymous sex. Mack and Amelia went at it like rabbits, which Nate knew because she was over at the apartment a lot and they weren't quiet. Jamie—well, maybe it didn't bear thinking about the way he and Sage used to make up after every time they'd been apart. Nate still wanted to throttle Sage.

When it came to sex, Nate wanted to know for sure. He wanted to be in love again. He swallowed, staring at himself in the mirror for a moment before fixing his hair. Did he love Izzy? They'd only known each other for a little over a month. In that time, so much had happened. Enough to make Nate need to be around Izzy as much as possible. All the time, if he could. Love, though? He wasn't certain. Maybe tonight would help him figure it out.

He rode in with Mack and Jamie in the van. They were early, but because of the First Night crowds, there were already a good number of people at Grand Slam. Nate helped Mack and Jamie unload the van, which gave him backstage access. While he was working, he caught sight of Izzy.

He was dressed much like Nate, and he had his bag and costume. He grinned and waved, making Nate's stomach flip. Nate waved back with his free hand. He was so lost in watching Izzy that Mack nearly ran into him from behind. Startled back into the moment, Nate turned around, apologized, and went back to giving the guys a hand.

Jamie and Mack joined Nate out in the bar when they were through, and Amelia tagged along with a friend of hers Nate had never met. Brandon, Jamie's cousin who happened to be engaged to one of their other bandmates, slid in beside Jamie. He'd brought his friend—Cian, Nate thought, the Irish dancer—with him. Mack was right about Cian; he was quite attractive, with midnight-black hair and twinkling light blue eyes. Nate noticed for the first time that his hearing aids looked like silver and black snakes.

As Cian sat, Jamie glowered at him, but he relented when Brandon gave him a shove and signed something angry at him. Cian didn't seem bothered by it in the least, but whatever he signed to Brandon made Jamie roll his eyes. Nate couldn't fathom what was so awful about Cian that Jamie gave him the cold shoulder every time they had to share space. Whatever it was, Nate wasn't going to ruin the evening pondering it.

The short queen with the turquoise hair got the crowd in the mood with her colorful commentary, and Nate relaxed as he watched the other acts. He couldn't wait to see what Izzy had come up with this time. The others at the table all seemed to be enjoying themselves as well, even Jamie, who had stopped shooting glares at Cian long enough to stay focused on the stage.

At last TaTa was up. She sashayed onstage in a black Ginger Rogers-style chiffon dance dress. Her partner, Chico, had on a slick Palm Beach suit. Nate only had to wonder for a moment what song they were about to perform. The music started, and within a few measures he recognized "You're the Top" from *Anything Goes*. He grinned, recalling how he'd told Izzy that was one of the first musicals he'd done in high school.

TaTa and Chico twirled around each other in expert dance moves, and Nate was swept up in watching them. TaTa remained perfectly in character and in sync with Chico until the very end. She looked over at Nate's table, made eye contact, and delivered the last line of the song, telling him if she was the bottom he was the top. She winked, and she and Chico dance-retreated offstage to the final notes.

Several mouths at their tables dropped open as they all simultaneously realized TaTa had done that specifically for Nate's benefit. He flushed, knowing she'd meant it literally, though he hoped it might be the other way around from what she'd suggested. Beside him, there was light laughter from his friends and the continuing applause of the crowd behind them. Nate's only thoughts were on TaTa; everything else faded.

Mack leaned in. "I'll take you back there to find her. Come on."

In a flash, Nate was out of his seat and winding his way to the back, following Mack through the performers' entrance. He slipped around several people, finally reaching the doors to the hallway with the dressing rooms. The queen with the turquoise hair stopped him.

"Please," Nate begged. "I need to see TaTa."

Turquoise arched an eyebrow. "Well, honey, you can wait until she's done changing into her street clothes."

"No!" Nate couldn't explain his desperation. "Can you tell her

I'm here?"

"That depends. Who shall I say is calling?"

"I'm—" Nate tensed. "I'm her man. Please?"

A slow, wicked smile spread across Turquoise's face. "Sure, sweetie. I'll be right back."

She disappeared, and a minute or two later, she was back with TaTa. Nate stepped closer, and TaTa's whole face lit up. She grabbed Nate and dragged him through the doors. She led him to a quieter section. Nate was done resisting. TaTa looked so gorgeous that he couldn't help himself. He pushed a little until he had her pinned against the wall where he could kiss her senseless. Behind them, he heard cheers and a few whistles.

They broke apart, and TaTa laughed. She wiped the smudged color off Nate's lips, and he shivered, liking the way she'd marked him. Breathless, he rested his forehead against hers.

"You want to get out of here?" she whispered in his ear.

"I can't." The word came out whinier than Nate had intended, and he cleared his throat. "I mean, I promised the guys I would stay and watch their band."

"I understand." TaTa stroked his cheek. "Let me get changed, and I'll come sit with you."

"Yeah."

Nate stepped back and let her go, waiting until she was inside the dressing room before he turned around and walked out. Turquoise gave him a leer as he passed, and he laughed shakily. There was no doubt in his mind now about where he wanted to be as soon as Mack and Jamie's band finished playing.

It was long after one in the morning when they stumbled into Izzy's apartment, a little tipsy and a lot ready to have their hands on each other. Nate had been about as patient as he could while listening to the Kreepy Krullers, but they hadn't improved enough for him to actually like them. He and Izzy only stayed long enough to be polite. By that point, he didn't care that every single person in his group knew exactly where he was going and why. Only the other passengers on the train kept them from doing more than letting their legs rest against each other under the pretense of leaving room for the other riders.

Inside the apartment, Izzy flicked on the light. The space was tiny and a bit messy, exactly the sort of place Nate imagined Izzy might live. Their need for contact had cooled somewhat on the chilly walk from the station, and Izzy offered Nate a drink. He declined, and Izzy stepped into his personal space.

"I meant it when I said we didn't have to do anything. If you want to sleep, it's all right."

Nate rested his palm against Izzy's soft beard. He wondered how he kept it from feeling wiry. The dark hairs tickled Nate's skin, sending a thrill through him. He responded to Izzy's statement by pulling Izzy closer for another long kiss. It was less frantic than the one he'd given TaTa after her performance. Long and slow, Nate explored Izzy's lips and tongue with his own.

When the two of them parted, Izzy said, "Bedroom?"

At Nate's nod, they joined hands and stepped around the corner to the single small room. Izzy closed the door, which made Nate chuckle. It wasn't as though there were other people or even pets they needed to keep out. They resumed kissing, Izzy taking everything gently. As much as Nate enjoyed it, Izzy's pace was frustratingly slow. Nate wanted the fire he felt with TaTa.

With a gasp, he pulled back. He wasn't supposed to admit that even to himself, not on their first night staying together. This was supposed to be what Izzy was going for, sweet and sensual and drawn-out. Not whatever it was Nate really wanted but didn't dare ask for.

A concerned frown crossed Izzy's face. "What's wrong?"

"N-Nothing," Nate stammered. He slid out of Izzy's arms and sat on the bed.

"Hey." Izzy joined him. "I didn't want to ask and upset you, but...is this your first time?"

"What?" Nate angled to face him. "God, no."

"Then can you tell me? If I've done something wrong—"

"No, it's not that." Nate squeezed his eyes shut. "Remember when you told me it made you hot getting me off in my clothes?" Nate's face flamed.

Izzy chuckled. "Yeah."

"Why?"

Izzy lay back on the bed, his feet on the floor and his hands behind his head. Nate turned onto his side and curled his legs behind him, propped on one elbow so he could see Izzy.

"Well," Izzy said, "the most I can tell you is that it's about control. There's something so sexy about having someone so into it, so ready, that they can't hold back. It feels a little dirty, too, but in a way that's almost hidden." He turned his head to look at Nate.

"What's this about?"

"What if I want something too?"

"Oh." Izzy rolled to face Nate and put a hand on his neck. "You can tell me."

Nate closed his eyes, thinking about the first time he saw TaTa, singing Annie Lennox for the Covers for Covers benefit. He recalled all the times he'd gone just to watch her, entranced and wanting something he couldn't name. Then there was the time they sang together, and tonight during the drag show when TaTa had been so cheeky with him. He wanted her, but he wanted Izzy, too, and there was no way to explain it.

"What does it feel like to be...*her?*" he finally asked.

Izzy's eyes widened. "You mean performing as TaTa?"

"Yeah."

Sliding closer, Izzy rested his arm on Nate's waist. "Are you asking if I feel like I'm expressing my gender? Or if it turns me on?"

"Both, I think." Nate pressed against Izzy's warm body.

Izzy moved his hand back up to touch Nate's cheek. "She is part of me, but only in the sense that I've created her—she's a character I play, even though I feel connected with her. And no, it doesn't really turn me on to become her. I simply like performing as her. Some people do get aroused by it, though."

"What if—" Nate stopped. He couldn't do it, confess to Izzy. Instead, he pulled Izzy to himself and kissed him, seeking the flames and the magic spark. He pictured Izzy in the chiffon dress, and the thought made him groan against Izzy's lips.

"You can tell me." Izzy kissed down Nate's neck, sliding a finger into the collar of his t-shirt and licking his collarbone. "Come on."

"I can't." Nate's breathing sped up.

"It's all right. Whatever you say, I won't be upset."

"Ungh!" Nate tipped his head back. "Please..."

"Please what?"

"Oh, god. Please...I need..." Nate was almost hyperventilating from nerves and arousal. "I want you to fuck me in that dress." He clamped his mouth shut, horrified at himself that he'd said it.

Izzy rolled them both so he was half-lying on top of Nate. He gazed down with his dark brown eyes shining in the dim room. Instead of shock or disgust on his face, he seemed excited. "You know there's nothing wrong with that, don't you?"

Nate's voice quavered. "I've never told anyone."

"I'm honored, then." Izzy pecked him on the cheek. "Do you

want me to wear the wig, too?"

"Yeah. And—and the lipstick. I want you to mark me as yours."

"Anything," Izzy said. He leaned in for a smoldering kiss before withdrawing and rising from the bed. He crossed to the closet and pulled out a red knee-length dress with a flared skirt. "Will this one do? The other one is a little tight in the hips for fucking. Also, it's my favorite, and I don't want it stained."

"Hell, yes."

Nate was almost dizzy. He couldn't believe Izzy was so willing to do this for him. Watching Izzy casually strip down and slide the dress over his head made him hotter than almost anything else he'd experienced. Izzy made it sensual, slowly pulling on a pair of thigh-high stockings and giving Nate a good look at his lean legs. They were muscular, and Izzy shaved them, which puzzled Nate since Izzy didn't shave his beard. Izzy took a wig off one of the foam heads on the shelf in his closet. When he was through, he crossed to the dresser and opened a makeup box. He removed a tube of the most obnoxiously bright red lipstick Nate had ever seen and applied it generously to his lips.

When he turned around again, Nate inhaled sharply. Izzy hadn't gone all out like he would if he were performing, but it was enough. Nate saw in him both the sultry singer and the handsome man. He slid back on the bed to make room for Izzy to join him. Izzy sauntered slowly toward him.

"What do you think?"

Nate had to take several breaths before he could say, "I want you."

Izzy crawled up the bed until his face was inches from Nate's. "I'm all yours, sweetheart," he cooed in TaTa's voice.

Nate moaned and pulled Izzy down into a fiery embrace. Izzy made a show of pressing firm kisses all over Nate's cheeks and neck, leaving lipstick prints wherever he went. Only when he set the tube on the nightstand did Nate realize he'd brought it over. He wondered what Izzy planned to do with it.

"Do you want me to undress you, or do you want to keep your clothes on?" Izzy asked. He palmed Nate through his jeans.

"I don't care." Nate arched his back. For Izzy, he would gladly ruin every pair of underwear he owned.

"I'll at least take your shirt off."

Izzy encouraged him to sit up a bit and pulled Nate's shirt over his head. After reapplying the lipstick, he began leaving prints all over Nate's shoulders and chest, kissing his way down until he tongued Nate's navel. Nate writhed, ticklish but turned on. Izzy popped the button on Nate's jeans and slid the zipper down. He reached inside, stroking while he continued to kiss Nate's belly.

Nate shoved at his jeans and briefs until they cleared his hips. Izzy sat up a bit and reached over to the nightstand. He grabbed the lipstick again as well as a condom and lube. All Nate could do was watch him as he put on more lipstick right before descending to engulf Nate in his mouth. With a cry, Nate dropped his head back and pushed his hips forward. He wouldn't be able to take much. He touched Izzy's head, causing him to look up.

"Stop. I'm too close."

Izzy pulled off, and Nate noted with a mix of shock and thrill that he'd left red stains behind from the lipstick. It was the most erotic thing Nate had ever experienced. He didn't even know what he needed anymore; his head was too clouded from being so close to the edge.

Sitting up, Izzy simultaneously yanked off the rest of Nate's clothes as he went. He tossed them onto the floor before straddling Nate and continuing to kiss him. The red dress fanned out around them as they thrust against each other. As good as it felt, Nate wanted Izzy to keep his promise. He pushed a little until Izzy shifted and Nate could roll over. He looked over his shoulder at Izzy, who nodded.

Izzy took his time, slowly preparing Nate until he thought he might combust. It had been months since he'd been with Rocco, and Nate knew it was better for Izzy to be careful. He still wished he would hurry. At last Izzy was sinking into him, and the only thing on Nate's mind was the way they fit together, the way Izzy adjusted and moved with him. It felt right, and with a jolt, Nate realized it was the first time he'd felt safe enough to admit what he craved.

A shiver rippled through him, and Izzy paused until Nate moved again, seeking to deepen their connection. Izzy leaned down over his back, pressing hot kisses all over Nate's shoulders. The energy increased between them, their pace urgent. Nate was almost there, needing one small push to go over the edge. Izzy's fingers found Nate's, linking at the same time he leaned to kiss Nate's ear. Nate turned a little, trying to join their mouths.

When Izzy's lips found his, Nate felt a wave of heat and pleasure rising. Something in the way Izzy had stripped away the shame Nate had carried around over his desires made him feel whole. He cried out, emptying himself onto the sheet underneath him just as Izzy's hips jerked against his ass.

Nate collapsed, breathing hard and not minding one bit that Izzy was heavy on top of him or that he'd landed in his own mess. He grunted when Izzy withdrew to shed the condom and lie down next to him. They didn't move for a few minutes after that, still and silent in the aftermath.

Izzy shifted and ran a hand down Nate's chest. "Are you okay?"

"Yeah."

Nate waited for embarrassment to return, for him to wish he hadn't opened himself up like that to Izzy. It never arrived. Izzy touched him, running gentle hands all over Nate's bare skin. He nuzzled Nate's neck and stroked a finger down Nate's cheek. After a few minutes, a low chuckle rose out of Izzy.

"You are absolutely covered in lipstick," he said. "It's surprisingly hot, but I'm guessing you won't want to sleep like that."

"Hot?" Nate half-sat, propping himself on his elbows.

"Yes." Izzy grinned. "Nearly as good as getting you to come in your pants. Want to shower?"

"Please."

He went to rise from the bed, but Izzy's hand on his arm stopped him. "It's all right if you want privacy, but I could join you and clean that off." He glanced down at his mostly soft cock. "I promise, I'm in no shape to start another round, if you'd rather not."

Nate's laugh was a little breathy. "It's all right. I could use the help."

They got up, and Izzy gathered towels while Nate fished in his overnight bag for a pair of pajama pants. He never would have imagined being here with Izzy would feel so right, but there was no denying it now. Nate was sure it wasn't only the rush of orgasm that made him decide he had indeed fallen in love.

Chapter Twelve

Izzy slowly returned to consciousness. Gray light filtered through the slats in the blinds, and he blinked in the semi-dark. He felt around and discovered the bed beside him was empty. A moment later, he heard the sound of singing coming from the kitchen. Something in Italian, and it was vaguely familiar. The scent of freshly brewed coffee drifted toward him, and the singing increased in volume. The deep, rich tones sent sensual shivers up Izzy's spine and made him smile.

Last night had exceeded Izzy's expectations. After showering, they'd gone to sleep, only to wake up for another round later on. Nate had certainly proved his tongue was good for more than turning those Italian phrases. Maybe there really was some magic at work between them. Izzy had never imagined Nate would open up to him about something so private the first night they spent together.

"Hey, babe!" he called, and the singing stopped. "Why don't you bring that sexy voice of yours back to bed with me?"

"In a minute!" Nate answered. The aria resumed.

A moment later, six-foot-three of shirtless man appeared in the doorway with a tray. Without missing a beat, he continued the melody, altering the words. "Wha-a-at would you like in your coffeeeee?"

Izzy laughed. "I take it black, thanks."

"As you wish!" Nate sang.

He stepped into the room and set the tray on the nightstand. He handed Izzy a mug and picked up the other one. He shoved his pillows against the headboard and slid back under the sheet with Izzy.

"What were you singing?" Izzy blew on his coffee and took a tentative sip. It was good.

"'Che gelida manina' from *La Bohème*."

"God, you're hot when you do that."

Nate chuckled. "Glad you think so."

"Is that the opera you're performing this spring?" Izzy curled his cold fingers around the mug.

"No. We're doing *Carmen*. Del, one of my cast members—the one whose place you took at the benefit—is ridiculously excited. What's not to love about sluttiness, bullfights, jealousy, and murdering your ex-lover after she dumps you for being a dick?"

Izzy nearly inhaled a sip of hot liquid. He coughed, and Nate thumped his back. "Oh, geez. Seriously?"

Nate nodded. "Did you not know that?"

"I don't know a lot about opera, to be honest." Izzy shrugged one shoulder. "I learned a few arias, but it's not like most high schools perform *The Ring Cycle* or whatever."

"Hey! You seem to know at least something. You like Wagner?"

"Actually, yeah."

"Interesting choice."

"Why?"

Nate set his mug down and turned onto his side. "One, *The Ring Cycle* is about sixteen hours long, and even I find it boring. I sat through the entire thing exactly once, and I will never, ever do it again. Two, Wagner may have been antisemitic, and at the very least his work was appropriated by the Nazis."

Izzy groaned. "Wow, I suck."

"You did last night, anyway." Nate gave him a wicked grin.

He shifted closer, and Izzy put his mug aside. Nate put his hand on Izzy's waist then slowly leaned in for a kiss. Izzy cringed, realizing he hadn't brushed his teeth and he'd been drinking coffee, but Nate didn't seem to care. The kiss was brief, but it sent a thrill through Izzy.

Nate pulled back. "I'm glad I stayed."

They curled against each other, talking quietly until the gray light brightened. Izzy had forgotten how good those easy mornings felt, with nowhere to go and only each other for company. It surprised him that Nate was so undemanding. He seemed as content as Izzy to take it easy, despite the heat between them the previous night.

Speaking of which, he took note of Nate's renewed interest, feeling his firm length against his hip. Izzy brushed his nose against Nate's cheek and went to shift so they could enjoy the other good parts of being able to stay in bed all day. His legs felt as though he'd remained in the same position too long, and he needed to move. When he rolled, he realized the odd lack of sensation wasn't dissipating. He frowned and flexed his feet. It wasn't complete numbness, and he could still move, but it wasn't going away like it should have. Not only that, there was no way he was going to be able to repeat last night's fun any time soon. He huffed in frustration.

Nate sat up partway. "Is everything okay?"

Izzy wanted to sink through the bed and into the floor. He turned over and buried his face in the pillow. As much as he would have loved to do pretty much anything Nate wanted, his body wasn't cooperating. He supposed he should be grateful he got in a couple of rounds last night, but it didn't stop him from being worried and embarrassed.

"It's fine," he mumbled into the pillow.

The bed moved, and Izzy thought Nate was getting up again. Instead, a warm hand brushed the bare skin of his back. Nate rubbed gently, and it relaxed Izzy to the point he almost fell asleep again. Nate's voice stirred him awake.

"Talk to me," he said.

When Izzy didn't respond, Nate began to sing. The words didn't matter—still in Italian—but the soft tone and gentle touch did. Izzy relaxed and closed his eyes until Nate finished the aria.

"Now," Nate said. "Are you going to tell me what happened?"

Izzy sighed. "It's nothing. I've been getting random things, probably stress-related. I thought it was from not being in shape, but I've been back into running, and it's not any better."

"Well, have you seen a doctor?"

"No." Izzy scowled at Nate. Val hadn't mentioned it in a while, but Izzy knew it was a matter of time. "Not you, too."

Nate only laughed. "I'm probably the last person to talk, but if it's that bad, you should get it checked out."

"Maybe." Izzy shrugged. He'd put it off for too long, but he was reluctant to admit it. "Speaking of seeing a doctor…"

"What about it?" Nate gave him a puzzled frown.

Izzy hauled himself up to sitting. His legs still felt weird, but it did seem to be less now. "I was thinking maybe we should, you know, get tested. We probably already should have, but I guess I'm still not used to this whole dating thing."

Nate paled. "I, um…okay."

"What is it?"

"Nothing. I'll take care of it."

"Why don't you want to get tested? You got upset when I suggested it."

Nate pursed his lips. "I told you, I'll go. I can do it at the clinic where Marlie works."

"Your friend with the baby?"

"Yes. They, um, have a sliding scale." Nate grimaced.

Ah, that explained it. Izzy would offer to pay, but he thought it might upset Nate. "All right."

Nate was quiet for a moment. "The last time I went, I was seeing this guy. He insisted on making it some big, romantic thing and waiting for sex until we had the results. We went together then set up a date for after." He smiled. "It was cute. We only dated a couple more months after that, but it was nice."

Izzy chuckled. "You want me to make you a candlelit dinner for Test Result Day?"

"No, not really."

Izzy ran a hand over Nate's arm. "I want to make love to you with nothing between us. Will that be enough?" He meant it in every way, and he hoped Nate understood.

"When you put it that way, it does sound nice." Nate leaned down and kissed Izzy. "And you can get it done when you go see a doctor about your stress thing."

Feeling better and a little more amorous, Izzy dragged them both down under the sheet. He rolled so he was pinning Nate. "Sounds like a plan. I promise I'll go to the doctor about the stress thing. Happy?" Izzy kissed him.

"I will be if you get over here and do something about this." Nate took Izzy's hand and slipped it under the waistband of his pajamas.

"I like the sound of that."

Despite his promise to Izzy, Nate waited a few days. Izzy was working his twenty-four-hour shift, and Nate had some extra hours in the cafe—still making up for time he'd taken off when he was sick and traded shifts. He didn't mind; it kept him busy until rehearsals began the following week.

He stopped at the clinic, and Marlie was at the desk. She handed him the paperwork. "Okay, I just need a copy of your insurance card."

Nate winced. "About that..."

She nodded. "Are you paying directly, then?"

"I can't really—never mind. Yeah." He would figure out what not to spend money on for the month later. He didn't feel right about taking advantage of the clinic, not with everything he knew about their financial troubles.

Marlie typed everything into the system. "Okay. Just pay on the way out, after they decide which tests. How do you want to receive the results? We'll send you a report either way, but we can call you as well."

"Sure. Can you be the one to call me?"

"That might be a violation of ethics, since I know you," Marlie replied. "Are you sure?"

"Positive. I'd rather have you looking at my chart. Not everyone needs to know why I was in here."

"No problem. I'll clear it with Dr. Joyce, then. Have a seat, and someone will get you."

When Nate was finished, as he was pulling on his coat, Andre emerged from the administrative offices. He waved to Nate to hold on. Marlie gathered her things and stepped out from behind the desk, replaced by someone else.

"Need a ride?" Andre asked Nate.

"Sure, yeah."

"You're welcome to join us for dinner. Trev's been home with the baby all day, so I think he'd like the company. Julian and Elisa are going to stop by too."

Marlie nodded. "Elisa promised to show me how to use this space-age breast pump before I go back to work and classes later this month."

Nate laughed. "I didn't even know there was such a thing."

"Oh, the things you learn when there's a baby in the house," Andre said.

They trudged through the slush to Andre's car, and Nate took the back seat so he could stretch crosswise on the seat. He texted Mack on the way to let him know he'd be out and they shouldn't wait for him to have dinner.

Back at Andre's house, Trevor greeted them at the door looking like he'd been through the ringer. He had dark circles under his eyes. He passed Aidan to Andre almost before he'd gotten all the way in the door.

"I feel like garbage. I'm so tired. Gonna go sleep."

Andre leaned in and kissed his cheek. "Go. We've got you covered."

"Aidan's in a fussy phase, barely sleeping," Marlie explained to Nate. "Trev let me sleep last night, I guess thinking he'd be able to rest today. Looks like that didn't work out." She stepped around Nate and Andre. "I'll go finish up dinner."

Andre took Nate's coat. Nate had only been inside the new house a few times, when he helped Trevor move the bulk of his things in and after the baby was born. The house had two bedrooms downstairs and two upstairs, with a full bath on each floor. On the way through the living room to the kitchen, Nate glanced at the hallway. He knew the room Trevor and Andre shared was back there, along with the bathroom and the room where they kept all their music. Marlie and the baby shared the second floor, and Nate had never been up there. A baby gate closed off both the top and bottom of the steps.

The house was still decorated for the holidays; they were clearly not the type to take it all down New Year's Day. Someone had strung lights everywhere, and a small artificial tree stood in the corner of the dining room. There weren't many ornaments on it. In the kitchen, all the usual towels and pot holders had been replaced with Christmas-themed ones. Nate would have thought Marlie had done it—he couldn't imagine Trevor decorating—but he wasn't sure if she would have been up to it with a new baby. Maybe Andre had put everything up.

Dinner was on the table by the time Julian and Elisa arrived. Trevor emerged long enough to eat and then went back to bed. Elisa and Marlie escaped into Marlie's room for their top secret breast pump training session. That left Nate alone in the kitchen with Andre and Julian.

It should have been awkward. Nate and Andre had never been close, and he barely knew Julian, other than his being Andre's best friend. It was all right, though. Nate started washing the dishes, figuring he'd help out and then get out of their way for the night. Behind him, the others talked while Nate scrubbed.

"Been meaning to get over here more often," Julian said. "Hard to get a sitter these days."

"You should call someone from our church. There are a few teens who could manage a preschooler and a toddler."

Julian shrugged. "I might try that. How are things going with you? Looks like being a daddy suits you."

Andre, who was holding a sleeping Aidan, laughed softly. There was a hint of bitterness in it. "It's going."

"What's that supposed to mean?" Julian asked.

Andre huffed. "I shouldn't be mad, but trips to see Marlie's family never include me. I mean, I know he needs to do things with just her, but she's always been welcome in my family's home. It's probably nothing, but it still bothers me. I don't know what they've told her parents about our relationships and how it works between us."

"Do Trevor's parents know?"

"Yeah." Andre's voice brightened. "They were pretty cool about it, more than I was expecting." He chuckled. "Or maybe it was the grandbaby who softened them."

Nate laughed and turned around. "Probably. I've known Trev's parents for years, and it wouldn't surprise me. They're good people, and pretty open-minded. I could easily see them being persuaded by Aidan."

Andre put on a pot of coffee, and the three of them sat around the table. Nate took a turn holding Aidan while his coffee cooled, and it was far more comfortable this time around. He enjoyed his nieces to an extent, but he'd never thought of himself as fatherhood material. Mercifully, Elisa rescued him just as he was trying to come up with a way to hand Aidan back. Elisa carried him upstairs, presumably because she and Marlie weren't interested in hanging out with all the men.

They were quiet for a few minutes, and Nate thought about what Trevor's life had become. His own, too, for that matter. He'd put a little space between himself and Izzy after their night together. It had been good, but Nate had been left with some lingering questions. He'd known exactly what Izzy meant by *make love to you with nothing in between us*. He hadn't only been referring to the condoms.

Nate glanced around the table like he was about to call a

meeting. Andre was looking at Nate over the top of his glasses, head tilted slightly. It was obvious he wanted to ask what was on Nate's mind but was waiting for Nate to bring it up. Drawing out a sigh, Nate wrapped his fingers around his coffee cup and peered down into the dregs. At last he looked up again, meeting Andre's assessing gaze.

"How—" he began then stopped and licked his lips. He tried again. "How do you know if you're bi?"

Andre's eyebrows shot up nearly to his hairline. "I gotta admit, I was not expecting that." He shook his head and gave a short, snorting chuckle.

Nate glared at him. "It's not funny!"

"It kinda is," Julian piped up from beside the sink. "I mean, you've been on these guys about not getting their sexuality or their relationship for how long, and now you're asking that question?"

With a frustrated growl, Nate sat back in his chair. "Well, I don't know, do I? See, this is exactly why I didn't talk to Trevor about it. You're no better, apparently."

Andre shot Julian an irritated glance, and Julian held up his hands in apology. Turning back to Nate, Andre said, "What brought this on?"

Ignoring Julian, Nate continued. "Izzy's bi. I've always only liked men. But Izzy...he's different. I've been watching him perform for months at Grand Slam, and..."

"You liked him when he was in drag, so you thought that was a sign?" Andre sounded incredulous.

"Yeah, partly. But..." Nate huffed, knowing his face had to be fire engine red. "I asked him to, you know, dress up when we were—when we had sex. So I want to know if maybe I'm not gay after all because I like it when he dresses that way. It's hot."

Andre reached across the table and put a hand on Nate's forearm. "You don't need to define yourself by what your partner does or how they dress."

"But...but how do I know for sure?"

Andre exchanged a glance with Julian, and Nate saw a question pass between them as well. He returned his attention to Nate. "Only you can answer that."

Nate took a few minutes to consider it. As much as he liked it when Izzy was in drag, he knew what he liked was the person underneath. Nate was a performer too, and what he connected to was Izzy's stage presence—his confidence, his graceful motion, his rich voice. Beneath the hair and makeup was a person Nate had grown to appreciate very much—the same man who had been there for a number of key moments in his and his friends' lives. Izzy was one of the most compassionate, gentle people Nate had ever known. What difference did it make what he chose to put on the outside? Nate had never been, and probably never would be, attracted to anyone who identified as a woman. That was answer enough for the time being.

Just as he was about to say he was pretty sure he wasn't bi after all, Julian said, "I was wondering the same thing." He said it so softly Nate almost missed it, but he didn't miss Andre's double take.

"What?" Nate and Andre said simultaneously.

Julian cleared his throat. "I don't know," he said. "I get...curious, sometimes. What it would be like." He wouldn't meet their eyes.

"What which part would be like?" Nate asked.

Shrugging one shoulder, Julian said, "I'm not sure. Sometimes I see a man I think is good-looking, and I wonder what it would feel like to...kiss him, maybe. Is it the same as with my wife? Or I want to see what his muscles feel like. His pecs, his abs...his ass. I like the energy of flirting or dancing with men, even though that's as far as it's ever gone." He set his cup on the counter and crossed his arms. "It doesn't matter, really. I'm with Elisa, and I'm not like Andre—I only want her. But still, I wonder."

"Haven't you two ever..." Nate gestured between Andre and Julian.

Andre gave Nate a horrified look. "You got brothers?"

"Yeah, one. Why?"

"You kiss him? Like, hot lip action, not a peck on the cheek."

"God, no." Nate chuckled, thinking about how Dean would react if he tried.

"Right," Andre said. "Now you know why Julian didn't ask me to be his experiment—and why I'd have said no if he had."

Nate shrugged. "You know Trevor and I messed around." He stood and turned to Julian. "I can help you answer at least one part of your question."

Julian's mouth hung open for a minute. "Uh...all right." He rose out of his chair as well.

Nate stepped into Julian's personal space, ignoring the amusement on Andre's face. He cupped Julian's jaw and leaned down, feeling the puffs of air against his nose as Julian's breathing sped up. "Close your eyes."

When Julian obeyed, Nate slowly narrowed the gap until he was a millimeter from Julian's lips. He paused then descended the rest of the way, capturing Julian's full mouth with his own. At first, Julian was frozen still, but then he recovered and kissed back. Nate drew it out, making his exploration of Julian range from sensual and lingering to greedy and devouring. He put out his tongue, seeking permission, but that was where Julian stopped him by pulling away.

"I don't think so," he said, panting as he drew the back of his hand across his chin.

Nate laughed, also a little winded. "Why not?"

Julian took a noisy breath. "Okay—don't get mad now, all right?—I can tell you're a pretty damn good kisser. But that did absolutely nothing for me." His shoulders slumped, and he looked defeated. "I think...I'm completely straight." He sank into his chair.

"You sure you don't need to test it out on me?" Andre asked, making no effort to hide his laughter.

"Aw, hell no. That would be worse than kissing your Grams."

"You sounded disappointed," Nate said as he sat back down. "Why?"

"I mean, I guess I wanted to know if it meant something that I can find a man attractive, you know?" Julian shook his head.

"It does mean something," Andre told him.

"Fill me in, then, 'cause I got nothing." Julian held out a hand to him.

"It means you've been hanging around us queers for so long you're not thinking like an average straight guy. You aren't straight 'cause it's what you grew up believing you were supposed to be— you're straight because you only like women. And you're comfortable enough in who you are that kissing another man didn't wreck you. That's all." Andre grinned at him.

Julian ducked his head, but he laughed. "Fair enough."

Andre turned back to Nate. "As for you, I don't think you were really asking about being bi, were you?"

It was Nate's turn to be embarrassed. "No, I guess not."

"So what is it you really want to know?"

"How do you do it?" Nate blurted. "This, what you have with Trevor and Marlie."

Andre sat back and fiddled with the handle on his mug. "If you're looking for something to validate your fears about dating a bi man, forget it. This is what works for us. I shouldn't have to tell you it's not for everyone. If you and Izzy feel differently from each other on the subject, now's the time to find out. If you're on the same page"—he gripped Nate's arm—"then you have nothing to worry about. He seems like a good man."

Nate blew out his breath. Andre had understood perfectly, for the most part. Nate didn't want permission to be worried; he wanted someone to tell him it was all right to fall. Andre might not have put it in those terms, but he was right. Nate nodded.

He didn't have a chance to say anything more on the subject. Zombified-Trevor came into the kitchen, yawned, and blinked in the bright lights. "Are you guys having a club meeting of some sort?"

Andre stood up and steered him toward the table. "Sit. I'll get you some coffee. I have a feeling we're gonna need it if the baby's up half the night again."

CHAPTER THIRTEEN

Nate couldn't muster the kind of enthusiasm he wanted for rehearsal. He'd gone to the theater early to meet Del and talk about the show. This was really Del's baby, and Nate thought he should have been the one putting it together. On the phone, he'd talked Nate's ear off about his ideas, all of which were far more fun and creative than anything Nate had in mind. Del wanted to give it an updated and distinctly queer feel, and he claimed he'd even done sketches for the costumes and sets. He was nothing if not wholly devoted to whatever he put his mind to.

They spent a good hour and a half going over everything, and slowly, Nate's excitement returned. After ditching the paperwork in favor of grabbing a snack in the break room, they sat down and propped their feet on the table.

"So, tell me about your new man," Del said.

Nate laughed. "Not much to tell." He certainly wasn't going to bring up his kink for Izzy in drag.

"You've been in a stellar mood lately." Del waggled his eyebrows suggestively.

Elbowing him, Nate replied, "It's not like that. Izzy's—" He paused. "Everything I was looking for."

They'd been out again on Izzy's day off, for a more mainstream movie and drinks before going back to Izzy's apartment. Nate couldn't underestimate the benefits of having an older and more financially established boyfriend. He lived alone, and there were never any nosy roommates hanging around.

Del grinned. "It's about time."

Before Nate had a chance to respond, his phone rang. He looked at the number, glanced at Del, and got up from the couch as he answered it. "Hello?"

Out of the corner of his eye, Nate saw Del rise and busy himself with tidying the room. Trevor would have been proud of his organizational skills, learned the hard way from Nate being too preoccupied with Izzy to pick up after the cast anymore. Nate turned his attention to the phone call.

"Hey, Nate. It's Marlie. You asked me to call with your test results."

Nate's heart thumped. "All right."

"Are you sure you don't want to do this in person?" Marlie's voice was quiet and calm—a little too much for Nate's liking.

"No, over the phone is fine." He paused. "Why do I get the feeling I'm not going to like what you tell me?"

Marlie was silent for several seconds. "I'll mail you all the results. Everything was negative except one."

Make it something simple. A round of antibiotics, and I'll be fine. No big deal. "Which one?"

"I'm sorry," Marlie said. "Nate, your HIV test was positive."

Nate held it together long enough to say, "Please don't say anything to Trevor or Andre. I need to do it myself."

"Everything we've talked about is confidential. I can't tell them a single thing without your written permission. Dr. Joyce asked you to come in and speak to her when you're ready. Do you want me to make an appointment?"

"No. I'll call later. I need some time."

"I understand." Another pause. "Take care of yourself, but don't wait too long. You have options, and you need to talk to a doctor, whether it's Joyce or someone else."

"Right, yeah. Okay. Uh...thanks, Marlie."

"You're welcome."

They hung up, and for a long time, Nate stood there, frozen to the spot, staring at his phone. It dawned on him the clanking of dishes had stopped, and he looked up to find Del watching him, his expression guarded. Nate wanted to throw his phone, but that wouldn't do any good. Instead, he gripped it so tightly it dug into his palm.

"You okay?" Del's voice cut through Nate's temporary paralysis.

"That was the doctor. Or, actually, the nurse. You know, from the clinic." Nate took a deep breath, straightened his shoulders, and jutted his chin. "Well," he said, "at least now I know my test results." The hand holding his phone shook violently. "I—I'm poz."

"Oh, Nate."

Del crossed the room and reached for him, but Nate pulled away. "Don't touch me!" he yelled. "Don't fucking touch me!"

"Come on. You need to sit. We can talk about this," Del pleaded.

Now Nate's whole body was trembling. "What am I gonna do?"

"You're going to come sit on the couch with me." Del put his hand on Nate's arm, and this time Nate flinched but didn't jerk away.

Del led him to the couch, and they sat side by side, facing forward without touching. Nate set his phone on the table. He propped his elbows on his knees and put his head in his hands. This could not be happening. He had too many things to figure out, too many decisions, too much overwhelming him to think clearly. He tried to breathe slowly to calm himself down, but he couldn't focus. His skin crawled, and he wanted to scrape it off in hopes of digging out the virus in his blood.

"Sh, honey," Del murmured. "Breathe. It's going to be okay. We'll get you some help, all right?"

"No one can help me!" Nate snapped. "I can't even afford meds."

Del reached over and rubbed Nate's back. "There are programs to assist you with the cost. Don't worry about that right now. We need to take care of you here first."

Nate closed his eyes and let Del's touch relax him. He had to think. It made sense now, the "flu" he'd had back in October and the lengthy recovery. Something else occurred to him, and his head snapped up. That had been when he was meeting up with Rocco, which meant—

"I have to tell the guy I was seeing last fall. Shit."

"What guy? I thought you'd been seeing Izzy for a couple of months now."

"I have. I didn't mean Izzy." Nate leaned back and slouched down so his head rested on the back of the couch. "Though I guess I need to tell him, too. I hooked up with a guy I used to date. It wasn't a good idea, so I broke it off. But we...we didn't...we weren't careful." He rolled his head to the side and looked at Del. "Don't say it, please."

"I wasn't going to. I'm not judging you."

"He was married—separated," Nate said. "He's a deeply closeted, very confused man who wants what having a wife and kids will get him but can't be honest even with himself. I knew, but I wanted to believe he might decide I was worth it."

"Been there," Del reminded him.

"I thought you were just being dramatic."

Del's smile was sad. "I really liked him."

Which brought Nate back to Izzy. "I don't know how to tell Izzy," he confessed. "I thought he might be it for me, you know?" Nate swallowed. "Now, I'm not sure he'll still want me. Maybe no one will."

"If he's a decent guy, this won't be the end for the two of you." Del took Nate's face in his hands. "You aren't a terrible person. Shit happens, you know? There are assholes out there, but anyone who's worth your time will want you for you. If they don't, it's only because they don't know how wonderful you are." Del pulled Nate's head down and kissed his forehead.

"You don't get it!" Nate snapped, jerking away. "How could you possibly know? You have no idea what I'm going through."

Del's expression turned hard. "You listen to me. I know exactly what you're dealing with. I've been there too."

Nate froze. "Wait, what?"

"Been poz for almost ten years."

"That would have been—"

"Yeah. In high school. I'm aware."

Nate whistled. "I'm sorry. I didn't know."

"You wouldn't have," Del agreed. "Life is on a need to know basis, and you weren't on the invite list. I only tell the people responsible for my health care and the people I'm interested in fucking. Which, let's be honest here, is a lot of people, but not you." He elbowed Nate and grinned, breaking the tension.

Nate snorted a laugh then sobered. "But—"

Del put up a hand. "I'm not saying it's all sunshine and hippie guitars. There are plenty of people who are nasty about it. But there are lots who aren't. I look for guys who say it doesn't matter or who are also poz, though I do avoid the fetishists—yes, they exist. I've been on a good regimen of meds for a long time, and I play safe. It's not stopping me from having wonderful, sexy men in my life, and it won't stop you either. If Izzy is an ass about it, then he's not someone you want to try to convince, trust me." Del squeezed Nate's hand. "Let me help you, okay?"

Nate took a deep, cleansing breath. "All right. So who do I tell first?"

"Has Izzy been tested?"

"Yeah, but it might not show up yet. We only just had sex for the first time last week." Nate's ears heated.

"Can you tell him in person? That would be better. You can let the clinic call the other guy."

Nate didn't want to think about how a conversation with Izzy might go. There were other people too. Nate thought about Trevor, wondering what he would say. Or his parents and brother, for that matter. There wasn't a good way to bring it up at a family dinner. He could picture it, the way each of them would respond. Once again, he was unable to live up to their expectations.

He leaned back against the couch. "He's going to blame me. He's going to sue me or something like those other guys who said they got tricked."

"Sh. No, he won't. He has no case. You only just got the test results today. He also probably won't know it's you, especially after this much time."

They were quiet for a few minutes. Nate's heart rate was still up, but talking to Del had helped somewhat. "I don't know where to start with all this."

"I promised to help you, and I will." He picked Nate's phone up off the table. "Start by calling the clinic back. Make an appointment, and give them the other guy's phone number. Just those two things. One step at a time."

Nate nodded. "One step at a time." He scrolled through his contacts to find the number and hit call. When Marlie answered, he said, "I'd like to make an appointment with Dr. Joyce."

After the kind of day Izzy had, all he wanted was to curl up with Nate, have a glass of wine, and get his mind off his worries. The doctor visit hadn't gone well, and he was still trying to wrap his mind around it.

Not stress. That was all his brain could grasp. It was too much to take in the blood tests, the MRI, and the referral to a neurologist. At least he'd been able to throw the STI panel in with the blood count and the ones indicating vitamin deficiencies and possible autoimmune disorders. Izzy didn't anticipate good news on any front. He hoped some time with Nate might cheer him up.

When he picked Nate up, his expectations were dashed. Nate looked like someone had stomped on his kitten. He wouldn't look Izzy in the eye, and he sat facing the window the entire time they drove. Izzy couldn't imagine what was on his mind, but whatever it was, they were a miserable pair.

They drove farther out of the city this time, to a cozy little place Izzy thought might help both of them relax. Nate still hadn't said much, but by the time they arrived, he appeared to have unwound somewhat. As they walked into the restaurant, Izzy put a hand on the small of Nate's back, but Nate jerked at the touch and Izzy dropped his hand.

Once they were seated, Nate opened his menu. Izzy could tell he was staring at it without really seeing what was in front of him. The tension was killing him. He was going to have a hard enough time talking about his appointment, knowing it meant Nate might not feel like there was a future for them. He was young, and he didn't need the burden of caring for someone who might be looking at something progressive and disabling. Still, Izzy owed it to him to explain, even if it meant they were over.

"I'm sorry," Izzy said. "I know I'm crappy company tonight." He wasn't ready to address the thing they weren't talking about.

Nate put down his menu, watching Izzy but saying nothing. He reached for his napkin, fiddling with the paper ring. "I'm not doing a whole lot to help."

The server appeared with water, ready to take their orders. Izzy glanced at Nate, who wasn't even trying to select something. "Give us a minute?" he asked.

"Sure. I'll be back to check on you." He disappeared.

"Look, this hasn't been a great day, but maybe we can set it aside until we've both had something to eat." Izzy reached for Nate's hand. Nate tensed, but he didn't pull away.

"I—" Nate drew his lower lip between his teeth. He looked like there was more he wanted to say, but something was holding him back. "My day wasn't great either."

Izzy took a deep breath. "Do you want kids?" he blurted. There went his mouth, shooting off before his brain caught up.

"What?" Nate's face scrunched in confusion.

Massaging his temples, Izzy said, "I'm not doing this very well.

Please, let's order, and then we can talk about it."

"Fine."

After they'd placed their orders, Izzy turned his attention back to his earlier out-of-the-blue question. "I'm trying to see where you think we're going, I guess. That's why I asked if you want kids."

Nate sipped his water, his eyes still on Izzy. When he set his glass down, he said, "No, not really. At least, I don't want babies." He half coughed, half laughed, adding, "I don't like them a whole lot."

"So you're not one of those settle down, get married, have kids and a dog types?"

"Where is this coming from?" Nate frowned. "I guess I'll answer that in order. I'd love to settle down and get married, but no kids and no dog—I'm severely allergic. To dogs, not children. You want to tell me what this is about?"

Izzy ran his finger through the condensation on his glass, trying to find the right words. "I don't know anymore if I can give you what you want."

When Izzy at last looked up, Nate's eyes shimmered. Izzy withdrew his hand from his glass. He had known this was going to happen, ripping Nate's future away just like he'd ripped Lynne's away. There was nothing more he could do but leave Nate to find someone who wouldn't eventually need care, someone with whom he could be happy and settled. Someone easier.

Nate spoke softly. "I don't know either."

Izzy sat back, perplexed. "What do you mean?"

"I need to tell you something." Nate's tone was pleading. "Please hear me out."

Izzy frowned, but he settled back in. "All right."

"Did...um...you get tested?"

"Of course. I was at the doctor today. I won't have the results for a few days, though."

"You need to call me when you get them. And you probably need to have it done again." Nate's face was strained.

Izzy shook his head. "What? Why?"

"I got mine yesterday." Izzy watched him swallow. "Iz, I have HIV."

"Oh," was all that came out of Izzy's mouth. His brain tried to keep up with what Nate was telling him.

"It's...you know...I know I dropped kind of a bomb here, but say something?"

Intellectually, Izzy knew it wasn't a problem. He had all the facts, all the data at his fingertips. When he and Nate were together, they'd taken care, and he didn't think his test results would show anything. He already knew he was negative before he was with Nate. Chances were good he'd been with someone before and simply hadn't known, back in his more open days before Lynne, but he'd always taken precautions. Still, he was enough older than Nate to remember a childhood of frightening news stories he couldn't shake off in one dinner date.

His heart wanted to reach out to Nate and say they'd do this thing together. He wanted to tell him it didn't matter, his own impending tests didn't matter. The only important thing was being together. Only he couldn't, not yet. He wasn't sure he could deal with both things at the same time. Once again, he was failing to provide for someone he loved, unable to send his emotional energy in more than one direction.

"I think we both need some time to process this." He glanced back up to see the utter devastation on Nate's face before he looked away again.

Nate put his elbows on the table and rested his head in his hands. The server arrived with the food and took in the awkward scene. He seemed uncomfortable and at a loss for what to do other than set the plates on the table. He asked if there was anything else then left them to it.

Around them, chatter picked up as more patrons entered. Izzy tried to think what to do, wanting to put an end to the tension, but it was a lost cause. Nate wouldn't even make eye contact, and he wasn't touching his food. No longer hungry, Izzy shoved his plate away.

"I'll ask if we can take this home."

He stood up and went in search of their server, needing something to divert his attention. When he returned to the table, Nate was gone. Izzy looked around for him, hoping he'd only gone to the bathroom, but there was no sign of him in there.

Hurriedly, Izzy paid for their food and took the boxes. He rushed out the door, still expecting he might see Nate somewhere close by. He'd disappeared without a trace. There were a number of shops and restaurants nearby. Izzy left the boxes in his car and took a look in a few, but he couldn't find Nate anywhere.

Crushed and knowing it was his own fault, Izzy climbed back into his car and drove home alone.

"Why did you need me to pick you up?" Andre asked as Nate climbed in beside him.

"Shitty date, and I needed to get out of there." Nate shivered.

Andre turned up the heat. "So you waited half an hour for me in the snow? That's not like you."

"Just get me home." He buckled his belt and turned away from Andre, not ready to explain what was going on.

"All right."

They drove in silence, and Nate tried to figure out if he should tell Andre the truth. Trevor would have pressed him, demanding to know, and Nate wasn't sure he was ready to take that step. Talking to Trevor had to wait until he wasn't so heartbroken, if that ever happened.

He'd known, deep down. As much as Nate had hoped Izzy wasn't one of the ones who would give him the boot as soon as he knew the truth, Izzy had made it clear he couldn't handle it. Now was as good a time as any to swear off dating for good, regardless of what Del had said.

Nate glanced at Andre, who hadn't uttered another word. He kept his eyes on the road as the snow flurries picked up. Andre was calm, seeming unruffled by having to drive out to rescue Nate from his awful evening. Whatever else had happened over the previous year, Nate understood now what Trevor loved about him. His quiet, gentle presence soothed the raw pain of Nate's conversation with Izzy. If anyone could be trusted, it was Andre.

"I called you because Trevor is too nosy," Nate finally told him.

"Yeah, I'll give you that one," Andre replied. "Especially when it comes to you."

"What did you tell him you were doing?"

Andre shrugged one shoulder. "You called while I was still at work. I told him I had some things to wrap up."

"Does Julian know where you went?" They worked together; technically, since it was Julian's company, he was Andre's boss.

"Naw. I told him I was taking off early. You sounded like hell, so I figured it was serious."

They fell silent again. After a few minutes Nate said, "Do you remember when I was sick last fall?"

Andre glanced sideways at him. "It would be hard to forget."

"Right."

"Something happen with that?" Andre was being casual, but Nate knew he had a good idea what was coming.

"Yeah." He sighed, and his breath made a foggy spot on the window. He wiped it with his sleeve. "I'm poz."

Andre nodded, but he didn't say anything.

"You guessed, didn't you? I thought you were pissed off because I went to your grandma's clinic to get a strep test instead of my own doctor. But you thought I should have listened to her and gotten tested then."

"Yes," Andre replied. "I also knew it wasn't my place to say. I've been volunteering there since I was a teenager, and Grams was never one to mince words. She talked to us about all kinds of things, and she's always kept up on her information. I recognized right away that it was a possibility, but you said you hadn't been seeing anyone."

Nate didn't want to get into the particulars of what happened with Rocco. "I told Izzy. On our date."

Andre frowned. "Why?"

Nate sighed. "He was talking about all this future stuff, like did I want to get married or have kids. I felt like I should say something. He said he needed time. You know, code for breaking up with me."

"Damn. I'm sorry."

"Whatever." Nate watched out the window at the snow rushing past. "He's the least of my worries."

"What do you mean?"

Nate ran a hand through his hair. "I have no health insurance. And also no money. It's been really tight with my opera company this fall, and my other job is only part time."

Andre took one hand off the wheel long enough to grip Nate's shoulder. "Did you make an appointment with Grams? I can stop by and give you a hand with the paperwork. There's a bunch, but we'll help you get it done."

Instead of responding to that, Nate said, "I'm an ass. I screwed up so bad. What am I gonna do?"

Andre didn't reply immediately, and shame rose in Nate out of fear that Andre agreed with his self-assessment. Nate shivered again despite the heat in the car. He wanted to demand Andre say something, but Andre was a man of few words. When he did speak, it usually meant something. If he planned to tell Nate the cold, hard truth, he would at least do it kindly. Nate braced himself.

They pulled up to the curb by Nate's apartment building, and Andre idled there while Nate collected himself. Andre put a hand on Nate's arm, stopping him before he got out of the car.

"You're not alone, and you're not an ass. Call me if you need anything."

Nate nodded and climbed out of the car, not trusting himself to speak yet. After a lungful of frosty night air, he leaned back in and said, "Don't tell Trevor." Without waiting for a response, he went inside, listening for Andre's car pulling away just as the outer door thumped shut. Nate trudged up the stairs, ignoring it when he saw Mrs. Crotchety stick her head out of her door on his way past.

Inside the apartment, Nate paused in the doorway, taking in the scene. Jamie was reading a magazine, and Mack was at the table going through the mail and separating it. Everything was so achingly normal, as though Nate's world hadn't just come crashing down around his ears. He was torn between pretending everything was fine and wishing he could make them see how it would never be fine again.

Mack turned up his nose at the kale chips Jamie was crunching. They were homemade, but not by him—Marlie's food cravings had apparently not disappeared after the baby was born, which Trevor had attributed to breastfeeding. At some point, she had gone into a frenzy of making snacks, which she sent home with anyone who came to visit. She claimed she had to test everything out before the baby was old enough to eat real food. The way Trevor told it, he'd been amazed she had enough energy to do it, given work, school, and a fussy infant.

"How can you eat those? They look weird," Mack remarked.

Jamie shrugged. "They're good."

"Ew." He tossed aside an envelope. "Still getting shit for Trevor," he said.

Jamie laughed, turning toward the door as Nate closed it. "Hey, Nate."

"Hey." Nate tried to walk on by to his room.

"Wait," Mack said, and Nate stopped. "I need to talk to you."

"Can we do it tomorrow? I've had a crappy night, and I want to go to bed." Nate was past caring what Mack had on his mind. Whatever it was couldn't be more important than what Nate had been through in the past few hours.

"At seven? Seriously, man, we have to discuss something."

"Fine." Nate turned around and returned to the kitchen. "What?"

"I'm not trying to be an asshole, but you're late on this month's rent. Second time in a row. We covered for you last time, knowing you were good for it. I know it's hard without Trevor's part, but I really need your share."

Nate's stomach clenched. "I'll get it to you. I don't have it right now."

"I'm serious," Mack said.

"Yeah, and I am too. I said I'd get it. My day went from bad to worse. Please fuck off until I get some sleep."

"I told you—" Mack started.

"And I told you to fuck off."

They glared at each other, and out of the corner of his eye, Nate saw Jamie back up against the kitchen counter. He looked like he was ready to run if things escalated any further. Mack stood up from the table.

"I know you told me to fuck off, but we weren't done. If something is going on, you need to tell me. We can try to find another roommate if we have to, but I'd like to know before they shut off our hot water."

"That's not going to be a problem. I'll give you the damn money. Just let me have a day or two."

"No. We have to pay the bill, and I don't have extra this month." Mack glared at him. "Maybe you were used to being all pampered, living with your parents, but you need to be an adult about this."

"Be an adult?" Nate snapped. "Yeah, let me tell you how much of an adult I had to be this week. I had to pay for a fucking blood test, and guess what? Now I have to find a way to pay for fucking meds that I can't afford. Because that's what you do when you have HIV and your boyfriend says he needs time to think about it."

Dead silence.

Mack and Jamie shared a glance. That hadn't been how Nate wanted to tell them. He leaned against the wall and ran a hand through his hair. For a long time, the others just stared at him.

Eventually, Mack said, "Shit."

Angry and embarrassed, Nate spun around and stormed into his room, slamming the door. He flopped onto his bed. It was easier to focus on Mack's demand for the rent money. Nate had part of it, if he pared everything down to the essentials. He couldn't count on

Izzy taking him out or cooking for him, so he would need to find a way to put money into the grocery fund. That meant he would need to cancel his appointment at the clinic or confess to Andre he couldn't pay. He mapped out the conversations in his head, concentrating on those worries rather than wondering what Mack and Jamie were thinking out in the other room after his revelation.

The knock on his door startled and annoyed him. He stood and crossed the room to open it. "What do you want?"

Jamie said, "Can we come in? Or can you come out?"

Nate gestured for them to join him. "Are you here to continue the argument?" he asked.

"No," Mack said. "We wanted to make sure you're all right."

"Do I sound all right?" Nate snapped.

"I guess not." Jamie sat on the bed, and Nate joined him.

"We'll cover for you," Mack told him. "I have some money saved up from our last gig." He plopped down on Nate's other side.

"Thanks," Nate said. "But you're right. I can't keep expecting you to do this."

They were quiet for a few minutes. Mack slid back on the bed until his back rested against the wall, and the others followed. Jamie rested his head on Nate's shoulder and took his hand. The soft gesture surprised Nate, and he glanced down. Mack rolled his head to the side and looked at Nate, but he remained silent.

Nate sighed. "Come on. Say something, you guys. Mack, you're always this fount of wisdom. Can't you come swooping in and tell us how it really is?"

Mack snorted. "Not this time, man. I've got nothing." He, too, laid his head on Nate's shoulder. "I'm sorry I was a dick to you just now. This is shitty, and for once, I don't think even my skills are a match."

"No, I guess not," Nate replied. "Not much we can do about any of it."

Sitting up again, Mack said, "Now, there's where you're wrong. I might not be able to tell you what to do, but we can at least figure out the rent thing. We'll get another roommate." He smirked. "Amelia might—"

"Hell no!" Jamie yelped. "No way. I can't live with the two of you."

In spite of himself, Nate laughed a little. "Me neither."

"Oh, fine." Mack pouted.

Jamie turned to Nate. "We have your back, you know."

"Right," Mack said. He became all business. "Listen, I'll go see what I can do, okay? Make some phone calls." He stepped out of the bedroom, leaving the door ajar.

Once he was gone, Jamie looked at Nate, and Nate could tell he wanted to say more.

"Go on." Nate sighed. "You wanted to tell me you knew, right?"

"Maybe." Jamie looked apologetic. "You were right, you know. About Sage." He curled his legs underneath himself. "I didn't want to listen."

Nate nodded. "Like how I didn't want to listen last fall. Except what difference would it have made?" He lay back. The difference was that he might never have gotten to know Izzy or gone out with him or had his heart shattered.

"You should have gone, but I get why you didn't." He studied Nate for a moment. "Does Trev know?"

"No."

"Are you going to tell him?"

Nate exhaled slowly. "I should."

Jamie nodded. "I used to talk to him, you know. About Sage."

Interest piqued, Nate angled toward him. "Yeah?"

"You and Mack were both on me about Sage and what I should do. Trev just...listened. He did tell me to leave, but it wasn't the same." Jamie wrapped his arms around himself. "He wasn't angry with me."

"We were never angry with you," Nate tried to explain.

"Maybe." Jamie shook his head. "You sounded like it. Anyway, I know Trev won't be mad at you."

Nate wanted to ask Jamie more about how he and Trevor had become so close recently. It wasn't adding up for him, and now that Izzy was out of the picture, Nate's jealousy flared again. He had no right to tell Trevor who his friends should be, but he felt as displaced now as he had when Trevor began seeing Andre. Still, Jamie was right, and he needed to tell Trevor what was going on. Marlie and Andre both knew, and Nate assumed they would both be gracious enough to accept his conditions. He couldn't ask them to keep silent forever.

"I'll talk to him," Nate told Jamie.

"We meant what we said." Jamie touched his arm. "We've got you." He stood up. "I'll let you get some rest."

When he was gone, Nate slowly undressed. He shivered as he slid between the sheets, no one to warm him. Wishing he could do the whole day—or maybe a lot of days—over, he buried his head in the pillow and closed his eyes, hoping for a dreamless sleep.

CHAPTER FOURTEEN

Nate didn't hold notions that he was obligated to tell his family anything, not then and not at some time in the future. They were no longer responsible for him, and the list of people he wanted involved in something so personal was limited. However, they were his next of kin, and that meant there was a small chance one of them might be called on in an emergency. If anything happened to him, he didn't want them to find out from anyone else. Despite knowing how they would react, he wanted to tell them. He still hadn't talked to Trevor, but that was neither here nor there in his decision to tell his parents and his brother.

Dean called mid-week to ask if Nate was going to Sunday dinner. He hadn't been to one in a long time, in part because he disliked having to play Happy Family when he was the only one not properly engaged in upper middle class marriage and kids. He couldn't relate when his mother and Corinne compared notes on how to socialize an infant or what classes were best for preschool education. He had no interest in discussing the housing market in the outlying suburbs with his father and Dean. And he wasn't particularly good with very small children, so he couldn't entertain his nieces while the others chattered on without him. He also hadn't wanted to subject Izzy to their brand of snobbery, and it was much more fun to spend their night off together just the two of them.

Swallowing his distaste, Nate agreed to go this week. He would tell them all at once, like having his wisdom teeth out. Better to do it in one shot than have to go back multiple times. If only he could work out the best way to open the conversation.

Nate was a wreck by the time Sunday rolled around. He wished now that Izzy would talk to him, but he hadn't heard back since he called and left a message. It was now clear they were over, the last spark of hope extinguished by the silence of his phone. Meanwhile, he spent the entire hour before heading to his parents' house rehearsing different scenarios. It was bad enough Mack told him to stop talking to himself, and Jamie only agreed to play-act with him once before he gave up and told Nate he was only making it worse.

He arrived with dessert, something he'd modified from one of the recipes they used at the cafe. It was somewhere between cake and cobbler, with a gooey, sweet berry filling. Mom accepted the still-warm pan and set it on the stove.

"Dinner's already on the table," she said.

"Sorry I'm late."

They sat down and began passing dishes. Almost as soon as they were in their chairs, the conversation turned exactly the way Nate had anticipated. Corinne began talking about their nearly three-year-old and some dance class she was registering for. Something about the studio being "partially competitive," whatever that meant. Nate tuned them out, but Dean and Dad's discussion wasn't any better. Silently, Nate stabbed things with his fork and tried not to think about what he would say when they inevitably noticed him and asked politely how the job they weren't interested in was going.

A nudge on his shoulder made him look up from his plate and over at Corinne. At first, she looked amused at his confusion, but then her brow furrowed. She rested her long fingers on his arm.

"You're quiet," she said. "Everything all right?"

Three more sets of eyes were on him. Bridget had gotten down on the floor to play after eating, and Margot was still feeding herself messy bites. The room was otherwise still. Nate took a deep breath; it was now or never.

"I have to tell you something."

His gaze wandered to the little ones, and Corinne nodded. "Do you need me to take them out of the room?"

"I don't know," Nate replied. "I don't think they'll understand what I'm saying, but it's up to you."

She looked over at Bridget and said, "She's not really paying attention."

Mom and Dad were sitting with their backs straight, eyes trained on Nate. Dean fidgeted with his napkin. Only Corinne seemed unfazed by everything. Nate was grateful for at least one person who wouldn't be ready to offer commentary the minute he stopped talking. He pushed his plate away so he could fold his hands on top of the table. There was no good way to do this.

"I'm positive."

There was a small pause, after which Mom—who still seemed confused—said, "Positive about what, dear?"

Nate clasped his hands tighter to stop the shaking. "I tested positive."

"For what?" Mom asked. God bless her for at least feigning innocence, unless she really was that clueless.

Corinne closed her eyes and bit her lip, looking like she was restraining herself from letting Mom have it. The muscle in Dean's jaw twitched as he clenched and released, but he said nothing. Dad frowned.

"Answer your mother."

"Oh, for crying out loud," Dean snapped. "Mom, he means he has HIV."

Mom looked like Dean had hit her. She startled, and then she turned her attention to Bridget, who hadn't moved or shown any interest in the adults at all. Mom's expression hardened, and she made a motion with her chin at Corinne.

"She's fine," Corinne said. "She's two—she doesn't even know what that is."

Mom and Dad both began talking at once. While Dad started verbally making a spreadsheet on what they should do, Mom retreated into her you-picked-a-fine-time-to-tell-us mode. They weren't saying anything of value, only giving their opinions on Nate's life yet again. He let them go for a couple of minutes and then put up his hand.

"I'm handling everything. The only reason I told you is if there's an emergency and you think someone taking care of me needs to know. That's all."

Mom huffed. "I always thought you were intelligent enough not to get yourself into this kind of situation."

Nate zeroed his attention on her, and she leaned back a bit. "'This kind of situation'? Really, Mom? What kind of situation would that be?"

Her eyes flashed. "The kind where you're going around doing whatever you feel like and not caring about the consequences."

"You don't care what's going on in my life, only that I messed up in a way that might make you look bad," Nate fired back.

"What are you talking about?" Dad snapped.

"Graduating with honors and being good on stage wasn't enough for you in the face of Dean's accomplishments. He made you look like stellar parents, the kind who raise their kids right. I was always one step behind, the kid you needed to apologize for."

"That's not true," Dad said, but his expression told Nate a different story—shock and regret.

Corinne looked around the table then got up and plucked Margot out of her seat. "I'm going to go give these two a bath," she said. She leaned over and kissed Nate's cheek. "We'll talk later, okay?" she whispered.

Nate nodded then turned away from her and back to the rest of his family. Out of the corner of his eye, he saw Corinne shepherding the little ones up the stairs. Across from him, Dean sat rigid and silent. Dad had developed a deep scowl, and Mom appeared scandalized by the whole thing. Nate took a deep breath and said what he'd been longing to for years.

"You were all right with it when I told you I was gay as long as you could pretend I was going to end up like the out-and-proud rich and famous. I was on stage, so I must be headed for Hollywood success, right? If I worked at it and did everything just like Dean, you'd look like parents of the year. Maybe I'd even shower you with gifts to show my gratitude for your undying support."

"Nate," Dad warned.

"Shove it, Dad. You were just as bad. Neither of you listened to what I wanted. Even when I started studying opera—at your request, not mine—you thought it meant at the very least I'd be performing at Carnegie or the Met, right? Not some tiny little company made up of the sorts of gay people you'd like to pretend don't exist. Be queer but not too queer. And for sure, don't do anything that might spoil your brother's reputation."

He pushed back from the table and stood up. Grabbing his plate on the way, he stalked to the kitchen and dumped it in the sink just to annoy his mother. For a moment, he thought about going home, waiting it out, and trying again the following week. They'd all have a chance to process it by then. Corinne had told him she would talk to him, though, so he would find something to do until she was free.

At the far end of the kitchen, a door led out to the garage. Without taking his jacket, Nate entered the garage and pulled the door shut behind him. He turned on a light and looked around. What remained of his childhood had found its way there, left on the shelves to gather dust. He spotted a stack of empty boxes in the corner and hauled it over to one of the shelves. Taking out a box, he began going through old toys and games.

He threw things into the box at his feet, taking out years' worth of frustration on deflated soccer balls and broken Frisbees. It wasn't his job to clean out his parents' garage, but he needed something to do. He couldn't go back in and face the people sitting at the table. Instead, he would stay until Corinne showed up and he could talk to her, someone who knew how his family was but hadn't survived their expectations only to come out as a failure after all.

That was it, wasn't it? He was a failure in every sense of the word. No one was taking anything away from him—he was too busy doing all of it on his own. He shivered, regretting leaving his jacket in the house. If his parents had ever looked at Nate with half as much reverence as they did Dean, maybe he wouldn't be out in the chilly garage putting leftovers of his youth in boxes.

The door creaked open and then shut. Footsteps on the concrete. Expecting Corinne, Nate didn't look up. The much deeper voice at his elbow surprised him.

"Need some help?" Dean asked.

"Not from you." Nate slammed an old bike helmet on top and pulled over an empty box.

"What are you planning on doing with that?"

"I don't fucking know, and I don't fucking care." Nate brushed past with the box, knocking into Dean's shoulder.

Dean grabbed his bicep. "Stop. Whatever your issue with Mom and Dad is, don't take it out on me."

Nate turned to face him, staring at his brother. "Take it out on you, my perfect, saintly older brother who married a perfect, saintly wife and produced perfect, saintly children and is successful at everything he does, ever? You who can do no wrong, not even to stand up for me when Mom and Dad are at their usual best. Meanwhile, I'm just the bottomless pit of disappointment, as always."

"What?" Dean backed off, confusion all over his face. "What

are you talking about?"

"My problem isn't with you! It's the way you were always their golden child, the one who did every last thing right. They don't care what's going on in my life. All they want is to hear about you. Then, when I actually need them to care for once, they're too busy mapping out what they think is my tragic fall into darkness. My life turned out exactly as they expected the minute I didn't live up to being their own personal gay celebrity. You, on the other hand, have made them proud."

"That—that's not true." Dean's voice shook even as he tried to deny it.

"It is," Nate confirmed. "Always has been. All through school, they went to every one of your games. Rewarded you for your hard work and paid you for every A on your report card. Me? They might have attended one school play in four years, and it was never enough for them that I was in the top ten. I didn't follow in your footsteps, Mr. Valedictorian."

Dean backed up. He looked pained, as though he didn't want to accept the truth. "You don't even know," he said.

"I don't know what? That I could never measure up? Hell, you're even taller than I am. Yeah, I knew. Loud and clear, message received."

"No." Dean shook his head. "I didn't...I'm not..." He swallowed. "It's not like that. They did what they thought they had to, and so did I."

Nate frowned. "You're right, I don't know. I have no idea what the hell you're talking about. Make some sense, or I'm going back to packing shit in boxes."

Dean slammed his fist against the shelf, making Nate jump. "I worked my ass off so I could stop feeling like a worthless piece of shit!"

Nate gasped, and they stood staring at each other. Dean's eyes were wet. He'd never cried in front of Nate, not even when they were little. Nate shook himself out of the trance first. He still had no idea what Dean was talking about, but slowly, fragments of conversations over the years drifted back.

"Tell me," he said.

"Mom and Dad thought they had to make up for it. They still blame themselves, you know."

"For what?"

"Do you remember when we were kids, and we were at that

church?" When Nate nodded, he continued. "They thought they should have stopped it. I don't know how they would have. What that priest did to me..."

He didn't need to finish his sentence. "Oh, god," Nate murmured. "Fuck, I'm so sorry."

"Yeah, well. Now you know why we left. The church didn't do a damn thing. Shuffled the priest off to somewhere else, where he could make some other boy's life hell, no doubt."

"I didn't know." But he had. Somewhere buried, Nate had guessed something had happened, even if he didn't know what it was. No one told him, but he'd seen clues.

Dean cleared his throat. "Did he ever—"

"No."

"I'm glad." He paused. "That's why they're like that, you know. They thought he did it to you too and you just weren't saying. Don't you remember?"

Nate frowned. "Not really. I was what, seven or eight? I think they asked, but the priest scandal was big news everywhere back then, so I thought that's why. Oh, my god. They think that's why I'm gay?"

Dean shrugged. "Probably, yeah. They're not exactly against it, but they think there must be a reason."

"And a reason why I'm such a fuck-up, too."

They stood there for a long time. Nate studied his brother. They looked so much alike that they'd been mistaken for twins despite their age gap. Nate wondered if it would have made a difference, knowing. If he'd have cut his parents some slack or tried harder to get along with Dean as a teenager. In fairness, their parents hadn't been upset when Nate came out, and they'd put him through college. They'd just expressed their disapproval of his profession the whole time. He wondered if things would have been different if they hadn't felt guilty about what happened to Dean.

Nate gave a sharp nod. There wasn't anything left to say. An understanding passed between them, and Nate turned back to his work. Beside him, Dean began clearing his end of the shelf into another box. He paused, and Nate glanced over.

"I went, you know," he said in a low voice.

"Went where?"

"To every single one of your concerts and plays. I sneaked in and hid in back. Last fall, I saw *Die Fledermaus* twice." The corner of his mouth lifted. "You're not a fuck-up. I'm really proud of you, little brother."

Nate ducked his head so Dean wouldn't see the tears forming. A warm hand ruffled his hair before disappearing. The thunk of something metal dropping into the box made Nate look up.

"What the hell was that?"

Dean bent and picked it up again. "Ancient roller skate. God, don't Mom and Dad ever throw anything away?"

They laughed, and Nate no longer felt the cold out in the garage.

Nate purposefully chose a night he knew Mack and Jamie were both working late to invite Trevor to the apartment. He'd stalled long enough on talking to him, and Trevor was the last person to find out. Nate was grateful to everyone for their commitment to letting him tell Trevor himself, but it wasn't fair to them to make them continue. He'd checked in with Marlie, and she was happy to take the baby to visit her sister for the night. Andre said he had plans as well, which left Trevor free to do as he pleased.

It was only Trevor, a person Nate had known for over ten years, and yet he was more anxious than he had been about talking to Izzy. With Izzy, he'd felt resigned—he had to tell the person he'd been intimate with, regardless of what it would mean for their relationship. None of the others were close enough to Nate for it to feel like he was baring his soul to them. Nate had mostly been grateful for Mack's financial support and for Jamie not unleashing his usual germ phobia. Izzy had already broken Nate's heart, so it shouldn't have mattered what Trevor piled on, but Nate was still tense.

In order not to sound like it was something major, Nate had called and told Trevor he wanted to "hang out." He'd only realized his mistake after he practically heard Trevor cringing on the other end of the line. That had been their code for "we're both single again, so let's relieve some tension." Nate had rushed to correct his mistake, saying he meant have a few beers and watch a game. Football was the only sport Nate liked, and the Patriots might provide enough background to keep the awkward tension at a minimum.

He fussed, taking out two beers and then putting them back in the fridge, not wanting them to be too warm. He rearranged the couch pillows six or seven times and eventually flung them all off into the corner to work off some of his nervous energy. He debated whether he should put chips in a bowl or if that would seem odd, like Trevor was a stranger he had to impress. Every little decision required close scrutiny to see if it would be obvious to Trevor this was more than a night in while everyone else was out.

The door buzzer was louder than Nate expected, causing him to jump and nearly spill the pretzels he was dumping back in the bag after all. It was still weird to let Trevor up that way rather than having him use his key. After a few minutes, Trevor's cheerful knock sounded on the door. When Nate opened it, his anxiety fizzled. This was only Trevor, his oldest friend, who had stood by him even when he was being an ass. He let Trevor in and grabbed his jacket to hang in the tiny coat closet.

They settled in on the couch to watch the Pats game. It was something they'd always been able to enjoy together. The other guys had no interest, and even Izzy had been passive about it. Trevor threw a pretzel at the television when a flag was called on a play, and it made Nate laugh.

"What?" Trevor asked.

Nate shrugged, not wanting to admit how much he'd missed nights like this. "You," he said.

"Whatever." Trevor threw a pretzel at Nate, who caught it and stuck it in his mouth.

Trevor propped his feet on the coffee table and drained the last of his beer. He stretched a little, revealing the blond fuzz on his round stomach. Nate had always liked how unselfconscious Trevor was about his body—he'd never been interested in sculpting it to have perfect abs or ass. Nate recalled Andre calling him "curvy" once, and it was obvious from his tone he found it sexy. Nate hadn't thought about it so deeply; he liked Trevor's confidence more than anything. It occurred to him he no longer felt jealous of Andre's place in Trevor's life.

"You want another one?" he asked, standing and picking up their empties.

Trevor looked up at him and tilted his head as though he were contemplating something more than merely whether he wanted another drink. "Sure," he said.

Nate popped the tops off two more and brought them out. He repositioned himself, reclining against the arm of the couch and wishing he hadn't tossed all the pillows on the other side of the room. Trevor glanced sideways at him. He tipped his bottle toward Nate in acknowledgment and took a sip.

An ad came on, and Trevor turned down the volume. "You're pretty quiet."

"So are you."

"I've been watching the game. You're barely paying attention." Trevor set his beer on the table. "I know we haven't really talked since last summer, but I thought we'd pretty well made peace about everything. I'm not still pissed, you know."

"I suppose I know that." Nate's palms were clammy, and he wiped them on his jeans.

"Are you still?"

Nate had no idea what Trevor meant. "Still what?"

"Upset. About Andre."

"No. I'm happy for you. You've found someone—well, two someones—you love." He bumped Trevor's foot with his own as reassurance.

"Ah, I think I see." Trevor angled to face Nate. "You never did tell me what happened with Izzy."

"It didn't work out." Nate wasn't ready to explain further, even though they seemed to be inching toward the conversation they needed to have. "We wanted different things."

"Oh, no. I'm sorry. Well, that's shitty. I suppose it doesn't leave you with a very good impression, does it?"

"What?"

"You know, that we can't keep our pants zipped. Izzy's bi, right?"

Nate couldn't help laughing. "Dude. You're assuming a lot. I've come a long way. For one thing, that's not the issue. For another, I already know that. I mean, look at Andre."

For a second, Trevor looked like he might share Nate's amusement, but his face fell. "Yeah."

"What is it?"

Trevor didn't say anything right away. He leaned back and ran a hand through his thick, blond hair, letting out a heavy sigh. Eventually, he rolled his head to the side to look at Nate. "Andre's been seeing someone."

Nate's eyebrows shot up. "I had no idea. He never—" He cut himself off, not ready to explain that he'd talked to Andre on his own but they hadn't discussed his love life.

"It was always part of our arrangement," Trevor said. "All three of us have different needs, and the only thing we asked was that we talk. He came to me a few weeks ago and said he'd met someone—a woman. Andre and Marlie have never been interested in each other, so it wasn't going to work out for us to make a triad. It made sense for him to find someone."

"But you're not happy."

Trevor shook his head. "It's not like you're thinking. It's…I don't know. Sometimes it feels like things are great—we both have each other and someone else. Perfect, right? Seeing him so happy should make me feel good too. Except instead I'm fighting so hard not to be jealous of the time he spends with her. I feel like I'm not enough, even though I know it's not true and Andre would tell me so if I talked to him about it." He scraped his teeth over his upper lip. "It makes me miss what I had with you."

Nate scowled. "Right. Because that worked out so well." He couldn't tell Trevor all the reasons it wasn't a good idea and maybe never had been.

"No!" Trevor exclaimed. "I don't mean we should go back. I mean I need that kind of friendship. Marlie is great, but I think she's probably the only woman I have or will ever love."

"So you want—what, an open relationship? Play with another guy?"

"I guess, but not with a string of strangers."

Nate sat back and considered what Trevor had said. It made sense, given their history. He'd been attached, but Trevor wanted someone willing to mess around occasionally. Nate reflected on their differing needs and how mismatched they'd been. Something small nagged the back of his mind, and he wondered if Trevor was already in such a friendship. He suspected there was more under the surface.

"Are you already—" he started.

"No, not yet. Feeling left out with Andre isn't a good enough reason to do it."

"You know it can't be me, right?"

Trevor nodded. "I know. You're a one-man kind of guy." He smiled.

"I am, but—" Nate swallowed, stalling. This was as good an opening as he would get. "I didn't just ask you here to drink beer and watch football and talk about Andre."

Sitting up, Trevor said, "Okay."

"I need to tell you something." More stalling.

"I got that impression." Trevor's shoulders slumped. "Sorry for sidetracking us. Whatever it is, I'm here. No matter what."

He knew. He'd guessed, even though Nate hadn't said yet. Nate saw it in his eyes, the moment it clicked. Because what else would Nate need to tell him and which he was avoiding doing? Everyone else had figured it out, most of them long before Nate was willing to admit it. The silence stretched, broken only by the faint sounds coming from the television. He had to say it, speak the words out loud. He'd done it half a dozen times already; why was this any different?

"I'm—"

"Don't," Trevor said. "Please. I already know."

"I need to," Nate said, low. "Trev, I'm poz. I have HIV."

Trevor nodded, losing the tension in his shoulders. He looked...relieved, oddly. "Not cancer, then."

"What?" Nate was momentarily thrown.

"I thought that's what you were going to say. You called me over to tell me you have six months to live or something."

"Oh, my god."

Nate's anxiety gave way to irritation that Trevor had assumed something more immediately catastrophic. He stood up and stalked to the corner where the pillows lay. He grabbed one and returned to the couch to smack Trevor soundly on the head with it. Trevor looked up at him, gaping.

"What the hell?"

"You thought I was fucking dying of cancer!" he yelled. "I would have told you that already, you meathead!" He thwacked Trevor again, catching his open mouth.

"Oh, you'll pay for that."

Trevor bounced off the couch and grabbed another pillow. He tried to hit Nate with it, but Nate was too quick and blocked the blow. When he pulled back to smack Trevor again, Trevor got him in the stomach. Nate tackled Trevor and dragged him down onto the couch. They play-wrestled, laughing and continuing to attack each other with the pillows until they were both out of breath. Trevor leaned back with Nate's head in his lap, and their panting laughter faded as they calmed down.

"Seriously, how are you doing?" Trevor asked.

"I'm...okay, I guess. I've had some time to process. I freaked out for about a week."

"Makes sense. It's heavy stuff." He paused. "That flu you had last fall—"

"Wasn't flu. Right." Nate twisted to look up at Trevor. "Andre already knows. I talked to him the night Izzy broke up with me."

"Okay."

"You're not upset?"

"Define 'upset.' There's no real reason to be, is there?"

"I don't know."

Trevor ran a hand through Nate's hair. "I'm glad you talked to him first. He's good with this kind of thing."

"Yeah." Nate cleared his throat. "I was so stupid."

"For talking to Andre?" Trevor's brow furrowed.

"No." Nate was silent for a long time. He closed his eyes, enjoying the way Trevor scratched his scalp lightly. "Everything. I trusted the wrong man. I should've listened last fall when all of you told me to go see a doctor. I didn't have one, and I don't have health insurance now. I made the clinic call the man who I think gave it to me. And Izzy..." He trailed off, suddenly fighting tears.

"Hey. Hey, it's okay."

Trevor pulled Nate up a bit so Nate could sob into his chest. He let out all the hurt and anger and confusion as well as relief at Trevor's casual acceptance. They stayed that way until Nate's crying quieted into soft hiccups. He tilted his head to look at Trevor, who took his face in his hands. Trevor kissed Nate's forehead the same way Del had, but with different emotions behind it.

"We'll get you help," he said. "I promise. You do need insurance, though. Why didn't you get MassHealth? You know there's a tax penalty for going without."

"There's a tax penalty for breathing wrong," Nate muttered. "I don't know...it just wasn't a priority. Andre said he and his grandmother will help me with all the forms and shit, and she recommended an infectious disease specialist for me. I'm seeing him next week."

"Good. You want to talk about it more or finish watching the game?"

"The game. I need a good Pats win to cheer me up."

"Pfft. Like that's even in question." Trevor grinned.

They leaned on each other, and Trevor turned the television back up. Whatever else happened, at least Nate knew he could count on Trevor.

CHAPTER FIFTEEN

Eema took the day off to accompany Izzy for his MRI. He drove, and neither of them said much on the way. Ma Rose would have been talking his ear off, but Eema was content to offer her silent support. She had her sewing kit with her, this time embroidery. She was putting detail on a gingerbread man applique, part of a baby quilt. Izzy wondered if it was for Lynne or one of the other young women; he didn't ask.

While they waited, Eema kept her eyes on her work, but she asked, "Where's your young man? Didn't he want to come with you?"

"He's probably working." Izzy would need to tell her eventually, but for now, he couldn't say more.

Eema sighed heavily. "Probably," she mused. "Interesting choice of words. Would you like to tell me what happened?"

"Not really."

"But you will." She put a hand on his arm.

Izzy said nothing right away. Around them, generic hospital sounds carried on—the soft voices of people checking in; magazine pages rustling; doors opening and closing. It was all muted by the atmosphere. Izzy closed his eyes, wishing he could do everything over again with Nate. He'd blown his chance, even if Nate were willing to cast his lot with someone likely to need a caregiver more than a partner one day. He might have been able to save their relationship if he hadn't been so needlessly cruel when Nate revealed his own diagnosis.

How could Izzy explain now that more than ever, he thought Nate deserved someone healthy? He would have enough to manage without adding Izzy's needs. He at least should have explained it instead of sounding as though he saw Nate as someone stained and unclean. It was too late now. Nate wasn't under contractual obligation to forgive Izzy for his thoughtlessness.

He turned to Eema. "I don't deserve him."

"Israel!" Eema exclaimed, causing a few people to look up. She blushed and lowered her voice. "What in the world would make you say such a thing?"

"I don't know. All I wanted was to tell him he shouldn't be with me out of sympathy, but then he started telling me things about himself too, and I couldn't—" Izzy slouched in his seat. "I didn't know what to do with it."

Eema nodded. "Do you remember when your father came to stay with us all those years ago?"

Izzy frowned. "Barely. I mean, I didn't want him there, so I think I shut it out of my mind."

"Right. At the time, you thought I was going to leave with him, that I would give up my life with you and your mother to go to New York. I never would have, of course. If anyone was looking for someone to be with them out of sympathy or caregiving, your father was it."

"Is that what it was?"

Eema nodded and pulled out a stitch to redo. "His partner had just died, and..." She looked at Izzy, and he knew what she wasn't saying. It wasn't her place, but she obviously hoped he would guess. He gave her a quick nod to show he understood, and she continued. "He did love me, you know, but he had no context for that. Not from the way we were raised. I had resigned myself to marrying him, and I certainly liked him, but I didn't love him. I wasn't going to leave my life to take care of him."

"He was fine, though. He didn't need you to."

"He did at the time he came to see us." She pulled out a new shade of embroidery floss and cut it to the proper length. "He wasn't well. Not because he was actually sick, though we made sure he saw doctors and got what he needed. He was grieving and alone. Jimmy's family had left their only son to die by himself, and then rushed in to claim everything as soon as he was gone. You were trying out college, so I'm not sure you remember or if your father ever told you. You certainly didn't know everything we did for him."

She was right. Izzy had taken a year deciding if school was right for him and concluding it wasn't. He'd spent extra time away, avoiding the strained relationships among the other people in his family. Somewhere in the back of his mind, he'd suspected there was more to the visit, but he'd never wanted to know or understand. He'd wanted his anger at his father leaving to take center stage. In his mind, his mothers were not to forgive either, not even if Izzy's father believed he was dying.

Eema set her embroidery on top of her bag and twisted in her chair to face Izzy. She clasped his hands in hers. "You're not asking the man you love—who loves you—to accommodate you. This is not the same situation." She gave him a pointed look. "It's not even the same as with Lynne."

"I don't know what—"

"Sha," Eema chided. "Yes, you do. I know I don't talk about it, but I know perfectly well what happened. Maybe I was wrong, keeping you up on Lynne's family. Maybe she was too. But we all needed you to know you didn't break her when you left."

"And what about Nate?"

"Your young man? I can't say, but I do know that at some point, Israel, you need to stop running."

She let go, and they were silent again. Izzy wanted to ask her more, but he didn't get the chance. A nurse appeared in the doorway and called his name. He stood then turned to look down at Eema. She smiled up at him and wished him luck. He nodded and faced the doors, not moving for a moment. At last he gathered his strength and walked toward the nurse, his fate in the hands of modern technology.

Nate was in the midst of organizing things which didn't need tidying, thanks to Del's hard work. The props room was already clean, and the library system had been revised over the summer. Mostly, he was finding ways to fill his now-empty social calendar. Izzy had said he needed time, but he hadn't given Nate any indication of how much or even what that meant. Nate took it to be code for ending the relationship without having to say so.

While he was attempting to keep so busy he wouldn't dwell on it, his phone vibrated. He pulled it out and frowned, seeing the theater's box office number. "Hello?"

"Nate, there's someone here to see you. Did you want to come down to the lobby, or should I send him upstairs? He says he knows how to get there."

Nate's heart thumped. It couldn't be Izzy; he would have called directly, wouldn't he? "Who is it?"

There was a pause and muffled talking. "Rocco Alessi."

Oh, hell. Nate went from confused but hopeful to panicking and sick. He certainly didn't want to have this conversation in public, so he did the only sensible thing. "Send him up."

A few minutes later, Rocco rapped on the props room door. He leaned against the wall, and Nate almost felt sorry for how tired and stressed he seemed. The only thing holding back his sympathy was how many questions he wanted to ask Rocco and how much he wanted to rage at the person who had repeatedly left him heartbroken. Nate glanced at him briefly then went back to not really sorting things.

"Can I at least come in?" Rocco asked.

"Suit yourself. I don't own the place."

Rocco didn't move from the doorway. "I didn't come here to watch you work. If you don't want to talk to me, I understand, but I needed to see you. To talk to you."

"Go on." Nate gestured at him but didn't pause in his non-work.

"Maybe I should have done this over the phone, but you need to know I tested positive for HIV."

"I'm aware." Nate put down a plastic pear and turned to face Rocco. "I had the clinic call you for a reason. The whole point was that I didn't want to have this conversation."

Rocco exhaled noisily. "That explains a lot. I obviously didn't know you were the one. They only said 'sexual partner.' Maybe I deserve your anger, but I'd like you to hear me out."

"Why? What could you possibly have to say to me? I hoped months ago that we were parting on good terms, but I didn't want or need you back in my life. Only it didn't work out that way, did it?"

"No." Rocco moved closer, but he stopped when Nate glared at him.

"Did you know?"

Rocco shook his head. "I promise you, I didn't. Please, listen to me."

Nate shoved the bin he was holding back on the shelf. "Fine. There's a lounge on the third floor. We'll be more comfortable there. I work with a group of high school students, and they'll be here in an hour. You have until then to say your piece and get out."

"Fair enough."

Nate led the way up the back staircase to the lounge. He sat on the couch, and Rocco pulled a chair over from the table. He sat across from Nate, running his palms over his suit trousers. He looked far enough out of his element that Nate's sympathy stirred again.

"Go ahead," Nate told Rocco, gesturing.

"I didn't know until the clinic called me," he said. "I swear it."

"That makes two of us," Nate snarled.

"I was pissed at you for not telling me when we were together, but I was still trying to get myself together."

Nate threw up his hands. "I already told you, I didn't know either. I was absolutely not the one who gave it to you. If you must know, I hadn't had sex since April, and I know for sure I was negative then because I'd been tested."

Rocco pursed his lips. "I know that now. Will you let me finish?" He folded his hands in his lap and looked down at them. "I got married too young. Did you know we were only nineteen? We had a baby by the time we graduated college."

"I didn't know. Is there a point to this?"

"Yes." Rocco stood up and paced. He turned his back to Nate; maybe that made it easier. "I started seeing someone. I was with him for over two years. When my wife found out, she called it quits. She told me she would keep me from our daughter unless I stopped seeing him." He spun around, and his eyes were red-rimmed. When he spoke again, his voice wavered. "I loved my wife and my daughter. I didn't only marry her to make our parents happy, even if we weren't ready yet. She wasn't going to accept that I loved someone else too, especially not a man."

"I—" Nate stared at him.

Rocco wiped his eyes with the back of his hand. "I was exclusive with both of them, but my lover—god, that sounds like an old-fashioned word—was uncomfortable with our arrangement. He wanted me to tell her. He was sure I was using her as a cover for us. I thought I could wait, be a good husband and father, and tell her slowly. She already knew I thought before that I was gay, but she's a good Catholic. She figured I'd changed."

Despite his anger, Nate was curious about Rocco's story. "You never told me any of this when you broke up with me. I assumed you were lying to your parents."

"I wasn't." Rocco shook his head. "I really was confused. If I was gay, and I was with you, then why did I still get excited by the thought of being with girls? I decided you must have been the problem." He came and sat back down. "I'm sorry for that."

Nate sighed. "I believe you, but it doesn't change what happened this time."

"I know, and I'm sorry about that too. When I wouldn't leave her for him, he threatened me too, and that's how she found out. After losing both of the people I loved, I didn't know what I was supposed to do. I didn't know if I was supposed to cure myself of being gay or being straight. I tried anything to do both, and I didn't make a lot of good decisions about how that was going to happen. When we had our chance meeting, I thought you might be the answer to all my problems."

"Those aren't the only options." Nate snorted. He couldn't believe he was the one to educate Rocco. He also couldn't believe how often he ended up attracted to bisexual men. Maybe the universe was trying to tell him something.

"I know. You said Trevor is bi?"

"Yeah." Nate hesitated. Trevor, Andre, and Marlie generally did not hide their relationships, but Nate wasn't in the habit of discussing them with anyone who didn't already know. He decided to make an exception for Rocco. "Trevor has a boyfriend and a girlfriend. And a baby."

Rocco's eyes popped. "He does?"

"They're not hiding it from each other. I didn't used to get it myself, but I think I do now. It works for them, and they're happy—at least, as much as any family is." Nate took a deep breath. "Look, I admit I was pissed at you, but this was never one-sided. I didn't want to talk to you because I thought you knew and didn't tell me. Now that I know the truth, all I want is to make sure you're okay."

"Not really," Rocco said. "It's a lot to deal with. I'm sure my ex will use it to keep our daughter from me, and I'm not sure where to go from here."

"It would help if you had someone to talk to." Nate kept eye contact. "But that won't be me. I need to take care of myself, and you need someone who wasn't involved."

"I know."

Nate stood, and Rocco followed suit. "I'm not trying to be a complete ass here. I know you only just found out, and trust me, I get how it feels. The thing is, I'm not in a place where I can be your friend right now. I should have been more careful, but so should you."

"You're right." Rocco looked crushed, but Nate only had so much sympathy to spare.

"I'll walk you out."

Nate headed for the door. Rocco hesitated for a moment as though he didn't want their conversation to end, but he eventually followed. Nate wondered if he was doing the right thing. He understood rejection, especially after Izzy, and he knew Rocco didn't have the kind of support Nate did. He had money, but his family wasn't likely to be much help. They were far less accepting than Nate's.

They reached the theater entrance, and Nate turned to Rocco. "Wait."

Rocco stopped walking. "What?"

Drawing on all his strength, Nate said, "I changed my mind. I'm here, if you need me. I can't speak for my friends—they might not be so welcoming. But I do care, and I don't want you to do this alone."

Rocco nodded and pulled Nate into a long hug. He let go and said, "I'll be all right."

Nate backed up and watched him leave, feeling his anger and disappointment follow Rocco out the door. One more step down, just like Del said.

The nurse had told Izzy not to change, since it was only a consultation to go over the results of the MRI. He sat in the chair instead of on the exam table so as not to tower over Dr. Levin. Three times, he stood up and paced before sitting back down. As he was on the verge of rising a fourth time, there was a knock on the door. Dr. Levin entered with Izzy's chart and reached out to shake hands. He sat on the rolling stool by the counter, chart open to the most recent visit's page.

Dr. Levin tapped his pen against his palm. "How have you been since last time?"

Izzy shrugged. "All right, I guess."

"A nurse called you about the blood tests you requested?"

"Yeah. All clear, but I apparently need a repeat." Izzy swallowed the rising ache in his throat when he thought about Nate.

"Oh?" Dr. Levin looked confused.

Izzy figured it wasn't breaking anyone's confidence to tell Dr. Levin the truth. "My last partner called me to say he has HIV. There wasn't enough time to know for sure when I had the previous test."

Dr. Levin nodded. "Check in with the nurse when we're through. She'll give you another form, and you can return to the lab for a follow-up test. How are you feeling otherwise?"

"Not bad." He shrugged. "Nothing new from the last time I was here, and I've at least been able to run."

"Excellent. Glad to hear you're taking care of yourself." Dr. Levin made some notes. "I wanted to talk to you about the results of the MRI, and I didn't want to do it over the phone."

That sounded as bad as Izzy had expected. He gripped the arms of the chair, struggling not to fidget. He licked his lips. "Well, that's why I'm here."

"Right." Dr. Levin nodded. "Izzy, there's not an easy way to break bad news, so I'm just going to get right to it. You have multiple sclerosis. The neurologist will run a few more tests to find out how extensive the damage is, but there's no doubt in my mind. The MRI showed marked lesions. At this point, we'll be working together to manage your care."

Izzy's head swirled. The possibility had occurred to him, but only as one of several potential diagnoses. He didn't even know anything about it, outside of a passing read on the internet. What did it mean? He wanted to ask, but his tongue was frozen. His fingers gripped and released the chair while he tried in vain to come up with at least one question to ask. Surely there were things he needed to know or do.

"I'm sorry," Dr. Levin said. "Maybe I should have done this differently. It's a lot to take in, I know."

Unsticking his lips, Izzy finally managed to say, "Is it—am I dying?"

Dr. Levin let out a long, slow breath. "The short answer is no. At least, not in the near future. There are several types of MS, and we need to determine which one you have. That will take time. For now, we're going to start with the tests I mentioned. The results will help us know how to proceed. We have a host of treatment and management options available to us, and with your otherwise excellent health, you already have a head start."

He was being overly chipper about it, even if he wasn't concealing anything. Izzy sat up straighter. "Be honest with me."

Putting his pen down, Dr. Levin swiveled in the chair to face Izzy straight on. "It's not good. You've probably had symptoms for a while, years maybe, some of which you may not have noticed or might have attributed to something else. We will keep you healthy and mobile for as long as we can, but MS is usually progressive unless it goes into remission. Over time..."

"It's permanently disabling." Izzy nodded. "So that's it, then."

Dr. Levin shook his head. "It's not. Iz, plenty of people live with this for a long time. There are some limitations, sure, but it doesn't mean your life is over."

"Not what I meant."

Izzy didn't know how to explain all the things he still didn't know, all the ways he was in the dark about how it would affect him. He reasoned he'd been right to let Nate go before he ended up spending his life taking care of Izzy, especially given his own recent diagnosis. Dr. Levin tilted his head, waiting, but Izzy didn't say anything more. There wasn't any point in discussing Nate with the doctor when their relationship had already become non-existent. Dr. Levin must have realized Izzy wasn't going to expand on his previous statement, so he continued with his own explanation.

"I'm sure you have a lot of questions, and we do have answers. The first thing I'm going to do is make sure you have good care, though I'm happy to continue being part of your team. I'm referring you to a physiologist who will be able to work with you on how to keep yourself in good condition. I'll give you some things to read which aren't written in medical lingo and should explain a lot of what's happening to your body. I'll have a nurse come in and go over it with you." He held Izzy's gaze. "I'm serious about this next part, and I want you to make sure you do as I'm asking. You need someone to talk to. I'm also referring you to a therapist." When Izzy started to protest, he held up a hand. "You only have to go once to start. You may like a support group model better, or you may prefer one on one, or you may end up deciding it's not for you right now. Don't make a decision while this is fresh. You're not alone—there are many people here to help you."

He ripped a prescription off his pad. He'd scrawled two names and numbers—the physiologist and the therapist. Izzy accepted the paper and folded it carefully to tuck into his pocket. Dr. Levin rose from the stool, shook hands with Izzy again, and left the room, closing the door behind him.

Izzy sat back in his chair and leaned his head against the wall.

He felt fine, but he thought he shouldn't. He thought he should notice new symptoms or at least some evidence of the ones he'd come in for in the first place. Instead, his pain was relatively low, and he wasn't fatigued. Emotionally, he thought he should have been freaking out. He wasn't doing that either. He didn't know what the right way to process everything was; there wasn't a handbook or a flowchart for receiving a diagnosis.

The nurse who had brought him to the exam room returned with a handful of papers. She closed the door and took over the stool where Dr. Levin had sat. She didn't start going over them right away. Placing her hand on Izzy's, she nodded in understanding.

"We don't have to start right away. When you're ready, I'll explain everything to you, and we'll go from there."

Only then did Izzy let his wall drop, leaning forward and putting his head in his hands. "Give me a minute," he said.

"Sure." She busied herself with writing some notes on the top of one of the pages.

Izzy thought about Nate and the easy way they'd come together since the night they sang for the benefit. He hadn't known at the time where they were heading, but he'd fallen farther and faster than he'd expected. When Izzy had asked him for time, he hadn't known what either of them needed; he still didn't. A lump formed in his throat. He missed Nate, but he couldn't ask a man he'd only been seeing for a couple of months to share the burden of a lifelong condition. Nate was young—still at an age where he could find someone his own age, someone he wouldn't have to eventually care for. He had his own needs now, staying healthy himself. Izzy couldn't promise to look after him and protect him the way he wanted to.

That was it, wasn't it? He felt like a failure, never living up to what he thought he should be. A small voice in the back of his mind whispered that Eema was right, he was running again. He'd never even offered Nate the option—he'd taken the choice away from him before telling Nate the truth. The least he could do was provide an explanation and see what Nate had to say about it. This was the same man who had stripped away his fear to confess his secret desires to Izzy. He might still reject him, but at least he deserved Izzy's honesty.

Izzy closed his eyes, hoping he would be able to find the right words. With a clear mind, he opened his eyes again and turned to the nurse. "Lay it on me," he said.

Chapter Sixteen

Izzy slid into the ambulance and shut the door. Val was already waiting for him, starting in on her report. She glanced over at him but said nothing. He didn't speak either, just pulled away and headed back toward the station. Val looked at him again, but he ignored her.

It took three more calls before she spoke. "All right, I'm done. I'll get it out of you eventually, so you might as well give in and tell me what the hell has had you in such a foul mood all week. I thought your vacation might be a chance to catch up on rest, or maybe spend some time with that cutie you've been seeing, but you came back more miserable than I've ever seen you. Come on, give." She crossed her arms and leaned back in the seat, her eyes trained on him.

She was right. Izzy had never been good at keeping things from her, not when they spent so much time in each other's company. He sighed loudly, more for her benefit than his. He at least had to give the impression he didn't want to talk about it, even though Val was the next best thing to calling a professional. The corner of Val's mouth lifted, and her posture relaxed.

Izzy said, "I know I've been awful the last couple shifts, and I'm sorry. Things are shit, and I'm trying to keep it together. Obviously I'm not being too successful."

Val nodded. "I guessed something was up when you took time off. You never take vacation, or hardly ever. Then suddenly you've got a week and a half off." Her voice softened. "What's going on with you?"

Everything and nothing, he wanted to say. "I finally went to the doctor."

"I take it you got some bad news." She sounded calm, but Izzy could tell she was worried.

"Yes and no. It's...bad? But I'm not dying." He took a moment to collect himself. "Multiple sclerosis. I'm cleared to live a long, healthy life, if not entirely the one I was expecting."

"Oh, Iz. So, what does that mean, exactly?"

It meant a lot of things Izzy didn't want to share with Val, so he explained the parts which affected her directly. "I have to keep an eye on my symptoms. For now, I can still work. But if it gets worse, I'm out of luck on that front. Running, performing at Grand Slam— those too. I do what I can until I'm not able anymore." He didn't tell her he was already trying to figure out what the next step was, for the day he couldn't work with her anymore.

"And what does Nate think about all this?"

There she went, poking the bear. Izzy didn't want to talk about Nate—not the way Izzy had treated him or the things Nate had shared. Izzy didn't respond to Val, which he supposed might be answer enough.

"Kaplan." She had that tone, the one she used when she was about to tell him what was what.

He glanced sideways at her. "Say it, Morales."

"You. Are. A. Damn. Fool." She crossed her arms again and glared at him. "Let me guess. You broke the poor kid's heart because you're feeling sorry for yourself."

"It wasn't like that!" Izzy protested.

"Then how was it?"

Izzy said nothing. Val harrumphed and fell silent until they'd pulled back into the bay. Izzy turned off the engine, but Val didn't make a move to get out.

"Well?" she demanded.

"He's dealing with a lot right now with his own health. I feel like I'd be breaking his confidence to say more, but I didn't think it was fair to put my needs on top of his."

Val trained her death glare on him. "Israel Kaplan, do you even know how relationships are supposed to work? My god, you are an ass sometimes."

"I know." He slouched in his seat. "I figured that out all by myself. That's not the trouble right now."

"Then what is?"

"I don't know what else to do. I finally got around to calling him back the minute my head was out of my ass, but he didn't pick up, and he didn't return my call." Izzy propped his elbow against the door and rested his head on his fist.

Val put a hand on her shoulder. "And that's where I come in."

Izzy eyed her. "Can't see what you're going to do about my mess. I own this one, and no one is to blame but me."

"Oh, my man. How long have you known me?" There was a wicked gleam in her eyes. "I think I have an idea. Call him and beg him to come watch you perform. I'll set the whole thing up for us. If he doesn't show, we can still make it work and it'll be fun for the audience. If he's there, well, I think you'll be able to convince him to at least listen."

The only sensible action was to agree. "All right."

"Good." Val grinned and climbed out of the ambulance. She turned to face Izzy. "And Iz? Make sure you say you're sorry this time." She slammed the door.

Izzy sat for another minute before following her out. He had one shot at talking to Nate, and he didn't want to blow it. Whatever Val was cooking up, it was still on Izzy to make things right. He trailed after Val into the station, his thoughts still on what he could possibly say to Nate to get him to come watch them.

The first time Izzy had called, Nate had let it go to voicemail and ignored it. It felt like too little, too late. He offered no explanation for what happened in the restaurant, and Nate didn't know what his intent was now. When Izzy called the second time and begged Nate to come watch him perform, Nate didn't trusted it would end well. Still, there was something in Izzy's apology which made Nate want to at least hear what he had to say this time. Izzy had promised they could talk after the show, although Nate wasn't sure what to say to him.

Del's advice so far had been fifty-fifty; spot on for not getting involved with married men, but Nate's problems definitely hadn't been solved by sex. So Nate figured it could go either way on whether he should try to persuade Izzy to see it from his perspective. He decided he could at least hear Izzy out before he concluded he wasn't worth convincing, as Del put it.

Nate sat wedged between Trevor and Jamie. They'd both agreed to come with him for moral support, though Nate still wasn't convinced he wanted to be there at all. The emcee, Brunhilde—she of the turquoise wig—delivered plenty of biting comedy, and the other performers were decent. Nate couldn't keep his mind on any of it. He was waiting for Izzy to appear. He fidgeted, tapping his fingers against his beer bottle until Jamie moved it out of his reach.

He was so tense he didn't hear Brunhilde announcing the next act. Trevor nudged him, and he looked up in time to see TaTa and Chico stepping toward the front of the stage and down off it into the crowd. Nate's mouth fell open at their costumes. He knew Chico was usually responsible for the designs, and he'd done a good job. They'd taken a page out of *Victor/Victoria*, and Chico was playing a man performing as a woman while TaTa was doing the same in reverse.

Chico was dolled up as a drag version of Elphaba from *Wicked*, which made TaTa into Fiyero. Nate wondered why they'd flipped roles, as it wasn't their usual. Something was different about their act which had Nate sitting up a little more in his seat. It happened to be one of his favorite shows, though neither TaTa nor Chico could possibly have known...unless someone told them. Nate glanced at Trevor, who shrugged, but Jamie blushed. Only a little exasperated, Nate bumped his shoulder. Jamie grinned and sat back to watch the performance.

They began to sing "As Long as You're Mine," and Nate was stunned by how gorgeous Chico's voice actually was. Nate was entirely focused on the vocals, and he almost missed how the two of them were moving among the tables. There was a quick exchange between them, so subtle Nate only noticed because Chico had been at their table, delivering a line to Jamie. Chico traded places with TaTa, and Nate looked up to find TaTa inches from him, her eyes on his.

She sang for his benefit, and Nate understood she meant every word. He sat mesmerized by her, even knowing probably every person in there saw what she was doing. His heart beat so hard he thought it might burst, and his stomach flipped. Being so close to TaTa reminded Nate how much he'd wanted her. But seeing her performing as Izzy was enthralling. This was the man Nate had given his heart to, begging in song for a chance to make it right.

TaTa dropped something out of her sleeve onto Nate's table.

She danced away, coming back together with Chico to finish strong. As they sang the final note, the applause around Nate was deafening. He tried to make himself join in, but all he could think about was the tiny piece of paper lying inches from him on the table. He reached for it and snatched it up.

Chico and TaTa were the final performance of the night, and chatter started in at the other tables. Nate slowly unfolded the paper with shaking hands. There were only a few words on it: *Meet me at my place for Shabbat meal on Friday. -Izzy*

Nate looked up at Trevor, and Jamie put a hand on his back. He blinked back tears. Should he go? He didn't know what Izzy wanted from him. Maybe this was Izzy's chance to say a real goodbye. Except from the way Izzy sang to him, it didn't sound like it. In fact, it sounded a lot more like an apology and asking for another chance. Nate had to decide if he was willing to give it to him.

"Are you going to go?" Trevor pointed to the note.

"I don't know," Nate said.

"Go," Jamie urged. "At least hear what he has to say."

But what if I'm disappointed all over again? Nate wanted to ask. He looked back and forth between his friends. They seemed to have faith that it would work out. "Okay. I'll go." Even if he was going to spend the days until Friday wondering if he was doing the right thing.

Izzy let Nate in and took his coat. He returned to the tiny kitchen and pulled the brisket out of the oven then put it on the table. He followed it with a loaf of braided bread and spiced oil instead of butter. He set a bowl of salad at each place and poured them both a glass of wine. He caught Nate watching, but neither of them said anything until the table was ready.

"I usually have Shabbat meal with my mothers, but I called them and told them we needed some privacy tonight. They understood." Izzy smiled. "I'm not as good a cook as Eema, but I'll do. I just have to light the candles."

He lit the candles the way Eema always did, wafting the slight smoke toward himself as he sang the blessings. At last he sat down and put his hand on top of Nate's. He squeezed a little and then let go.

"Eat up," he said.

Nate put food on his plate, but he didn't touch it. Instead he looked down at his lap or up at the candles or across the room to the clock on the wall—anywhere but right at Izzy. It was awkward and frustrating, but Izzy didn't know what else to do. He ate in silence until at last Nate began to pick at his meal. It did nothing to ease the tension between them, even though Izzy noticed Nate had begun to relax.

Izzy set his fork down. "We need to talk about this before the tension reaches critical mass."

Finally Nate looked at him. "I know. I'm not sure where to begin. I'm still getting used to my new reality." He propped his elbow on the table and rested his cheek on his fist. He poked at a leaf of lettuce then looked up at Izzy. "It bothers you, doesn't it? My HIV status."

"I would be lying if I said it didn't." When Nate's gaze dropped back to his plate, Izzy touched his arm. "Let me explain."

Nate twisted his napkin in his fist. "Explain why we can't—"

"No." Izzy held up his hand. "Not like that. I never would have asked you here if I was only going to tell you we can't ever be together."

"I'm listening." Nate finally raised his eyes.

Izzy blew out a breath. "Around nineteen ninety-eight, my father came to stay with us. He'd been living in New York." He sighed. "I guess I should start at the beginning. I don't know the whole story, but my parents all left an ultra-Orthodox community. Eema was pregnant with me, but she and my father weren't married. It would have been terrible for them. They came to Boston with Ma Rose, who is my father's cousin. When I was very small, my father left." He swallowed around a sudden lump in his throat. "His partner passed away in the mid-nineties. So my father came back to us to die."

"Oh, God!" Nate exclaimed. "No wonder—"

"Wait. My father is still living. When he came here, he wasn't sick, but he decided it was a matter of time. He thought there was nothing anyone could do for him. I think he was too devastated to look into his own future—he didn't want to live without the man he loved, and to him, death was inevitable anyway. I doubt his partner was the first one he witnessed. He stayed with us for about a year, and my mothers helped him find doctors and better care. I was eighteen at the time, and I couldn't bear being around him. It's why I did an ill-advised year of college as an escape. He was in such deep denial. He'd referred to his partner even to us as his 'roommate' or his 'friend.' After he moved out, he hung around for a while but eventually went back to New York. To my knowledge, he's remained in stable health since then."

Nate's voice was small. "You know it's not like that anymore."

"Not for people like us," Izzy agreed. "But if you worked in my profession, you would know that's only true for those of us with access to care."

"I do know." By that time, Nate's eyes were full of tears.

Izzy reached across the table for his hand. "I don't know how to be the boyfriend you need. But that doesn't mean I'm not willing to learn. I loved you before we knew. Why should this change anything?"

"It might," Nate said, wiping his eyes. "I thought maybe you saw me as dirty. Do you?"

"No." He sighed, knowing he had to tell Nate the truth. "I wasn't upset with you when you told me."

"So why did you tell me you needed time?"

"Because I didn't want to burden you with my problems when you had enough of your own to work out. It was stupid, and I'm sorry." Izzy ran his thumb across Nate's knuckles.

"That doesn't make sense." Nate frowned. "What problems? I knew something was wrong, but I thought it was work, like a bad accident."

They'd arrived there at last. "I wasn't ready to talk about it. I wound up in my doctor's office that day facing test after test."

Nate frowned. "What?"

Izzy withdrew his hand. "We had an agreement. You would get tested, and so would I when I went to find out why I was going numb. It turns out it wasn't stress."

Nate sat back. "Why didn't you tell me instead of letting me think you were angry with me?"

Heat flooded Izzy's face and spread down his neck. "I was worried about you, and I didn't want you to feel obligated to me once you knew what I was facing."

"I don't understand."

Izzy ran his finger around the rim of his wine glass. Nate deserved the truth. "Do you know why my marriage failed?"

"You never said, not really."

"I couldn't have kids. Ten years of testing, a surgery that was supposed to 'fix' the problem, rounds of fertility treatments. Even in vitro didn't work. Lynne was open to letting it go and building our family a different way, but I wasn't. Everything became my fault, and I felt like a failure as a man and as a husband. I couldn't provide what she wanted, even after she assured me her dreams could change." He couldn't look Nate in the eye.

The pressure of Nate's hand on his caused him to glance to where their fingers were joined. "I have a feeling there's more, since obviously that's not the concern with me."

"Do you remember when I asked you about having kids?"

"Sure, of course."

"I was trying to find a way to let you out of being with me, hoping maybe if our goals were different we could part ways. If you wanted something I couldn't promise to give you, it would make it easier to let you go." Izzy took a deep breath and exhaled slowly. "I have multiple sclerosis. That's what they found. It's progressive. So you would be stuck with someone who might one day need care."

"So you let me think it was my fault?" Nate stared at him.

"No!" Izzy almost shouted. He gripped his hair. "You threw a wrench in my plan to leave you a way out. I didn't want you to have to worry about me on top of everything you were going through. Am I wrong? Would you have taken it well at the time?"

"I don't know." Nate sat back. "I'm not even sure exactly what multiple sclerosis is."

Izzy nodded. "It affects the nervous system. That's why I was going numb and having all that pain. Eventually, I might not be able to walk anymore." He took a deep breath. "I have to ask you the same question you asked me earlier. Does it bother you to know what life with me will be like?"

Nate's face crumpled. "I would be lying if I said it didn't," he said. "I'm sorry."

"We're on equal footing then." Izzy squeezed Nate's fingers.

"But you can't give me what you have. That's the biggest difference."

Izzy frowned. "Is that what you're worried I'm thinking? Because I'm not. I didn't tell you about my father so I could make excuses for being an ass. You asked me how I felt, and I told you. I wasn't upset with my father for coming to us when he thought he would need us to look after him. I was angry that he couldn't even speak the words. He wouldn't say he was gay or that his partner of almost ten years died from complications of AIDS, choosing to use coded words like pneumonia." Izzy made his way around the table and knelt beside Nate, even though his knees protested. "I told you all this because I wanted you to know why I left the first time. I was afraid of putting you through all that with my health. I am not now nor will I ever be ashamed or afraid of you."

Nate pulled his hand away and put his head in his palms. He shook, and he wouldn't meet Izzy's eyes. "I don't know where we go from here."

"I don't either, but I know for sure I want us to do it together. We both needed someone, and I failed you then. Maybe I don't deserve you, but I hope you'll give me another chance." He paused to get up and sit in the chair next to Nate's, inching it closer so they could touch. "I already talked to my doctor about PrEP. He doesn't usually prescribe it—not all doctors do—but he's looking into how it might interact with my other meds. If I didn't want to be with you, there is no way I'd have gone to the trouble."

Nate cupped Izzy's cheek. "Sometimes, I'm okay," he said. "And sometimes, I'm scared. I need you to understand."

Izzy closed his eyes and leaned into the touch. "Can you do the same for me?"

"I never wanted anything else," Nate said quietly. "When you left, I felt like no one else would ever want me if I couldn't even trust you."

"Then let me show you how wrong you were." Izzy stood. "Come on."

Nate glanced at the hand Izzy extended then peered up at him, waging an internal war. Everything felt tipped sideways, and he had nothing to anchor himself. He'd barely figured out how to navigate his own situation, and now Izzy had told him about his uncertain future.

He looked back up and said the only thing that came to mind. "What about dinner?"

Izzy's eyebrows rose. "We can reheat it or put it away in a bit."

Nate shook his head. He wanted to let Izzy touch him, to ground him and reassure him they would be okay. Only he couldn't let go. He stayed where he was, caught between the need for Izzy's warmth and the worry that he would only end up hurt again. He closed his eyes.

The soft notes surprised him, and he slowly opened his eyes again. Izzy was singing, the way Nate had done that morning in Izzy's bed when they'd first talked about being tested and Izzy seeing his doctor. Nate knew this song. He stood slowly, and Izzy took his hands while he continued singing about love changing everything. Nate stepped closer until they were chest to chest. Izzy wrapped his arms around Nate, still singing, his lips against Nate's cheek.

When the song was done, Nate shifted so he could look into Izzy's eyes. He was right; they'd both been changed. Nate put his hand on Izzy's neck and rested their foreheads together. "Thank you," he murmured.

Izzy took Nate's hand. They retreated to the bedroom, and Izzy shut the door. He pulled Nate in for a long, slow kiss. They didn't do anything else, just stood in the middle of the floor exploring each other's mouths. Izzy opened to let Nate's tongue in, sliding deliciously against his. He made a sound of pleasure in the back of his throat, and the vibrations made Nate shiver. He ran his hand up and down Izzy's spine, and their bodies gravitated toward one another until they were pressed flush against each other chest to hip.

Their kisses grew more eager, and Nate longed to be even closer, to lose the clothing separating them. He trembled, and Izzy stood still. He didn't undress or make a move to take Nate's clothes off, as though waiting for Nate to decide. Instead he ran his hands gently up and down Nate's arms, offering loving touch and breathless kisses, making Nate's skin heat with desire.

Nate pulled away. "Can I—?" He touched the buttons on Izzy's shirt.

"Yeah."

Izzy allowed Nate to undress him, pushing his shirt off his shoulders and unfastening his pants. When Izzy was down to his socks and underwear, he stepped back to look at Nate.

"Your turn," he said.

When Nate nodded, Izzy used the same care to undress him. As he did, he placed soft kisses down Nate's cheek to his neck and across his shoulder. Each one chipped away at Nate's self-consciousness, shedding it along with his clothes. Izzy ran his fingers lightly over each newly bared bit of skin. At last Nate stood before him in nothing but his boxer briefs and his socks.

They lay down on the bed, facing each other. Nate closed his eyes and pressed into Izzy's touch as he continued to caress Nate's body. Nate's cock thickened and strained against his underwear, and Izzy gazed at it like he wanted to devour it. Remembering previous times together sent a flash of heat downward from Nate's scalp. Izzy made Nate's whole body come alive. Wanting to feel Izzy too, Nate reached over and ran a hand between his legs. Izzy was only partially hard, but his cock twitched when Nate's hand came to rest on it.

"I want to show you how loved you are," Izzy said. "How wanted."

He bent to kiss Nate's chest, moving his mouth down to lick and suck at his nipples. He ran his tongue slowly down and lapped at Nate's navel. He placed kisses along the trail of hair disappearing into Nate's underwear. At last he lifted the waistband and held still, poised and ready to tug them off at Nate's go-ahead.

"Would it be all right to take these off?" he asked.

"Please."

Nate lifted his hips, and Izzy dragged them off, allowing Nate's cock to spring free. It lay on his belly, heavy and hard. Izzy's breathing sped up audibly, and he ran his fingers up the underside. Nate groaned. Izzy bent forward again and put his lips to the tip. He looked up at Nate, asking the question silently. Nate breathed faster too, but for entirely different reasons.

"Aren't you worried about—"

"Sh," Izzy responded. "No, I'm not. This is perfectly fine. Trust me."

It took everything in Nate to say, "I trust you."

At those words, Izzy engulfed Nate in his mouth. Nate moaned at the feel of his tongue and the way his girth filled Izzy's mouth. Izzy began to move, bobbing his head in rhythm. Beneath him, Nate's hips jerked, and he made subtle thrusting motions. He was holding back, not wanting Izzy to gag, but it was all right. Izzy relaxed his muscles to take Nate deeper, causing a long, shuddering groan to escape from inside Nate. He made no other effort to speed up or slow down or change anything. This was about enjoying the moment and about reconnecting.

Nate's legs shook under Izzy's palms. "God...stop...I'm really close."

Izzy took his time pulling off. He stretched out next to Nate and kissed him, letting Nate taste the flavor of his cock. He put his hand between Nate's legs, cupping his balls. "What do you need?"

Nate shifted a little and palmed Izzy through his briefs. "You're not—" he started but cut himself off with a frown. "Sorry."

"It's all right." Izzy kissed him. "This happens sometimes. It feels good, doing this with you. It's enough for now." He stroked Nate's erection, slowly and with only light pressure. "Do you want me to finish you off like this, or do you want me to fuck you with my fingers?"

Nate took several shuddering breaths before he answered. "I'm...god." He groaned when Izzy pressed behind his balls. "Fingers."

"Whatever you like."

Izzy reached into the bedside drawer and extracted the lube. He slicked his fingers and rested one lightly on Nate's hole. He rubbed gently until Nate shifted against him in an effort to get Izzy to put it in. Izzy pushed inside until Nate's muscles gave way. Slowly, he moved, each glide making Nate more slick and loosening him. Izzy added a second finger. He adjusted his hand position, crooking his fingers and finally brushing the spot which made Nate's hips rise off the bed.

Nate rocked against Izzy's hand, and they found each other's mouths again. Nate wrapped a hand around his cock and tugged furiously. He panted against Izzy's lips, and the whole frenzy sent shivers of pleasure through him. He hovered on the edge until Izzy pressed a little more firmly, and Nate opened his mouth in a choked-off scream.

He gasped and writhed through his orgasm, thick jets of come shooting onto his chest and up to his neck. Izzy held his hand still, but he didn't remove the fingers from inside Nate right away. He waited until Nate relaxed back onto the bed, still quivering. Nate cried out softly when Izzy pulled his fingers out, feeling their sudden loss.

They lay together, Izzy curled around Nate with his ear resting next to Nate's heart. The rapid thumping gradually slowed back to normal as Izzy ran his palm up and down Nate's arm. The room was still and quiet around them.

After a few minutes, Nate opened his eyes and touched Izzy's face. His fingers trembled, and Izzy took Nate's hand. In the light from a street lamp outside the window, Izzy's face was partially illuminated. Nate's eyes blurred with the tears he was holding back. Izzy kissed him over and over, whispering words of reassurance in between. Nate's unsteady breathing wasn't arousal this time but fear. Izzy tried to pull him closer, but Nate jerked away.

"I'm sorry," he said, his voice breaking.

"For what?"

Nate rolled onto his back and stared up at the ceiling. "I feel like everything we do is some kind of danger to you."

Izzy touched Nate's shoulder then ran his hand down to where Nate's fluids were drying on his stomach. He put his fingers in it, rubbing it around. Beneath his hand, Nate's muscles tightened.

"See?" Izzy said. "Nothing to worry about. It's just a little come."

Nate put his hand on Izzy's wrist, stilling him. "But what if—"

"We'll be careful. We were together before we knew, remember? The only thing that's changed is how we both know more about each other than before."

In an effort to stop the intrusive anxiety, Nate said, "What about you?" He slid his hand down, but Izzy was still almost completely soft.

Nate felt Izzy's half smile against his cheek. "You have no idea how good it felt to touch you like that."

Curious, Nate asked, "What do you mean?"

"It's hard to explain," Izzy said. "It happened once before. When we were making out in the theater. It's...intense, but different from coming like usual." He was quiet for a minute. "Does it bother you? That I can't, sometimes."

"I thought it would, but it doesn't, as long as it doesn't bother you." Nate nuzzled Izzy's nose with his and kissed him.

They fell silent. Izzy kept up his intimate touch, no effort to renew arousal but everything aimed at closeness. He reached over Nate to pick up the box of tissues on the nightstand. Carefully, he wiped Nate clean, remaining pressed up against him the whole time. At last he tossed everything in the trash and settled down with his arm and leg draped over Nate's body. Nate twitched, but he relaxed into Izzy's arms.

"I love you," Izzy murmured into Nate's chest.

"I love you too," Nate answered.

CHAPTER SEVENTEEN

Nate flopped onto the couch in the break room, exhausted from all the hauling he and Del had done. They'd put everything back in place after the weekend's final performance of *Carmen*. Del had been absolutely wonderful, and the show had been popular enough to draw in a standing room only crowd both of the last two nights. Nate couldn't have been more proud of his cast and crew.

They had one more opera before summer, and Nate had chosen *The Pearl Fishers*. It seemed fitting for a number of reasons. Nate thought his final opera as creative director should be one which paid tribute to the first song he'd ever performed with the love of his life. Breaking it to Del and the rest of the company that he was stepping down was much harder than picking the opera.

Del sank down next to him and handed over a bottle of water. He unscrewed the top on his own and took a long drink before saying, "How's it been going for you?"

Nate slouched so he could rest his head on the back of the couch. "Going well. I have another appointment scheduled this week, so I'll talk to my doctor." He rolled his head to the side to look at Del. "Thanks. For everything."

"No problem. What about some of the other stuff?"

"It's going. I still need another job. The turnout for this show was great, but I've had to depend on everyone else while I get back on my feet."

"I think I can help you out there." Del grinned.

"Oh?" Nate sat up. "What have you got in mind?"

"Position just opened up at work. I can put in a good word for you, if you want." Del patted his knee.

"Doing what, exactly?" Nate frowned. In all the time he'd known Del, he'd never bothered to ask what else he did.

"I'm a librarian," Del said. "We need someone part-time to cover a few shifts doing basic things. You don't need to have a degree or anything, and it's not that exciting, but it's a job."

"I'm in," Nate said.

"I'll send you the application. No guarantees, but I'll see what I can do."

They were quiet for a bit. Nate thought carefully about how he wanted to explain why he couldn't keep putting his energy into something which no longer made him happy. He wanted to go back to singing, and he wasn't really good at directing anyway. He'd already relied on Del for the bulk of what he did.

"I'm quitting," he blurted.

Instead of acting shocked or upset, Del angled toward him. "I was wondering when you'd say that."

Nate chuckled. "Pretty obvious, huh?"

"Hon, you have hated this job since you took it. I know I teased you about needing to find a man, but seriously? It's been bad. So, what's the plan?"

"I don't know," Nate admitted. He eyed Del. "You wouldn't want to take over for me, by any chance?"

"Ha! Hell, no." Del paused. "Actually, maybe I can do you one better."

This had to be good. "Go ahead."

"You and me." Del's smile was wicked. "Think of all the mischief we could make if we shared the job."

Laughing, Nate replied, "Oh, god. That would be..." He stopped. It would be brilliant, is what it would be. "Fantastic."

"The way I see it," Del continued, propping his feet on the table, "is filling both jobs. I don't want to completely give up performing, and you want to go back to it. So we work together. I'm already helping you out, and you know I couldn't do all the organization and keeping everyone in line. But let's be real, I'm a lot better with the staging and all the creative stuff. So what do you say? Can we make this work?"

"Yes, absolutely." He held up his water bottle, and Del tapped it with his.

"We start again next Monday?"

"Nope," Nate said. "I'm going to go watch the marathon in person."

Del laughed. "Oh, that's right. Next Sunday is Easter. Why are you watching it?"

"Izzy's running it."

Nate couldn't help his smile, somewhere between lovesick and proud. After everything else between them, they were in a good place. Izzy's health was stable for the time being, and he'd been able to continue training for the marathon. He'd done less dancing on stage at Grand Slam, but it was all right. Nate had been the beneficiary of many delightful private performances in Izzy's apartment. Even thinking about it made him blush, but he was a man in love, and he didn't care who knew it.

"That's good enough reason in my book," Del said. "Tuesday is plenty soon enough to get ourselves together. Do you two have plans after it's over?"

"Let me show you."

Nate stood, knowing his face had to be bright red. He wanted to let Del in on the secret, though. He crossed the room and pulled out the poster he'd hidden behind one of the shelves. Turning around, he showed Del, whose eyes nearly popped out of his head.

"Oh, my god!" he squealed. He jumped up and bounced over to hug Nate. "Good luck, honey. I hope he knows how lucky he is."

"I definitely know how lucky I am," Nate replied.

He rolled the poster, ready to take it home now that he'd finished it and shown Del. The others didn't know yet, but he'd convinced them to come with him to watch Izzy run. They were all about to find out.

They threaded their way through the crowd toward the finish line. They wouldn't be able to get right to it, but they'd be close. Nate kept his poster folded shut. Next to him, Jamie shivered and zipped his jacket shut.

"You okay?" Trevor asked.

"Yeah."

Jamie appeared better than he had last winter, but there was still a hollow look in his eyes. He hadn't gotten back together with The Boyfriend this time, which was a good thing, but he hadn't really seemed to recover, either. This was the longest they'd gone without starting over. Nate wondered how much Trevor had to do with it. He glanced at them out of the corner of his eye, and he couldn't quite place the brief understanding which passed between them. A few short months ago, it would have bothered him to have his best friend holding something back from him. Now he understood that whatever Jamie had shared with Trevor was between the two of them and not something he should interfere with.

"What's that for, anyway?" Trevor pointed to the poster.

"It's a surprise for Izzy."

Mack's eyes narrowed. "You've been hiding that in your closet for over a week. Come on, man. Give."

Nate opened the poster far enough for the others to peek at it. Jamie's eyes grew big, and his mouth dropped open. Trevor grinned. Mack let out a loud guffaw.

"You devil," he said. "I hope he doesn't puke all over you. Heard some poor guy did that to his girlfriend last year."

Nate rolled his eyes at Mack. "He didn't literally puke on her. Besides, Izzy's a seasoned runner. He's done this a whole bunch of times."

Nate thought about Izzy's health. He'd been doing well, but some days were better than others. Nate hoped this was one of the good ones. Izzy had said this would be his last marathon, but Nate couldn't imagine Izzy sitting around afterward, never running again. He supposed it was an issue to bring up with the doctor, and he wouldn't push Izzy either way.

A woman next to them with flame-red hair turned to them. "Here to see someone?"

"Yeah," Nate said. He paused, deciding what to tell her. It was hard to tell what reaction he might get. He figured in a crowd this size, the worst she could do was to sneer at him if she didn't like it. "My boyfriend is running."

The woman's face lit up. "My daughter and her wife are both in it. My daughter is in the wheelchair division."

"Cool," Nate replied. "She'll be by toward the beginning, so let us know and we'll yell for her."

"Will do," the woman replied. "So, what's the poster?"

Nate showed her, and she grinned the way Trevor had. She winked at Nate and went back to watching the road. It was good to have his friends at his side. At some point, Andre showed up with Marlie, the baby, and a woman Nate thought might have been

Andre's girlfriend. Izzy's coworker Val arrived with her fiancée.

It felt as though they watched an endless stream of runners passing. The red-haired woman had already left to greet her daughter and daughter-in-law, both of whom had finished. Tension coiled in Nate's gut as he kept an eye out, fearful he might miss Izzy in the herd of people going by.

"There he is!" Trevor's voice startled Nate.

Scanning the runners, Nate finally spotted him. He wriggled his way closer to the edge of the sidewalk, much to the consternation of several much shorter people. When one woman complained, Nate showed her the poster. She grinned and shoved him forward.

Izzy was now close enough to yell to him. Nate cupped a hand around his mouth and shouted, "Izzy! Israel Kaplan!"

Trevor, Jamie, and Mack hollered as well, but Izzy still didn't seem to have heard them. Nate resorted to plan B. He cleared his throat, took a breath, and began to sing.

Izzy was in the home stretch, his lungs and legs burning. Almost there. He was so focused on finishing that he was momentarily confused when he heard his name. He looked around, but he didn't see anyone. As he was returning his full attention to the road ahead of him, he heard Rodgers and Hammerstein in Nate's rich, beautiful baritone voice. Izzy almost laughed. When he was within a couple of yards, he turned his head to look. Nate musically informed him that people would say they were in love. With the people around them watching, Nate flipped the poster in his hands around and held it up.

Will you marry me?

Izzy's lips silently formed the words as he read. Warmth blossomed in his chest which had nothing to do with the miles he'd just run. He raised his eyes to Nate's, his mouth open. He jogged in place until there was a break then played Frogger with the other runners to get to the side of the road. He stopped in front of the spectators, and they parted so Nate had room to get down on one knee. His hand trembled as he took Izzy's and fumbled around in his pocket with the other. He withdrew the rainbow ring and slid it onto Izzy's finger.

"A placeholder until we get real ones," Nate said. He cleared his throat. "Will you marry me?"

Izzy pulled Nate to his feet and wrapped his arms around him in a crushing hug. "Yes. Oh, yes."

They pulled apart to the sound of cheers all around them—some for the runners still streaming past, some for Nate and Izzy. Nate wiped at his eyes, and Izzy grabbed his free hand, pulling.

"Come on," he said.

He dragged Nate with him onto the road, and together they ran the short distance left to the finish line. When they crossed, there were people there to meet Izzy and check him over. He was breathing hard and soaked with sweat, but otherwise he felt all right. He cringed at the shape some of the runners were in. Nate didn't appear fazed, but there was more puke than he'd probably ever been around in his life. Izzy tugged him to where they had a bit more privacy.

When Izzy was less winded, he drew Nate in for a brief kiss. He ran his finger down Nate's cheek and jaw.

"I love you," he murmured. "So much."

"I love you too."

"I don't plan to ever let you go," Izzy said.

"No matter what," Nate agreed.

There were still so many things they would need to work out, but they would do it together. Izzy thought back to when he was worried their relationship might be too complicated, and it made him exasperated at his former self. He and Nate had complications to spare, but it wouldn't hinder them any more than any other family.

He took Nate's hand in his, and they headed toward their friends. Before they got far, Izzy heard someone else calling his name. Three people were coming their way. Izzy stopped walking, effectively halting Nate as well. Eema and Ma Rose were there, along with a man Izzy hadn't seen in years—not that there was any mistaking him. Izzy stared, and Nate glanced between them, trying to puzzle out what was going on.

"Israel," the man said, his eyes softening. "We were looking for you."

"Dad."

Nate was now staring as well. Surely he wouldn't have missed the resemblance, the features Dad and Izzy had in common. The man looked exactly how Izzy might in another twenty some years. He had the same tall, athletic build, the same deep brown eyes, the same hair and beard, though his was salt-and-pepper instead of dark brown. He was darker than Izzy, but his skin had the same olive tone.

Izzy wasn't going to pretend for him. He drew himself up to his full height and said, "Dad, this is Nate. My fiancé."

"We saw!" Eema said, joy written all over her face. Ma Rose kissed Nate's cheeks.

Dad looked Nate up and down then turned his attention to Izzy. "Is he at least Jewish?"

"Dad!" Izzy yelped.

"A father can hope, can't he?" Dad smiled.

Nate was laughing, and Izzy elbowed him. He changed the subject before anything else could be said on the matter. "I don't mean to be blunt...wait. Yes, I do. Dad, what are you doing here?"

"I came to see my only son run his marathon. Is that so bad?" Dad rested a hand on Izzy's shoulder. "I'm proud of you." He turned apologetic. "I shouldn't have become such a stranger. I'm sorry."

Izzy almost told him it was okay, but it wasn't. Too many years and too many emotions lay between then and now. But his father's presence made him hope one day it might be all right.

"Why don't we all go home, and I'll make us something to eat?" Eema suggested. She looped her arm through Nate's, and Ma Rose put her hand on Izzy's back.

"Sure," Izzy said. He turned to Dad. "Are you coming too?"

"If it's all right with you."

"It is," Izzy assured him. "Give us a minute. I think some of our friends are waiting."

Eema nodded and let go of Nate. Izzy's mothers and father stepped aside, and Izzy took Nate's hand. They made their way back toward where Nate had left the rest of his group.

"I'm sorry for the surprise," Izzy said. "And for Dad being so forward. Guess you know where I get it from."

Nate laughed. "I'm not mad."

Chuckling, Izzy said, "Think you'd be willing to convert?"

It surprised him when Nate said, "I've thought about it, yeah. If it's important, I'll at least study and see where it goes. I'm not sure how I feel about religion, but I'm clear on how I feel about you."

Izzy stopped walking. "Oh, yeah? And how's that?"

"Like this."

Nate put his hand on the back of Izzy's neck and pulled him into a long, passionate kiss. He'd been right, people would definitely say they were in love.

About the Author

A.M. Leibowitz is a queer spouse, parent, feminist, and book-lover falling somewhere on the Geek-Nerd Spectrum. They keep warm through the long, cold western New York winters by writing about life, relationships, hope, and happy-for-now endings. In between noveling and editing, they blog coffee-fueled, quirky commentary on faith, culture, writing, books, and their family.